PRETEND TO BE YOURS

ALEXA RIVERS

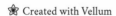

To the gorgeous, retro redhead
who inspired me to write Faith.
Keep being you.

FAITH ST. JOHN STARED AT THE INCOMING CALL ON HER mobile phone with trepidation. The caller ID read Molly & Arthur Weasley—the codename she'd assigned her parents. Faith's mum and dad never rang after 9:00 p.m. unless something was wrong, and she had a bad feeling about this.

She glanced at Dylan, the eleven-year-old she was babysitting, who lay sprawled on the couch beside her, having fallen asleep while waiting for his dad to get home. She stood and took herself to a different room so she wouldn't wake him up.

She slowly raised the phone to her ear. "Mum? Dad?"

"Faith!" her mother, Katherine, exclaimed.

She yanked the phone away, wincing. Her mother had one volume. Loud. A trait Faith had inherited.

"Hey there," she said, switching the phone to speaker so she could talk without risking her eardrums. "To what do I owe the pleasure?"

"We're here!"

Faith's eyebrows knitted together. "I don't follow. What do you mean?"

"Well...." Katherine dragged the word out, clearly wanting to deliver her news with a punch, as per usual. "You'll never guess, but we came to town a week early to spend time with you. We drove up after work. Surprise!"

"Oh, my gosh." Faith smiled. Her parents may be full-on and meddlesome, but she rarely saw them since they'd moved to Wellington, and she missed them. Her cousin Erica's wedding was next Saturday, but she hadn't expected them to be in town until then.

"I know. Isn't it exciting?" Katherine's voice sped up, and Faith imagined her father, Darren, was hurrying her along. "We were supposed to be up earlier but got stuck in rush hour traffic, and you know how long the drive is at the best of times. Anyway, we've arrived now, and we're parked outside your house. Where are you?"

"I'm babysitting Dylan and Hunter. Shane Walker's boys. Feel free to come over. Shane should be home before long."

It was nearly midnight, and Shane typically returned from playing poker with his friends just after twelve on Fridays because he took four-year-old Hunter on daddy-son DIY dates the next morning and didn't want to risk oversleeping. First and foremost, Shane was an awesome dad. That was one of the reasons Faith adored him. Well, that and he looked like a young Mark Ruffalo playing the role of hot professor. *Yum.* Unfortunately, he'd never seen her as anything other than a friend who sometimes watched his kids. Probably just as well. She wasn't exactly stepmum material.

"Remind me what his address is," Katherine said.

"10 Guinness Street."

"We'll be there soon. And darling, we have another surprise for you too."

Faith didn't ask what the other surprise was. She found it best to take things as they came. "Bye, Mum."

Ending the call, she made her way back to Dylan, who thankfully hadn't awoken. In fact, she was pretty sure he'd leave an imprint on the couch at this stage. She settled beside him. When she'd first started babysitting the Walker boys, Faith had tried to get Dylan into bed earlier, but she'd given up long ago. Perhaps it was something to do with his mother walking out on them, but he couldn't sleep until he knew the whole family was where they were supposed to be.

The tabby cat, Tinkerbell, butted her head against Faith's shin and she bent to pat her. "Who's a pretty girl?"

Faith opened her magazine and picked up where she'd left off, reading an article about the latest celebrity scandal. She knew most of the stories were patently false, but they entertained her, and she enjoyed seeing who was wearing what. Of course, she had to skim every magazine before taking it to the Walker residence in case it contained a photograph of, or story about, Diana Monroe—Shane's ex-wife who'd walked out on her family to become a Hollywood starlet. Prior to leaving New Zealand, she'd had a few guest roles on soap operas but hadn't achieved the level of success she'd craved. These days, she wasn't an A-lister, but was on her way up.

A while later, there was a soft knock at the front door. Faith closed the living room door behind her to muffle any noise so they wouldn't wake Dylan and trekked down the hallway to the front entrance. She opened it to let her parents in, but then stopped, her mouth forming an O of surprise because they weren't alone. They were accompanied by a cute guy about her age, with an easy smile and messy blond hair.

"Hello," she said, scanning their expressions, which ranged from guilty (Darren) to eager (Katherine) to nervous (the stranger). "And who might this be?"

"Darling." Katherine reached for Faith's hand, but she backed up, eyes narrowed. Something was going on here, and she didn't think she was going to like it. "Can we at least come in before the interrogation begins?"

Faith sighed. "I suppose so."

Standing aside, she let them in. They filed past one by one, and she didn't care for the way the stranger's gaze lingered on her cleavage. She had a damn good set of boobs and didn't mind them being ogled, but not when she had a sinking sensation about the reason for his presence. She led them to the spare bedroom, not wanting to disturb Dylan.

Hands on hips, she stared at her mother, then her father. "Explain."

The stranger offered a hand. "It's lovely to meet you. I'm Leon."

Faith eyed the proffered hand the same way she might a rattlesnake. "Nice to meet you, Leon." She studied him. He was a Niall Horan, she decided. Cute in a boyish way. "What brings you to the bay?"

He smiled, blue eyes twinkling. "You."

Faith's jaw dropped. "I beg your pardon?"

Katherine grabbed her hand, snatching her attention away from the boy-band lookalike. "Leon is from your father's church."

Faith looked to Darren for confirmation. Her father worked as an Anglican minister and had a wide social circle as a result.

He nodded. "It just so happens that Leon's parents are also invited to the wedding. They're family friends on the groom's side. Your mother and I discussed the matter

4

and decided we'd like you and Leon to meet. We thought he could be your date to the wedding."

A flush crept over her cheeks until she was sure they mirrored her hair color. She couldn't believe this. Her parents had brought her a blind date. One that she'd be stuck with for a week—because no question about it, they'd be staying at her place.

Oh, God.

She face-palmed. Could this get any more embarrassing? And why on earth was Leon going along with it? She couldn't believe any sane man their age would encourage a ridiculous, parent-sponsored matchmaking scheme.

Finally, she dropped her hands and looked from her mother to her father. "I don't need you to introduce me to a man."

No, she met plenty of those herself. Just not ones she'd ever spend more than a few nights with.

Darren cleared his throat. "Clearly, you do. You're twenty-seven and haven't snagged one yourself yet."

Snagged. What kind of person said that? Made it sound like she was fishing for a husband.

"I—"

"Just give Leon a chance," Katherine said.

Mortification threatened to swallow Faith whole. She squeezed her eyes shut, and words burst from her mouth without any warning. "You didn't let me finish. I don't need you to introduce me to a man because I already have one."

She opened her eyes to find all three of them watching her dubiously. Damn. Why had she said that? If they asked around, it'd be easy enough to refute.

"Who's that, dear?" Darren asked.

At that moment, a key rattled in the lock outside.

Faith groaned. As if the situation couldn't get any worse, the object of her unrequited crush had arrived.

"Shane," she muttered.

Her mother's eyes widened and darted to the bedroom door. "Oh, Faith. You're seeing Shane? Why didn't you tell us?"

Of all the slips of the tongue.

But then an idea occurred to her. Why couldn't she be with Shane? Her parents would be gone in a week. She'd babysit his children free of charge for a whole freaking year if he got her out of any awkward matchmaking attempts. She had all of twenty seconds to make up her mind, and then the front door opened.

With enthusiasm she didn't have to fake, she ran into the hall and launched herself at him, seeing the whites of his eyes as they widened, then she dragged him into a thoroughly dramatic kiss.

SHANE EXPERIENCED A MOMENT OF UTTER PANIC AS A BODY flew toward him, and then he was in paradise. Faith was in his arms. She was kissing him. He had no idea why, or whether it was even real—perhaps he'd drifted off to sleep on Logan's couch—but he wanted it to go on forever. He'd dreamed of this moment since he first hired her to watch his kids and found her dozing in the armchair with Hunter curled on her lap and her spectacular cleavage displayed to full advantage.

Faith was everything Shane wasn't. Vibrant, young, passionate, funny, and completely gorgeous. Now she was kissing him. Realizing he'd yet to respond, he looped his arms around her waist, pulled her tight against himself, and deepened the kiss. She gasped into his mouth, and he took the chance to taste her. She was sweet and addictive, as he'd always suspected.

Was this really happening?

But then she pulled away and hugged him, her cheek pressed to his. In his ear, she whispered, "Please play along."

What?

He blinked as she released him, baffled by her words, and struggled to collect himself. He adjusted his spectacles, which were askew, and when his vision cleared, he noticed three people standing behind her. Two he recognized as her parents, whom he'd met a couple of times, and the third was a young man he'd never seen before. Shane was good with faces—as a teacher, he had to be—but he was coming up empty.

Then it struck him. The kiss hadn't been real. Oh, it had happened, but it had been for show, not because she truly wanted to kiss him the way he'd longed to kiss her. For some reason, she wanted her parents to believe they were a couple. As if anyone could possibly think that. She was so far out of his league, he'd never even bothered stepping up to the plate.

Disappointment settled in his gut.

"Mum, Dad," she said, threading her fingers through his and standing shoulder to shoulder with him. "You remember Shane."

"Of course." Katherine threw an arm around him. She couldn't hug him properly since Faith refused to let go of his hand. "It's lovely to see you again."

"You too, Katherine."

Darren reached over to shake his hand. "How are you?"

"Good, thanks. I didn't know you were in town."

"We just arrived." Katherine's statement was followed

7

by a beat of awkward silence. She turned toward the stranger, wearing the oddest expression. "Shane, this is Leon." Her voice was high, and she cleared her throat, her cheeks coloring to match her hair. "Leon's parents are friends of ours. They attend the church." She glanced from Leon to Faith and, if possible, flushed even harder.

"Nice to meet you," Leon said.

"Likewise."

Shane got it now. They'd brought this guy, Leon, to town in the hopes of setting him up with Faith. This in mind, he studied the man with fresh eyes. He was good-looking, with floppy hair and one of those faces that looked like he was always on the verge of saying, "Aww, shucks" while shuffling humbly from foot to foot. But wasn't he too young for Faith? While Shane had five years and a whole lot of life experience on her, Leon could have walked straight out of a university lecture theater. She needed a man with more character than that. Apparently, she agreed, or she wouldn't be trying to avoid him.

"Would you like a drink?" he asked, envisioning the contents of the refrigerator. He didn't have any alcohol, but perhaps he had a carton of fruit juice and one of milk. Real, grownup options.

"No, but thanks for the offer," Darren said. "We just need a key so we can make ourselves at home at Faith's place."

At his side, Faith stirred, fishing around in the wallet tucked into the pocket of her dress. She held out a key, and Darren took it. "I wasn't expecting you, so nothing is prepared, but it shouldn't take too much effort to get things sorted, and I won't be far behind you. Just help yourselves to the chamomile tea and I'll be there in no time."

Chamomile tea? People actually drank that? He fought the urge to cringe.

"We'll do that." Katherine eyeballed them in a way that made Shane squirm. "I'll have a mug ready for you."

"Thanks, Mum." Faith kissed her cheek. "See you soon."

The three of them trailed out, and Shane closed the door behind them. Finally, he and Faith were alone.

He turned to face her and ran a hand through his perpetually messy hair. "Well, that was unexpected."

A massive grin split her face, displaying perfect white teeth. The kind of grin that showed she was nervous. He noticed now that her lips weren't as red as usual. In fact, her lipstick seemed to be smeared. Groaning, he realized the rest of it had probably been transferred onto him. He wiped his mouth on the back of his sleeve and prayed Dylan—if he were awake—wouldn't notice anything amiss.

"Explain," he ordered, leaning against the wall for support.

She shrugged, one strap of her vintage dress slipping off her shoulder. "You've probably pieced most of it together. Mum and Dad decided to come to the bay a week early. You know it's Erica's wedding this weekend?"

He nodded. Faith's cousin, Erica, worked with his friend, Jack, at his outdoor adventure company. Everyone in Haven Bay knew she'd planned a big wedding in the town hall.

Faith fidgeted with the hem of her dress. "Apparently, they decided I'm so hopeless they need to supply me with a date. Hence, Leon." She sighed. "It's a shame, because he's got an adorable One Direction thing going on, but if I give them an inch, they'll have arranged the marriage before Erica's wedding is over."

9

He folded his arms across his chest, his T-shirt pulling tight. Her eyes dipped, and he thought he saw appreciation flicker in them, but it was gone so fast he might have imagined it. After all, Faith wasn't shy about her sexuality. If she found him attractive, surely she'd have told him by now.

"So, you said you're dating me?" he asked.

She nodded, looking miserable. "I'm sorry. I just couldn't think of anything else." She grabbed his hand and made big puppy eyes from behind her glasses. "Will you pretty please be my pretend boyfriend and come to the wedding with me next weekend?"

"Uh...." Under normal circumstances, he'd be able to list a dozen reasons why that was a bad idea, not least of which was that he didn't want to confuse Dylan and Hunter, but when she fluttered her thick black lashes at him, all of those reasons fled his conscious mind.

"Please, please, please."

The sight of Faith begging did curious things to his insides. He was a disturbed man. "I don't think—"

"I'll do free babysitting for six months," she interrupted. "A year—whatever it takes."

"Huh." The shrewd, calculating part of his brain kicked into gear. "Make it every Friday for a year, and perhaps some other days if you're free."

"Done."

"This situation can't affect the boys."

"Of course not."

"Then you have a deal."

They shook on it, and to his surprise, she jerked him forward and planted a kiss on him. "Thank you."

Two kisses in ten minutes. He needed to have pretend girlfriends more often. This was the most man-on-woman action his lips had seen in years. He'd bet Leon had seen action recently. Heck, the guy had probably intended to get a nice taste of Faith, church-going parents or not. Shane could easily understand why he'd come. Faith's parents would have showed him her picture, and he'd have jumped with excitement at the thought of getting his hands on her. Probably promised them he had nothing but marriage on his mind. And why wouldn't he? She was pretty, quirky, and clever enough to run a successful business.

In other words, a keeper.

And now she was going to sleep in the same house as the other man. That didn't sit right with him. What if Leon won her over with his youthful energy and the cuteness she'd mentioned? She wasn't actually with Shane, so there was no reason she couldn't see where things went.

Not on my watch.

"You're welcome to stay here," he told her, and cleared his throat. "It sounds like it will be a full house at your place."

She smiled. "Thanks, you're sweet, but I like my house full. I'll grab my things and be off."

He trailed behind her into the living room. Dylan was sleeping on the couch, and Shane bent to ruffle his son's hair. "Wake up, champ."

Dylan stirred, blinking sleepily. He sat up. "Did you bring home the M&Ms?"

Shane had been at his weekly poker game with his friends, but these days they usually bet with candy rather than money. They'd found that it evened things up since they had everything from a millionaire computer genius to a pub owner to a librarian among their numbers.

He retrieved a paper bag from his pocket. "Unfortunately, not an impressive haul. Sterling made away with most of it."

Dylan pulled a face. "Why? It's not like he eats them himself."

"No," Shane agreed. "But he has a competitive streak, and he shares them with the children at the lodge, so it's not as though he's selfish. He wins them fair and square."

Dylan sighed. "Yeah, I know." He took the bag and opened it. "I'll split these up so Hunter can have his in the morning."

"Good plan."

Dylan was a responsible kid and took fairness very seriously. Sometimes Shane feared he was raising a mini adult, but then his son would get in a temper because something didn't go his way, and he'd be reminded the boy was only eleven. Still, his brother was much younger, and Dylan seemed to view himself as a second father to Hunter.

While they'd been talking, Faith had gathered her belongings, and she now gave Dylan a hug and patted Shane's shoulder. "See you later, sugar."

He didn't read into the endearment. She doled them out freely to everyone she met. "Thanks for watching them. Have a nice night."

She left, and he couldn't help but wish he'd received a hug the same way Dylan had. He envied his son. How ridiculous was that?

2

Thank God for Shane Walker. He was going to save Faith's bacon. When the door of his 1920s villa closed behind her, she let the tension ease from her shoulders and glanced up at the sky. Tonight the stars wove between the pink and purple twists of the milky way. The sight of the night sky had always soothed her.

A cool breeze stirred her hair, and she continued down the drive to her car, a retro VW Beetle she'd had restored. She slid into the driver's seat and started the engine. A couple of minutes later, she arrived outside her cottage on the opposite side of the Haven Bay township. She slung her bag over her shoulder and made her way up the path, then let herself in the front door. The cottage was cozy and opened into a small hall, with her bedroom on one side and the living room on the other. The spare bedroom came off the living room, as did the kitchen. She didn't have a dining area—she ate on the couch most nights, or at the kitchen counter.

She dropped her things in her bedroom and found her parents in the living room, side by side on the couch, with Leon on the armchair. Since there were no other furnishings—at least not that she could sit on, she perched on the arm of the couch.

"Did you find everything you needed?" she asked, wondering for the first time what they intended the sleeping arrangements to be. There were only two beds and too many of them to fit.

"Sure did," Katherine replied. "Your father and I made the spare bed, and Leon has a sleeping bag, so he can sleep in here."

Faith sized Leon up. He was all of six feet, and her couch wasn't much more than five. He wouldn't be getting a lot of sleep this week.

She sighed. "Why don't you take my bed, and I'll take the couch?"

His eyes widened. "That's kind of you, but not necessary."

She shook her head. "I insist. I couldn't live with myself if you came all this way for nothing and then had a miserable time."

A smile curved his lips. "Okay, then. Thank you, Faith."

"No problem. Would you like fresh bedding?"

One corner of his mouth hitched up higher. "I think I can survive your secondhand sheets."

Glancing at the ceiling, Faith cursed inwardly. Leon was looking at her the same way most guys her age did: like she'd given them the all-clear to strip her naked and take her for a spin.

This was why she didn't do relationships.

"So, Faith, how long has this affair with the teacher been going on?" her father asked. He was one of those pleasant sorts of people who was hard to ruffle and rarely had a bad word to say about anyone. He also tended to use outdated language, like "affair."

She smiled. "Only a couple of months. It's still early days."

He nodded. "You could certainly do worse. He has a respectable job, and from what I understand, a good standing in the community."

Oh, yes. Because those were the metrics one should use to find a suitable spouse. She resisted the temptation to roll her eyes or make a sassy comment about how well that had turned out for her sister.

"That he does."

"He also comes with two sons and quite a history," Katherine reminded her, as if she'd ever forget.

"Two lovely children," Faith replied. "And it was hardly his choice to be abandoned by his wife."

Leon watched this back and forward with interest. Her mother seemed to notice this and stood. "Faith, can I speak to you in private?"

Faith led her into the kitchen and closed the door behind them. "What is it?"

Katherine wrung her hands and took a few moments to put her thoughts together. Faith gave her time, familiar with her mum's need to have a fully formed idea before verbalizing it.

"This is terribly awkward," she said eventually. "We should have asked if it was okay to bring Leon before just turning up with him. Would you like us to find somewhere else for him to stay? I'm sure he'll understand if you or Shane are uncomfortable with him being here."

Faith considered the question. It would certainly make life simpler if she said yes, but Leon had come all this way to meet her, and it would be rude to kick him out. She'd made it clear there would be no romance between them, which meant there wasn't really a reason to ask him to leave. A few wisps of red hair tickled her nose, and she blew them aside.

"No, he can stay."

Katherine's expression softened in relief. "You always did have a kind heart."

She'd often wondered if it was too soft. "Shall we rejoin the men?"

Back in the living room, Darren and Leon were debating the merits of golf versus tennis. Faith, who preferred to watch shirtless men play sports rather than actually participate, listened to the sound of their voices without paying attention to the details.

When they stopped for breath, Katherine took advantage of the reprieve to ask a question Faith suspected she'd been dying to all night. "How did you and Shane get together, darling?"

Faith shrugged. She and Shane hadn't discussed the specifics, but she should have guessed her parents would ask. "Nothing special. I've been babysitting his boys for a couple of years now, and we just grew closer. Not long ago, we decided to date."

Katherine looked disappointed there wasn't a more exciting story. "That's nice, I suppose." She brightened. "Why don't you invite them to lunch with us tomorrow? Shane and his sons. It would be lovely to get to know them."

Uh oh. Faith froze. They couldn't all go out together. Not when the boys didn't know about their deception. Dylan would give them up within the first five minutes. Worse, she didn't want to confuse the kids. Especially not Hunter, who had no recollection of his mother and had referred to Faith as "Mum" in the past, setting Dylan off on a temper tantrum.

"Maybe," she said, thinking on her feet. "But Shane

usually takes Hunter to DIY Saturday at Sanctuary, and Dylan has cricket."

"We can go after they finish."

Her stomach tied itself in knots. This was why she ought not to lie. It was far too easy to get caught. "I'll talk to Shane and see if he's free."

Katherine smiled. "Good."

They spoke for a while longer, and then, worn out, Faith climbed into her makeshift bed on the couch. She'd almost drifted to sleep when she remembered she needed to contact Shane. She whipped her phone out, selected his name, and typed a message.

Faith: *My parents want to have lunch with you and the boys tomorrow. I'm so sorry.*

When she didn't immediately receive a negative response, she wondered if he was already asleep, but then a message popped up.

Shane: *We can make it work. 1pm at Cafe Oasis? Hope they don't mind if we're sweaty and dirty.*

Faith tapped a reply. *I'm sure they won't, but aren't you worried about the boys?*

Shane: *Yes, we'll need to be careful not to cross any boundaries.*

Faith: *Easier said than done, but I promise to come clean if needed. Thanks for being such a good sport.*

Shane: *No problem. Good night, Faith.*

She sighed, wriggling further down beneath her bedding. Was it wrong that she wished, just a little, that their lunch date would be real? She had a big old crush on Shane. Always had, and probably always would. Unfortunately, he'd never be interested in her. Judging by his ex-wife, he preferred petite blondes. The opposite of Faith. Even if, by some miracle, he was attracted to her, she wasn't relationship material. Enough men had told her she was fun but too full-on to have around permanently that she had no choice but to believe them. If three people told you to sit down because you were drunk, you should sit down... right?

SHANE WASHED PAINT FROM HIS HANDS AND SCRUBBED Hunter's fingers while Dylan regaled them with a full rundown of his cricket match. He played on a team with his friends, and one of the mothers kindly took him to and from matches when Shane wasn't able, but he tried to attend at least every second week. He dried himself, then Hunter, and they walked out to the car.

"Can I have cake at the cafe?" Hunter asked, not for the first time.

"You can share a piece with Dylan," Shane replied, also not for the first time, and made sure Hunter was belted up.

"Why do we have to go out for lunch with Faith's mum and dad?" Dylan asked, belting himself into the passenger seat.

Shane had given a lot of thought as to how to explain the lunch to his boys and had arrived at the conclusion that it would be best to keep it as simple as possible. "Well, you know how when you stay over with Josh, you have to eat dinner at the table with his parents?"

"Yeah."

"Faith is my friend, just like Josh is yours, and sometimes even adults have to sit at the table with their friend's parents."

He could tell by the way Dylan rolled his eyes that he wasn't buying it, but Hunter seemed satisfied by the explanation. The fact was, his friendship with Faith was usually pretty one-sided—something he was well aware of. She was always giving him her time and attention. This was his chance to do something for her, and he was determined not to mess it up. Also, he had to admit, he was flattered she'd chosen him to play her fake boyfriend. Either one of the Pride brothers would happily have filled the role, as would a number of other men.

They drove into town and parked on a side street, then walked together to Cafe Oasis where he'd arranged to meet Faith and Mr. and Mrs. St. John. Checking his watch, he noted they were five minutes late. Not bad for him. Usually, he was running at least fifteen minutes behind. An old-fashioned doorbell signaled their arrival, and he scanned the wooden floor, searching for familiar flame-red hair. There she was. At the table by the window. As were her parents and the interloper. Shane's teeth gritted. Her parents had brought the blind date to meet his family? If they were actually together, he'd see that as a declaration of war.

But you're not, he reminded himself. *Faith isn't yours.*

That didn't stop him from striding directly to her side and dropping a proprietary kiss on her cheek. For today, at least, he got to pretend she belonged to him.

"Hello," he said to the group as he sat. Dylan slouched into the chair on his other side, and there wasn't space for Hunter, so Shane hefted him onto his knee. "It's nice to see you again, Mr. and Mrs. St. John. These are my sons, Dylan and Hunter. Boys, these are Faith's parents." He ignored the interloper. The man should have known better than to come on a lunch date with them.

"Please, call us Katherine and Darren," Faith's mother said. "We're so delighted to meet you."

Dylan glanced at the door like he wanted to run. He

wasn't a fan of attention on the best of days. But he mumbled a greeting, and for that, Shane thanked his lucky stars.

"Buddy, what do you say?" he asked Hunter, who'd turned his face into Shane's chest. His youngest could be painfully shy and only came out of his shell around a select group of people he trusted. Faith was one of those, but her parents didn't make the cut.

Hunter peeked around. "Hi." Then he buried his face again.

Shane expected them to dive into questions, such as how long they'd been seeing each other and why they hadn't told anyone, but Faith must have fielded those already because instead Katherine launched into a monologue about the upcoming wedding, and weddings in general, and how wonderful and uplifting they were. Shane didn't necessarily agree. His had been expensive and had provided an excuse for Diana to act like a diva for months.

Faith slanted a cheeky grin his way. "This is her way of dropping hints. Subtlety is not a family trait."

Katherine waved a hand. "I have no time for that. The only one of us who ever has is Charity."

"Charity?" Shane asked.

Katherine's eyes widened, and she shot Faith a look. "Faith's sister."

"Oh, of course," he said, wincing at how thoughtless he'd been. Faith never mentioned her sister, but he could remember the scandal from when she'd left. Everyone in the bay could.

"Leon, have you met our Charity?" Katherine asked, a calculating gleam in her eye that made Shane think she might have a new matchmaking plan in mind.

"Dylan, Hunter," Darren interrupted. "Why don't you

come with me, and we'll order some food? Shane, would you like anything?"

"A long black, please." Shane tried to lift Hunter from his knee, but the kid clung to his leg. Bending over, he murmured, "If you want cake, you have to go with Mr. St. John, okay?" Reluctantly, Hunter released him and let Dylan take his hand and lead him away. Shane's heart squeezed to see the two of them together like that. Dylan was insanely protective of his little brother, and Shane couldn't have asked for a better sidekick in raising him.

Katherine followed his gaze. "They're darling."

"They're very sweet," Faith agreed. "Do you like children, Leon?"

Leon ran a hand through his mop of blond hair and aimed his bluebird eyes at Faith. Now that his sons were distracted, Shane had no compunction about sliding closer to her and resting his hand on her thigh. It was warm and soft, and her breath hitched in response. Everyone at the table followed the movement, and from the way Leon's nostrils flared and his eyes narrowed, Shane knew he saw it for the claiming it was.

Leon's eyes flickered back to Faith's, away from Shane's hand on her leg. "I love kids. I help run the Sunday school program at your dad's church, and it's a joy to be able to spend my time with the young people of the parish." He turned to Katherine, bestowing such a blazing white smile on her that Shane almost needed to shield his eyes. "And no, I haven't had the pleasure of meeting Charity yet."

The way he said "Yet", as if it were only a matter of time, and followed it up with a wink in Faith's direction, had Shane seeing red. Sure, Faith wasn't actually his girlfriend. But if she was, and this guy had the audacity to flirt with her in front of him, he'd want to wring the little shit's neck. Never mind that Leon had the benefit of youth.

Shane smoothed his palm up and down Faith's thigh, taking comfort from the knowledge that for now, he was allowed to touch her and Leon wasn't. Unfortunately, when the boys returned, he'd have to let her go. Faith's hazel eyes met his with a question in them. God, she was so gorgeous, with her creamy complexion, crimson lips, and soft features. He wished he were allowed to kiss her again.

"We'll have to introduce you to Charity," Katherine said, breaking the moment.

"When do I get to meet Charity?" Shane asked, knowing he was behaving poorly but not really caring.

"This weekend," Faith said, a smile quirking her lips. "She's coming to the wedding."

"She is?" Katherine's hand went to her chest. "Oh, that's wonderful. She never told me."

Faith shrugged, and he tried to ignore the way her breasts lifted. Her cleavage was temptation incarnate. "You know how she is with this town. She's hoping to slip in and out without anyone knowing she was here."

Based on what he knew of Faith's sister's past, that didn't surprise him.

"Faith, I've heard you own an ice cream parlor," Leon said, changing the subject. "I'd love to hear how that came to be."

Forcing himself not to stare down his opponent, Shane instead looked at Faith, only to find her already looking at him. Behind her, he could see his sons on their way back and knew he'd have to stop touching her soon, but for a few seconds, he let every bit of yearning he felt for her show in his eyes, and he was pleased to see her pupils dilate in response. She drew in a shaky breath and started to answer Leon's question, but she didn't take her eyes off Shane.

"As soon as I was old enough to be allowed in the kitchen by myself, I loved making dessert for other people. It's so lovely to see them enjoy what I make. Especially ice cream. People don't give it enough credit, but ice cream can make a bad day so much better. It provides comfort, but it can also be fun or playful." She shrugged. "I like to care for people, and to delight them with something new. The Shack is a great fit for me."

3

SHANE WAS DRIVING HER CRAZY WITH HIS HOT LOOKS. Faith fought the urge to fan herself and hoped that whatever words were tripping off her tongue made sense, because her brain wasn't processing them. She was floating in the depths of his dark eyes and wondering, for the umpteenth time, what it would be like to have him look at her that way for real. It was a good thing he never dated because if she saw him gaze adoringly at another woman, she'd poison the bitch's ice cream. But then his sons rejoined them, he blinked, and their connection was lost. She felt like he'd severed a cord between them, leaving her disconcerted and a little confused.

"Faith?" Leon asked.

With a great deal of effort, she forced herself to look at him. "What's that?"

His brows pulled together. "You were saying something about experimenting, but you kind of drifted away."

"Oh." Lucky she didn't blush easy. A fact that, considering her complexion, often surprised people. "Was I telling you about my experimental flavors?"

He snapped his fingers and grinned. "Yes, that's it."

She went on to explain how she rotated new flavors in and out of the parlor, but all of her focus was on Shane's conversation with her father. She couldn't believe her parents had actually brought Leon on their lunch date. When she'd arrived and seen him there, she'd been horrified. They were trying to be nice and include him, she understood that, but surely they could see how inappropriate it was.

A warm palm settled on Faith's leg, and her breath seized in her lungs. She stole a peek down, and now she was officially blushing. Shane's thumbs drew small circles on her inner thigh, and her body wanted to open up to him in a way that definitely wasn't appropriate when his sons and her parents were around the table. She glanced at him, but he was speaking to Dylan and didn't look her way. Was he trying to turn her on, or was this all for show?

All for show.

It must be. But dang, it was hard to remember that when his hand curved around her knee. Who the heck knew a knee could be an erogenous zone? Not her, that's for sure, and she barely refrained from moaning. With an act of willpower she didn't know she possessed, she shot to her feet. Everyone stared.

"I, uh, need to use the ladies' room," she said.

Her mother stood. "I'll join you."

Faith marched to the toilets, but before they entered, Katherine stopped her with a hand on her arm.

"Honey, there's something you need to know."

Faith glanced around. No one seemed close enough to overhear them. "What's that?" Katherine bit her lip, and Faith frowned. Her mother was rarely hesitant to say anything. "Mum, whatever it is, I can handle it."

She sighed. "We didn't only bring Leon because we thought you might get on well. We brought him because Mason is going to be at the wedding, and we didn't want you to be blindsided."

"Oh, fuck." Her heart thumped erratically, and her legs turned weak.

"Language!"

"Sorry." No, she wasn't. The situation warranted a curse word or two. Maybe even ten.

Mason.

She hadn't heard that name in years. No one was cruel enough to say it to her face, although the few people who knew what had happened no doubt gossiped behind her back. But why would Erica invite Mason to the wedding? She and her cousin had gone to school together. Erica knew what Mason had done to her. How he'd broken her heart and decimated her self-esteem all at once by sharing the intimate photos she'd allowed him to take with people who in turn used them against her. She felt good about herself now, but she'd had to claw her way out of a deep pit of crappy self-esteem when, previously, her confidence had come naturally. She pursed her lips. Mason should stay in Auckland where he belonged. Why would he come back here?

"How long have you known?" she demanded.

Katherine studied her face, ignoring the question. "Are you okay, honey? I know this must be a shock."

She could say that again.

"I'm okay. Promise." Faith gave a tremulous smile. "It was a long time ago, and I've grown up since then. I can deal with him. But why is he invited?"

Katherine grimaced. "Turns out he's the groom's cousin."

"Oh." So he had as much right to be there as she did. "What luck, huh?"

"We'll be with you. Your father and I may not approve of the decisions you made when you were younger, but we'll stand by you through anything."

Tears burned Faith's eyes, and she removed her glasses and carefully wiped them away so as not to smudge her eyeliner. Then she placed them back and yanked Katherine into a hug. "Thanks, Mum. Love you lots."

"Love you too." Katherine stepped away and adjusted her shirt, which Faith had ruffled. "Now, go pee."

"You don't need to?"

"No, I just wanted to talk to you in private."

Faith ducked her head closer to her mother's and confessed, "I don't either. I just needed to get away from the table for a moment."

"Because Shane was groping you?"

Faith's jaw dropped. "Mum!"

Her mother grinned. "I may be old, but I'm not blind. That man can't keep his hands off you."

How much Faith wished that were true.

"Let's head back then."

They finished lunch without further issue and then split into two groups, her parents having promised to show Leon the sights. Faith suggested that Shane and the boys get ice cream, so they strolled to The Shack. As they walked, they talked. Dylan told Faith about his cricket match, and Hunter explained how he'd learned to help hang wallpaper. Faith smiled at the image, certain the adorable kid had been as much trouble as he'd been assistance, and the look she shared with Shane reinforced her suspicions.

When they arrived in the familiar peach-and-green

retro-flair parlor that was Faith's home away from home, the boys hustled to the freezer to look over the choices. She was about to follow, but Shane drew her to the rear of the shop.

"I need to run something by you," he said, his expression serious.

"Sure thing."

He opened his mouth, seemed to reconsider, closed it, then started again. "While we're... pretending... to see each other, I don't think we should be involved with anyone else."

"Okay," she agreed readily. It was a single week. Did he really think she had so many men lining up for her that it'd be a hardship to sleep alone?

His eyes narrowed behind his glasses. "That was too easy."

She burst out laughing, and everyone turned their way. She waved off the attention, well aware by this point in her life that she had no volume control.

"Do you see hunks hiding in the corners waiting to sweep me off my feet?" she asked. "Because I don't."

He cocked his head. "I know you like to flirt with the tourists."

"And what?" She rolled her eyes. She liked to sleep with some of them too, but that was none of his business. Why would he even care? Unless.... Was it possible he was jealous of the men she'd been with? No, it couldn't be. She shook off the bizarre thought. "For this week, we're pretend exclusive. Done and done, sugar."

He still didn't look like he believed her, so she patted his chest and sashayed up to the counter, where her business partner and best friend, Megan, was serving the boys.

"These ones are on me," she said.

28

Megan nodded. "How'd lunch go?"

Faith shuddered. "Ugh, not amazing, but could have been worse, all things considered, so I'll count it as a win."

She wasn't ready to share the news of Mason's impending visit with anyone, not even her best friend. For one thing, Megan didn't know what had gone down in senior year, and Faith would rather keep it that way. Yeah, Megan had made her share of poor life choices, but nobody had ever circulated naked pictures of her among the most popular crowd at school purely for the sake of humiliating her. Megan's mistakes were tragic and understandable, whereas Faith's were just embarrassing.

"Faith!"

She glanced over her shoulder at the sound of her name and smiled. "Betty White, as I live and breathe."

Betty beamed, taking the comparison to the actress with the same pride she usually did. "I just saw your parents with a young man. Any idea who he might be?"

Faith's lips twitched. "Why? So you can add him to the sweepstakes?"

Betty and her friends had an ongoing sweepstakes as to which people would couple off next.

"I'm questioning whether I should change who my money is on when it comes to your romantic future," Betty said. "Is he a special friend of yours?"

Faith laughed. "No, not at all. He's only here for Erica's wedding. My parents are trying to set us up, but I'd rather not be set up, so Shane has kindly volunteered to help me stave them off."

"Oh, really?" Betty's eyes twinkled. "So you and Shane are pretending to be an item? How daring. I'll spread the word."

Faith hid a smile. If Betty promised to spread the

word, she meant it. Everyone in town would know before dinner, and then they wouldn't need to worry about anyone accidentally outing them.

Betty winked. "Nice seeing you, dear." She turned to leave, then seemed to think better of it and shuffled closer, murmuring under her breath, "I always thought I saw something between you two."

"Oh, n-no," Faith stammered. "It's just—"

"Pretend?" Betty asked, cackling. "You keep telling yourself that, dear. Goodbye, now." With that, she trotted off, leaving Faith a little concerned about exactly what story she'd be spreading.

AFTER FAITH AND THE WALKER FAMILY PARTED WAYS, Shane dropped Hunter off to play with his friend Izzy, then took Dylan to karate in the town hall. The class was run by Hugh MacAllister—the town councilman—and his daughter, Nadia, each of whom held a black belt, although Hugh was too frail to practice beyond the basics anymore. Shane greeted Hugh with a nod and a handshake, while Dylan bowed to him, then Shane took a seat against the wall to watch.

Most of his life was spent working, doing housework, and managing the boys, so when other people were responsible for his kids, he took advantage of the opportunity to have a catnap. He'd become adept at napping on command and drifted off within minutes of closing his eyes. He awoke to a hand on his shoulder.

"Shane? You all good, man?"

He blinked the blurriness from his vision. "Logan?"

His friend hovered in front of him, water dripping from his hair onto a towel wrapped around his shoulders. He wore board shorts and no shirt. In another life, Logan had been a professional surfer, and these days, he was still in the water every chance he got. He ran a surf school and had likely just come from a session at the beach.

"I hear you and Faith are a thing now."

It took a moment for his meaning to sink in. Shane groaned. "Who told you?"

"Nell." Logan flashed white teeth and knelt beside the chair. "She dropped by during my last class to share the gossip."

Nell was a friend of Betty's and a fellow member of the Bridge Club. He'd seen Betty speaking to Faith at The Shack but hadn't thought much of it at the time. Perhaps he should have taken more notice.

"Just for the week," he muttered, scanning the kids until he found Dylan, who was executing some kind of kick. His son was sporty, something Shane personally didn't have much experience with.

Logan's smile broadened. "So she said. But she was a little confused as to why."

"Faith's mother brought her a blind date for Erica's wedding."

Logan laughed but smothered it rapidly when Nadia glared at him across the sea of small people. He lowered his voice. "So you're her human shield against the match-making power of her parents?"

"Basically."

"Huh." Logan side-eyed him, and Shane was afraid to ask what was going on in his friend's head. "You know, I always thought you and Faith would make a cute couple."

This time, it was Shane's turn to laugh, and to receive a glare from Nadia in return. He ducked his head in apology. "Faith is so far out of my league, it's crazy anyone is buying this story in the first place. I'd never have a shot with her."

"And that," Logan said meaningfully, "Is exactly what makes you a good match."

"Yeah, right." He couldn't believe they were having this conversation. Surely Logan knew how absurd it was. "Get your head out of the clouds. The last time I got involved with a woman who was out of my league, she ran off to L.A. to become a movie star. I'd rather not sign up for a repeat."

"Faith isn't like Diana," Logan reminded him, his tone gentle.

Shane tilted his head back to stare at the ceiling and rubbed his eyes. "I know she's not, but she's still too good for me." With a sigh, he met his friend's sea-glass-blue gaze. "Let's say I was interested in her. What do I have to offer? I'm older—and not only in years. I have two children, and a home in dire need of upgrading. I'm perpetually tired, haven't bought a new outfit in as long as I can remember, and any abs I had are long gone." Letting his arms fall to his sides, he scowled at the sad picture he'd painted of himself. Logan was trying to be a good friend, but Shane didn't need that. He needed to keep his feet firmly on the ground. Faith was off-limits to him as anything more than a part-time nanny.

Logan whistled. "Whoa, dude. Didn't realize you felt that way." He shook his head, flicking Shane with droplets of saltwater. "You need to reevaluate yourself. Half the mums at school have the hots for you."

Shane huffed, exasperated. "No, they don't. It's ridiculous that you all insist otherwise."

"On days when you're the traffic warden, there's twice as many mothers who walk their little monkeys all the way to the gate, just for the chance to flirt with you."

"How would you know that?"

"Bex told me."

He should have known. Bex, who taught art classes at the school several days a week, was always giving him grief about the mums who supposedly hit on him.

"She's mistaken." Sweet, but misguided.

"If you say so." Logan's watch beeped and he glanced at it. "I need to head off, but think about what I said. Faith might play the field, but eventually, someone will snatch her up for good. If it isn't you, it'll be someone else." He raised a golden brow. "You reckon there's anyone in the bay who's good enough for her?"

Hell, no. But he just grunted.

Logan's lips pursed as if he were trying not to smile. He knew he was getting through to Shane, the jerk. "Actually, you know what? I can think of one guy who might deserve her." He paused for dramatic effect.

Shane's teeth ground together. "Who?"

Logan resembled a cat with the cream as he announced, "Kyle."

And there it was. Shane's heart sank. Logan actually made a good point. His younger brother, Kyle, was a librarian, practically a monk, and an all-round good guy. He didn't have baggage. What he did have was hoard of female library patrons slipping him their numbers. Ones he kindly let down because he was only interested in finding his true love. How could any guy compete with that? He pictured Kyle hand in hand with Faith, and his stomach knotted. He could hardly stand it. He wanted to be the only one she touched. Even imagining it made him feel sick.

Logan clapped him on the shoulder. "See you, man. Enjoy your week with Faith."

33

4

FAITH SUNK INTO THE HOT, SCENTED WATER OF HER BATH and relaxed for the first time since she'd arrived home to find her parents going through old photo albums with Leon. They meant well, but they didn't seem to see the way their friend kept eyeing Faith up like she was dessert, even when she supposedly had a boyfriend.

Resting her head against the end of the tub, she closed her eyes and released a long breath. Thank God for bathrooms with locking doors. For a while, she just lay there, enjoying the peacefulness. Then her phone rang. She considered ignoring it but decided she'd best check who it was. Sitting up, she dried her hand and reached for the phone, a smile passing over her face when she saw Shane's name on the screen.

"Hi," she answered. "Fancy hearing from you."

"We need to get our stories straight," he said, getting right to the point.

She smiled. He wasn't much of a talker, and she didn't recall him ever ringing her except to arrange babysitting. "Is that so?"

"Yes."

Her body heated. Hearing his voice while she was naked turned her on like crazy.

"Details like how we got together," he continued. "When we first kissed, what made us change from friends to lovers—things like that. They might ask, and I want to be prepared."

"You're such a boy scout." Her smile widened. "I should probably be clothed for this conversation. Do you mind if I call you back soon?"

He coughed on the other end of the line. "You're, uh, naked?"

So much for not making the conversation weird. "I'm in the bath," she explained. "I just got in, but I can wash up and call you back in ten minutes."

He made a strangled sound. "No, no, I don't want to rush you. This is fine."

"Are you sure? Because you don't sound okay."

For a few seconds, he was quiet, then he said, "I'm only human, and thinking about you naked isn't helping my concentration, but that's not your problem. Stay where you are."

She bit her lower lip, secretly thrilled that she was affecting him that way. Was her sweet, clueless Shane flustered because she was undressed on the other end of the call? How flattering. Except for returning her kiss, which could have been more out of shock than anything else, it was the first time he'd given any indication he was attracted to her. But then, he wasn't a particularly open person, and she knew it wouldn't have been easy for him to admit, so she didn't push for anything more.

"Okay, thanks." She shifted, warm water gliding over the length of her body. "As far as our story goes, I suggest we stick as close to the facts as possible. I've already told my parents it's a new relationship. We've been seeing each other for a couple of months."

"I can work with that," he said. "Perhaps we could say I've always admired you from a distance, but I was finally brave enough to make a move."

She smiled. "I like it. We could say we fell for each other a little bit more every time I watched your kids." The twang of her heartstrings told her the statement hit a little too close to home. After all, wasn't it true that she looked forward to those brief moments when they were alone more than nearly anything else?

"How about our first kiss?" he asked. "And are we sleeping together?"

"Hmm." Faith thought on this. "We kissed on the doorstep one evening as I was about to leave your place." She closed her eyes, imagining herself in the moment. "You couldn't bear to let me go without finally getting a taste of me. And as for sex...." She laughed. "We want to tear each other's clothes off so badly, but we're waiting for the right opportunity to have an evening away from the boys before we do."

FAITH'S WORDS ECHOED IN SHANE'S MIND.

You couldn't bear to let me go without finally getting a taste of me.

Did she know how close to the truth she'd struck? Every time he saw her, he grew more desperate to touch her. To taste her. Fortunately, he had the strength to resist. If she ever found out how he felt about her, she wouldn't be comfortable spending so much time around him and his sons. Hell, even just talking to her now, knowing she was nude and thinking of him, had him painfully hard. He chose to ignore the erection because it was horribly inappropriate, and also because it had been years since he'd had sex, so it wasn't unusual for him to be hard at the thought of Faith. She awoke the primal part of himself he preferred to keep under wraps.

That said, his condition had been ten times worse since she'd kissed him. Now that he knew how it felt to hold her, to rub against her, to sweep his tongue inside her mouth, he wanted to do it again and again and again until he'd memorized her.

He cleared his throat. "That sounds believable."

Except... it didn't. Not to him. If Faith were his, he doubted he'd have the mental fortitude to hold out for a suitable opportunity. He'd probably lure her into a coat closet and have his way with her the first chance he got. If possible, he grew even harder, and buried his face in his pillow, groaning.

"Shane, you okay?"

"Fine," he muttered, because he didn't want her to hang up. Strange as this conversation might be, he wanted it to continue. It had been too damn long since he'd spoken with an adult one on one without having to rush off to do something with Dylan or Hunter. "How's your family?"

She laughed, and the sound warmed him from the inside. There was just something about her. Her mood was infectious. "They're good. Mum spent the day dragging Leon around the shops, and Dad escaped to play golf with a couple of old friends. They're watching a movie at the moment, so I snuck away for quiet time."

She wanted quiet time?

"I thought you liked to be around people."

He heard her release a breath. "I do, and I absolutely

adore my family, but I'm also used to having the house to myself, so it's a big change."

"I can see that."

It hadn't crossed his mind that for all she chatted, gossiped, and flirted all day long, she went home to an empty house. Frankly, it sounded lonely. He couldn't imagine living in a place that didn't have the bustle and buzz of other people. He'd gone straight from living with his family to flatting with friends to renting with Diana. He'd never experienced the solitude of life as a single, childless person.

"Do you ever think of getting a roommate?"

"I had one for a little while. Until Tione stole her. It was nice, but I wouldn't want to invite just anyone into my home. It would need to be someone special."

"It's just as well Tione took Megan away," he said. "Having the two of you living together is too much culinary goodness concentrated in one place. Hardly fair to the rest of us."

She laughed again, and his heart skipped. "The rest of you need to up your game. It's not our fault we're awesome."

"Touché."

"Hey, Shane?"

Rolling onto his side, he cupped the phone close to his ear. "Yeah?"

"Thank you for going along with all of this. I know it's crazy."

"You're welcome. You've been helping me for years; it's about time I return the favor." Footsteps padded down the hall outside of his bedroom. "Hang on a moment."

A couple of seconds later, Dylan appeared in the

doorway, his face sleepy and pajamas rumpled from being in bed. "Is that Nana and Granddad?" he asked.

Shane shook his head. "It's Faith. Don't worry, kiddo. You're not missing out."

To his surprise, Dylan frowned. Then he mumbled something, rubbed a hand over his face, and carried on to the bathroom.

"Dylan?" Faith asked in his ear.

"Yeah," he confirmed, only now realizing how late it was. "I'd better go. Goodnight, Faith."

"Night, gorgeous."

His stupid heart swelled at the endearment, regardless of the fact she handed them out to everyone.

It doesn't mean she's into you, he reminded himself. *That's just the way she talks.*

Nevertheless, as he brushed his teeth, checked on his sons, and climbed into bed—dislodging Tinkerbell from his pillow and shifting her down by his feet—he couldn't help but wish it did mean something. He lay on his back, staring into the dark, and imagined how lovely it would be to have Faith curled beside him, her head on his pillow as they debriefed each other on the day that had passed. He'd stroke her hair, cup her cheek in his palm, and kiss her softly. She'd snuggle into his body, and he'd wrap his arms around her and tug her close.

When he finally drifted off to sleep, he could have sworn he smelled ice cream.

5

FAITH WAS SERVING THE AFTER-SCHOOL RUSH ON MONDAY when Dylan wandered into The Shack and lingered in the back. She hadn't seen him there alone before. Usually he came with Shane, Bex, or a couple of his friends. Keeping an eye on him, she scooped ice cream onto one cone after another until the line of kids and parents cleared out, leaving only her, Megan, and Dylan in the shop. Still, he didn't make a move to approach the counter, nor did he make eye contact.

"Dylan," she called. "Where's your dad today?"

He took a deep breath, almost as though he were psyching himself up, and lifted his head, meeting her gaze head-on. "He's at work, but I'm allowed to be here."

"Sure you are." Although the very fact he'd felt the need to tell her that made her doubt it. If Shane was working, he should be with Bex, or visiting with a friend, not wandering around town. "Can I get you an ice cream or a cupcake?"

He crossed his arms and stuck his chin out. "No."

Wow, that was blunt. Dylan was a polite kid. Usually he'd have added a "thanks" on the end. What was up with him? And if he didn't want ice cream or a cupcake—the two things they sold in The Shack—then why was he there?

"What did you come here for, then?" she asked, baffled.

He shrugged but didn't say anything. Okay, this was too weird.

"Meg, why don't you give us a moment?" she suggested to her friend, who'd been watching the exchange with interest.

"Okay, I'll be in the back if you need me." She left the room, closing the door gently behind her.

"What's wrong?" Faith asked, coming around the counter to sit at one of the stools in the front window, hoping he'd join her. He didn't.

"People are saying you're dating my dad."

"Oh." She winced. While she and Shane had been careful about how they behaved in front of the boys, it hadn't occurred to her that the gossip might get back to them. "Well, people shouldn't believe everything they hear."

Dylan grunted, sounding far more like a teenager than an eleven-year-old boy. "I hope it's not true, because Dad can't love you."

Her jaw dropped. "Excuse me?"

He narrowed his eyes, looking so much like a minia-ture version of Shane that it made her heart ache. "Caleb's parents broke up for two years, and they just got married again because they still love each other. You can only be in love with one person, and Dad must love Mum since he married her." His hands fisted at his sides. "It doesn't matter if you're his girlfriend right now. Mum will come back when she gets too old for Hollywood, and then we'll be a family again, just like Caleb's family."

Whoa. Faith's hands trembled. Where had that come from?

He'd never spoken to her like that before, and she didn't know how to react. She was used to taking heat from some of the more conservative older folks around town, as well as the people she'd gone to school with, but a child had never spoken to her so bluntly. Especially not Shane's child. She had to admit, it hurt. She'd thought they were friends of a sort.

His words also made her sad for him. She could tell he honestly believed that his mother was coming back and that his parents would reunite, just like his friend Caleb's had, but Diana had been gone for four years, and during that time she hadn't visited once. Faith sincerely doubted the woman was ever returning.

"Honey," she said gently, trying to mask her shock because some things were more important than her feelings. "I really think this is a conversation you need to have with your dad."

He paled. "Are you going to tell him?"

She sighed, weighing the pros and cons. "I don't want to get you into trouble, so I'm going to pretend this never happened, but you should talk it through with him. It's important that he know how you feel."

"It should be obvious," he mumbled. "And you should remember that he loves my mum."

Ice pierced Faith's heart. The worst part was, he could be right. Shane hadn't dated since his wife left, and it was possible he still had feelings for her despite everything. Faith shouldn't care about that because this was all pretend, but she did. That wasn't important though. The biggest thing was to make sure that if or when Shane started dating again, he knew what kind of headspace his son was in.

"Talk to him," she said firmly.

"Fine." He rolled his eyes. "Okay, I will."

She questioned whether he meant it. But since she'd be seeing him plenty, she could remind him until he did. Perhaps once he realized there really was nothing going on between her and Shane, he'd warm toward her again. One could hope.

As soon as he finished marking his students' math tests, Shane grabbed his keys and left the school. He headed straight to Bex's place to pick up the boys, parking a block away and walking the distance to The Hideaway. He let himself in the front entrance and turned right to knock on the door of Bex's private apartment. She lived there with her daughter Izzy, but he expected to hear any day now that she was moving in with her boyfriend—his boss—Michael Briggston.

He knocked once, then entered. "Hello, everyone."

"Daddy!" Hunter flew around the corner from the living room and wrapped his arms around Shane's legs.

"Whoa, there, Buzz Lightyear. You'll knock me over."

He giggled. "Sorry, Daddy."

Shane scooped him up into a hug, then lowered him back to the floor. Hunter was getting too heavy to carry around the way he used to.

"Where's Dylan?" he asked Bex, who'd followed a few steps behind Hunter.

"Toilet," she said. "He's done his homework." She glanced over her shoulder, then said, "Come and sit down." She led him to the dinner table, and he took a seat, concerned by her expression.

"What's wrong?"

43

Bex's lips pressed together. "I don't think it's anything to be worried about, but Dylan was late home. He walked from the bus stop, but I think he might have stopped somewhere along the way."

"Okay, thanks for telling me. Otherwise, they were all good?"

"Just like always." She smiled. "I swear, your boys make Izzy look like a terror."

"It's because Hunter follows her lead. Isn't that right, Hunt?"

Hunter nodded, and they both laughed.

"Speaking of, where is she today?"

Bex crinkled her nose. "With her father."

"Ah." Izzy's father had only recently entered her life. Shane knew Bex was having a hard time sharing her with him after having had Izzy to herself for so long. He could sympathize. God knew how he'd feel if Diana reappeared and insisted on sharing custody of their kids.

Bex propped her elbows on the table and leaned forward. "I hear you and Faith are fake dating."

"Has everyone heard that?" He raked his fingers through his hair. "It's only for a week. I'm going with her to Erica's wedding."

"To keep the matchmaking sharks away?"

"Yeah."

Hunter's eyes widened. "What sharks?"

Shane ruffled his hair. "Not real sharks, buddy."

"Oh." He deflated. "I wanna see a shark."

"Maybe someday." From a safe distance. Preferably on land.

"Okay."

Bex's mouth curved into a sly smile. "Has it occurred to you to wonder why Faith chose you? She could have

44

asked Logan or Kyle, and they'd have done it, no questions asked."

He shrugged, uncomfortable with the way she was looking at him like she knew more than he did. "Right place, right time. I turned up just a few minutes after her parents arrived."

"Perhaps," Bex allowed. "Or perhaps you're the only one she could actually imagine being with."

"Yeah, right. Because sleep-deprived single dads are such a catch."

She rolled her eyes. "You're oblivious. Forget I said anything."

The toilet flushed, and a moment later, Dylan appeared in the doorway.

"Ready to go?" Shane asked, trying to put Bex's comment to the back of his mind—and failing. Was she suggesting that Faith was interested in him? Because that was crazy talk.

"Yeah." Dylan shouldered his backpack and made for the door.

"He's been in a mood all afternoon," Bex murmured. "No idea why."

"Sorry about that."

She waved a hand. "No problem."

Shane waited for Hunter to gather his things, and they followed Dylan out of the apartment. "That was rude," Shane told him. "You didn't say goodbye to Bex or thank her for having you over."

Dylan shrugged, his expression sullen. "She knows I meant to."

"How's she supposed to know that if you don't say the words?"

He didn't respond. Shane unlocked the car and climbed in. He didn't know what was going on with his son lately. He was getting perilously close to being a teenager, and sometimes Shane wished he came with an instruction manual. They drove home with Hunter filling the silence with chatter about the painting he'd done at kindergarten. Shane parked outside their villa, grabbed his work gear from the back seat, and walked inside with Hunter. By the time they reached the door, Dylan had let himself in with the spare key and was shutting himself in his bedroom. Shane hovered outside, palm on the door, wondering if he should knock and find out what was wrong. Or was this the time to give Dylan space? Who the hell knew?

With a sigh, he opted to leave the kid alone for a while. He changed out of his work clothes, put the TV on for Hunter, placed a casserole in the oven to reheat, and fixed the boys and himself packed lunches for tomorrow. While dinner cooked, he did a few chores around the house, and when it was ready, he dished up three servings, handed one to Hunter and went to let Dylan know it was time to eat. As he approached the bedroom door, he heard voices and paused. Then, glancing around to make sure Hunter hadn't followed him, he set his ear to the wood.

"...just for a bit?"

Dylan was on the phone. But with whom?

"I know it's late, Mum. Can I just have two minutes?"

Ugh. Closing his eyes, he rested his forehead against the cool wood of the door. *Diana.*

Trust her to find a way to mess with her son's head from the other side of the world. No wonder he was in a difficult mood. Shane dithered over whether to interrupt, but he didn't want to put Dylan on the defensive. His son knew Shane didn't like it when he spoke to his mother, although he'd never come straight out and say it.

She may be a manipulative, self-centered diva, but she was still a parent. Retreating to the dining table, he sent Dylan a text, knowing he'd get it immediately. Thirty seconds later, Dylan joined them, eyes ringed with red. Shane pretended not to notice because acting concerned would only serve to alienate him.

Dinner passed without incident, but he couldn't get that phone call, or Dylan's behavior, out of his head. Hours later, he lay in bed, mulling it over, wishing he had someone to talk to. He considered calling Bex, but she had enough problems of her own.

What about Faith?

Once the possibility occurred to him, he couldn't shake it.

He shouldn't. But damn, he wanted to. She didn't have kids, so she couldn't relate, but she was so good with his, and he wanted the closeness he'd experienced during their previous late-night conversation. He reached for his phone and sent her a text.

Shane: *Are you awake?*

A moment later, he received a reply.

Faith: *Sure am, sugar. What's up?*

Without pausing to give himself time to think, he dialed her number.

"Hi," she said, voice warm and husky, giving him the impression she was snuggled beneath the blankets, same as him.

He petted Tinkerbell's head, enjoying the way she purred, then replied, "I hope it's okay to call."

"Of course it is. Was there something you need to talk about?"

Now that he had her, he hesitated, unsure how to proceed. "It's about Dylan."

"Dylan?"

Was it just him, or did she suddenly sound wary? "I'm worried about him."

"Oh." She seemed to relax. "Why's that?"

He rolled onto his side, holding the phone to one ear, and Tinkerbell puffed her fur up in response, then rearranged herself into the crook of his body. "He was late to Bex's after school today, and as soon as we got home, he called his mother."

"Is that unusual?"

"Not in and of itself," he admitted. "But he just feels... off. He's usually a level-headed kid, but he's worked up about something."

"Hmm." Faith was quiet for a few seconds. "I think I can ease your mind on one count. He dropped by The Shack after school. That's probably why he was late to Bex's."

Shane's heart lightened. His son had gone for ice cream, that was all. Suddenly, he felt silly for worrying. "That's a relief. Thanks for letting me know." He sighed into the phone. "I suppose you think I'm a helicopter dad?"

"Not at all." She came through louder than she'd probably intended, and he had to lift the phone away from his ear. "I think you're a wonderful dad, and those little boys are lucky to have you."

Her words warmed him from the inside out. "Thank you."

"No problem." She yawned. "Sorry, it's been a big day."

Guilt weighed down on him. "Sorry, I shouldn't have called."

She laughed breathily. "It's no bother. I like talking to you."

He was certain he wasn't supposed to feel quite so

pleased to hear that. It was also surprisingly nice to know she was there for him to talk to, if he needed. It had been a long time since someone had been there for him in that way.

"Seriously, Faith. Thank you. Goodnight."

"Dream of pleasant things."

6

CHOOSING THE RIGHT GRAPEFRUIT WAS A TRICKY BUSINESS. Faith weighed one in her hand, tested it for firmness, then swapped it for another. Even though she wasn't technically supposed to manhandle the fruit in the mini-mart, no one complained because they were used to her eccentricities. It didn't hurt that the locals wanted to have the best possible ice cream available at The Shack. The better the produce she purchased, the tastier her final product.

Selecting three perfect grapefruit, she added them to a basket and moved over to view the feijoas. Many tourists to the bay enjoyed sampling her feijoa-and-ginger ice cream because the fruit was something of a local treat. She added several to her basket and rounded the corner to the refrigerated section, where she helped herself to a couple of blocks of butter to use for frosting. Ever since Megan had moved to town a few months back, The Shack had been serving specialty cupcakes in addition to ice cream.

"Faith?"

Raising her head, she turned and found Shane, with

his two boys, immediately behind her. He was wearing a scarf, his cheeks and ears flushed, and looked positively edible.

"Oh, hey there. Fancy running into you."

Hunter raced over, and she set her basket down and hefted him into a hug. Dylan scowled, and the expression bothered her. She recalled the way he'd warned her away from Shane and wondered if that's what he'd been talking to his mother about the night Shane had called her, concerned about him. If so, she knew Dylan hadn't raised the matter with him like she'd suggested he do. Not that she was surprised. Typical tween boy. Thinking he knew better than everyone else. To be fair, he was a clever kid, but he hadn't grasped what difference a little life experience could make.

Arms aching, she lowered Hunter to the ground. "Are you helping your dad do the shopping for the week?"

"Yup. He reads the list and I find the things." Hunter's dirty blond hair fell over his eyes, and he had to tilt his head back to see her. So. Freaking. Cute.

"I bet you're super helpful."

"He can't reach the high things," Dylan broke in. "I have to get those." Based on his petulant pout, he wanted her to butt out. Well, too bad. She was doing her own shopping, and they were the ones who'd approached her. If he had a problem with her, he'd just have to get over his budding male ego and talk to Shane about it.

"Then you're a great team," she said evenly.

"They are," Shane agreed, scanning her from head to toe in an absent-minded way that made her doubt he was aware of even doing it. Unfortunately, her body was aware enough for the both of them. It heated as his gaze passed over her chest, which was covered by the bodice of the maroon dress she'd chosen to pair with her calf-hugging boots. After Mason ruined her senior year of high school, Faith had lost a lot of confidence and she'd avoided wearing anything this eye-catching so as not to attract unwanted attention to herself. These days she gave a one-fingered salute to anyone who said redheads shouldn't wear red and did her own thing.

"I meant to ask, are you free to come over this Friday so I can go to poker?"

"Absolutely. Same time as usual."

"Thanks." He smiled, and her silly knees became weak. "You're the only reason I have any semblance of a social life."

I wish your social life included me.

She didn't say it. He had enough on his plate without a woman he considered his friend throwing herself at him. Although from what he'd said during their phone conversations, the attraction wasn't entirely one-sided. Perhaps he wouldn't mind going beyond friendship with her.

Stop dreaming. You're not relationship material, and he's not the kind of guy who has casual affairs.

"You're very welcome. It was lovely to see you all, but I had better...." She trailed off at the sight of a familiar pair of broad shoulders entering the mini-mart. Shoulders that were topped by a crazy-handsome face with a square jaw and carelessly styled brown hair.

Oh, God. It couldn't be.

Not here. Not yet.

The man turned toward her, and his green eyes locked with hers. She massaged a hand over her heart, which was going absolutely bananas. He started her way, and she shuffled back a step, bumping into the chiller. She whimpered.

52

"Faith?" she heard Shane ask, as if from a distance. "Are you okay?"

No, she wasn't. She was very much not okay. What was Mason Delphine doing in the mini-mart in Haven Bay? He hadn't been to town in years, and that's how she'd liked it. This was her turf. And yeah, maybe he was returning for Erica's wedding, but he shouldn't be here yet. She hadn't had time to mentally prepare.

Mason didn't stop until he was directly in front of her, standing shoulder to shoulder with Shane. He was a few inches taller and broader, but thankfully his mere presence didn't send her hormones into a meltdown anymore. No, instead of the magnetic pull she used to feel toward him, he simply brought back awful memories she'd done her best to suppress.

"Hi, Faith." His voice rumbled exactly as she'd recalled.

"M-Mason. You're here." Her lips trembled and her words tripped over each other. "Hi."

He smiled, and twin dimples popped in his cheeks. He'd always had those, the bastard. There had been a time when she'd playfully licked those dimples and told him how sexy they were. She'd thought she'd had something special with him, and then he'd tossed her heart aside and humiliated her.

"It's really great to see you," he continued, apparently oblivious to her inner turmoil. "You look spectacular, as always."

Yeah, he'd been obsessed with her body—no surprise that hadn't changed—but it had taken her a while to realize that he was embarrassed by his obsession, because she wasn't the kind of girl his friends had considered suitable for a high-profile athlete. Her throat threatened to close over, and her cheeks burned with a rising tide of mortification. She glanced at the exit, willing it to suck Mason back out and deposit him on the street. Better still, in the middle of the countryside, with no car and no wallet.

When that didn't happen, she searched the people around them, many of whom had paused to watch. Tears burned in her eyes. They'd all be gossiping after this. Usually, she loved a bit of gossip, but this level of interest felt threatening and malicious. A hand alighted on Faith's arm, and she flinched.

Shane snatched it back. "What's wrong?"

She couldn't tell him. He didn't know what had happened to her, and for her dignity's sake, she'd prefer to keep it that way.

"I know this must be a shock." Mason's expression had softened. "But I'd like to speak with you in private."

—————

SHANE'S MUSCLES STRAINED FROM HOLDING BACK HIS desire to take Faith in his arms and shield her from this guy, whoever he was. He'd never seen her like this. The moment the stranger approached, she'd shut down. Her face had become even paler than usual, and her shoulders had rolled inward like her subconscious was trying to help her disappear. She didn't want anything to do with him, that much was obvious, but she wasn't acting anything like he'd have expected her to. She had no sassy quips or condescending brow raise. Instead, she looked to be on the verge of tears.

Who was this guy? An ex?

He couldn't think of anything else that would make sense.

"Faith, can I talk to you in private?" the man repeated when she didn't answer.

With apparent effort, she straightened her shoulders, her eyes continuing to dart around like a scared rabbit's. "No, I'd rather not."

Shane's concern faded. That was more like the Faith he knew. Little arms wrapped around his leg, and he looked down to see Hunter hanging off him, biting his bottom lip. Shane stroked a hand over his head. His son hated conflict and could no doubt sense the tension in the air. If he didn't move on before long, Hunter might start crying, but he didn't want to abandon Faith when she clearly needed support.

"I get that," the guy said, although his frown indicated he didn't like it. "But I need to talk to you, and I really don't think you want to do this in public."

"Do what in public, Mason?" she asked sharply, anger flashing in her eyes. "From what I remember, making things public was always your thing. *Especially* when they ought not to be."

The man—Mason—flinched as though she'd slapped him across the face. Shane had no idea what was going on here, but he felt like Faith had scored a point in some kind of ongoing battle. He wanted to cheer her on.

"Don't be like that," Mason said. "Come on. Just give me ten minutes. For old time's sake."

Shane could see her wavering. She scanned the onlookers as though wary of the attention they were garnering. She didn't want to make a scene, which was interesting in and of itself because Faith never feared making a scene. He could also tell that she wanted this encounter to be over and might agree so it would end sooner. But she shouldn't have to do something she didn't want. He weighed the pros and cons of intervening. He'd never been particularly aggressive, and Mason had thirty pounds and several inches on him, but he didn't think the guy would retaliate physically in public. Even if he did, Shane couldn't stand to see Faith hurting.

Still…. She was usually so self-assured that he didn't want to interfere if she really did have everything under control.

"Faith," he said quietly. "Do you want this guy to leave you alone?"

Her eyes caught his, and she gave a slight nod. Sucking up his courage, he put himself between Mason and Faith. "Back off. She doesn't want to talk to you."

Finally, Mason seemed to notice him after ignoring him even when they'd stood near enough to almost touch. He'd had eyes only for Faith. He sneered down at Shane, and the expression twisted his handsome face, adding a hint of nastiness. Shane stood firm and prayed to God he didn't look as petrified as he felt. Oh well, at least he was teaching his sons a valuable lesson about standing up to bullies.

"Who are you?" Mason demanded, stepping closer.

If Shane had harbored any delusion that he might be Faith's type, it vanished in the shadow of this Greek god who obviously had a past with her. He was Shane's complete opposite. But regardless of that, she needed a friend, and that job fell to him.

"I'm the man who's looking out for Faith's best interests. I want to keep her happy, and seeing you has upset her."

Oh, Mason didn't like that. His eyes narrowed, his nostrils flared, and he took another step forward. Shane refused to back down, even though they were now standing chest to chest like a pair of gladiators sizing each other up. Then Mason shook his head and looked over Shane's shoulder.

"Faith," he said. "Call off your attack dog. I never meant to upset you. I just want to talk." He smiled, and Shane wanted to plant a fist in his face to wipe that tender, too-knowing grin away. "It's been years. Surely we can be civil about this."

"Leave. Her. Alone," Shane growled. He could really use backup right about now. Unfortunately, none appeared.

"Shane is right," Faith said, her voice stronger. "Please go away."

He wanted to turn and see how she was doing but didn't dare remove his attention from Mason.

"Go on," she continued, with a dismissive hand gesture. "Shoo."

Cursing under his breath, Mason swung around and stalked off, glaring at everyone he passed on his way outside. Shane released the breath he'd been holding and shrugged, working the stiffness out of his shoulders. Summoning another burst of courage, he faced Faith. Now that Mason had gone, she'd deflated.

"Are you okay?" he asked.

"Fine."

More than anything, he wished he could take her into his arms and comfort her, but that wouldn't be appropriate.

"Dylan," he said, getting his son's attention. "Can you please take the grocery list and finish packing the shopping cart? I need a minute with Faith." When Dylan hesitated, he added, "Choose a chocolate bar each for you and Hunter."

Dylan didn't dally for a moment longer, taking the

cart and his younger brother and hurrying away before Shane changed his mind.

"What just happened?" he asked, drawing her aside so they could talk without an audience. "Who was that guy?"

She shrugged. "An ex from a long time ago. High school, actually."

And they still had that much unresolved tension?

"Is there anything you need from me? Would you like me to finish your shopping or call Megan?"

"No." She appeared to pull herself together and ran a finger beneath each eye, careful not to smudge her makeup. "I'm fine, but thanks for your help."

"Are you sure? I can—"

She cut him off. "Shane. I appreciate your help. Really, I do. But I'm okay now."

7

FAITH LONGED TO DUMP HER SHOPPING BASKET, HIGHTAIL
it out of the mini-mart, lock herself in her bathroom, and
soak in a hot bubble bath. Unfortunately, that was not to
be. Worse, Shane didn't seem inclined to leave without
some kind of explanation. And yeah, he probably
deserved one after standing up to Mason on her behalf,
but she couldn't handle the questions right now.

"That's interesting," Shane said, following her as she
picked up her basket and continued down the aisle,
"Because you're white as a sheet and your hands are
shaking."

Why must he choose now to become observant? He
was freaking clueless about most things most of the time,
and that was how she preferred it.

"I need to finish shopping and get back to work," she
said without looking at him. "You're welcome to make
yourself useful, but I've already wasted too much time."

"Okay." He kept pace with her. "What do you need?"

She rattled off the items on her list and together, they
collected them from the shelves. When they reached the

counter, Dylan and Hunter were waiting for Shane to pay the bill so they could go.

"Thanks for your help." She unloaded the contents of her basket onto the counter. Realizing she'd sounded like she was blowing him off, she took a deep breath and made an effort to be more sincere. "Really, thank you. That encounter with Mason could have gone poorly if you weren't around."

"No problem." He paid for his family's groceries, and Dylan wheeled the cart through toward the exit, clearly ready to leave. Shane hesitated before following. "If you won't talk to me, you should consider talking to one of your friends."

Faith nodded. "I'll take that under advisement. See you around."

"What was that about?" Wendy, the cashier, asked, lowering her voice so no one else would hear.

Faith just shook her head. She didn't have the energy to explain. "Bad day, that's all."

Wendy looked disappointed, but Faith wasn't about to grease the gossip wheel any more than it already had been.

"Well, I hope it improves," she said.

"So do I."

Faith carried her purchases the few blocks to The Shack, unloaded them, and returned to work. Later in the evening, she drove home. Her house, a small weatherboard place painted cream and navy, was blessedly empty. Her parents must be out with Leon. She let herself inside, crawled onto her sofa bed, and hugged her knees to her chest. While she wasn't one to let negative experiences get the best of her, Mason Delphine was a festering wound that had never healed. Lowering her forehead to the tops of her knees, she sighed, releasing all the tension from her body.

God, she wished she had someone to talk to, but she'd rather keep her bestie, Megan, in the dark about her past, and none of her other girlfriends had been in town at the time everything went to hell. Maybe that said something about her. Was it possible she'd intentionally distanced herself from anyone who might remember the lies Mason and his girlfriend, Gigi, had spread?

She could always call Charity.

The thought took root, and she fished her phone out of her purse and found her sister's number. Instead of calling, she typed out a message.

Faith: *Hey, babe. Guess who I just ran into? Mason, that's who. I have zero luck.*

While she waited for a reply, she sprawled out and buried her face in a pillow. What a mess. Mason Delphine. She'd have been happy never to see him again, but the universe worked in strange ways. A buzz signaled Charity's reply. Faith opened one eye and checked the response.

Charity: *I hope you neutered him.*

A laugh gurgled up her throat. Trust her sister to say exactly the right thing. When it came to men, they shared the bond of having epically awful taste. Other than that, they didn't have much in common. Back in the day, Charity had been popular, petite, and pretty—the opposite of her older sister—and had distanced herself from Faith because of their differences. At the time, the rejection had hurt, but they'd made their peace since then. After all, the scandal that resulted in the ruination of Charity's marriage had been much further reaching than any high school drama. Was it wrong that Faith was a little grateful about the awful things that had happened in Charity's life to bring her sister back to her?

Faith: *Not this time. Maybe next. He'll be at the wedding.*

Charity: *I'll bring a scalpel. I'll strap it to my thigh and go all Bond girl on his ass.*

Faith snorted, her hand flying to her mouth so she didn't goober all over the sofa.

Faith: *Has anyone ever told you that your name doesn't suit?*

Charity: *Only a million times.*

Faith: *Make it a million and one. Anyway, how are you doing?*

It took so long for Charity to reply that Faith began to think she wouldn't.

Charity: *About as well as I deserve.*

Faith: *You deserve awesomeness.*

Charity: *I call bullshit.*

Heart heavy, Faith stared at the ceiling and wondered how long it would take before her baby sister stopped holding herself accountable for someone else's wrongdoing. Three years had passed, and she'd still not been back to the bay. This weekend would be the first time she visited since her divorce. Hopefully, it wouldn't be another three years before her next visit.

SHANE AND THE BOYS LOADED GROCERIES INTO THE BACK of their car. Hunter was thrilled by his chocolate bar, but Dylan was in a sour mood, and Shane didn't know why.

"What's on your mind?" he asked as they drove to their villa near the waterfront.

Dylan shrugged and grunted in the way only boys of a certain age could.

"Sorry, I don't speak grunt."

Dylan glared, his lower lip thrust out. "It's weird that Faith just happened to run into us there," he said with the same enthusiasm he might use to talk about an upcoming dental appointment. "Isn't it a bit strange that she was there at the same time as us?"

Startled by the topic, Shane took a few moments to collect his thoughts. "I don't think it's particularly strange," he said, wondering what had brought this on. "We live in a small place. We're bound to run into people we know when we do the groceries. Especially in the evening, after most people have finished work for the day."

"If you say so." Dylan didn't seem convinced.

Shane pulled into their driveway and parked, turning to face his son. "Well, what do you think?"

Dylan picked at the sleeve of his shirt. "I dunno. She just seems to have a lot of drama."

"Who? Faith?" He frowned. He'd never thought her particularly dramatic, and the comment was rich coming from Dylan, considering who his mother was.

"Yeah."

It seemed like something about Faith had really gotten under Dylan's skin today.

"I thought you liked her."

Looking out the window, Dylan refused to make eye contact. "I did when she was just the babysitter."

What's that supposed to mean?

Had Dylan gotten wind of their fake relationship? They'd been careful, and he'd made sure not to say or do anything the boys might misinterpret. Whatever the case, they weren't having this conversation in the car, in front of Hunter.

"All right, time to head in. You boys going to help me? I reckon we can make it in one trip."

"Yeah!" Hunter cried, running around to the trunk. Shane followed, waiting for Dylan to begrudgingly leave his seat so he could lock up. With a team effort, they managed to get everything inside and packed into the pantry.

"Dylan, can you help Hunt pack his school bag for tomorrow while I make dinner?"

Behind him, the refrigerator door slammed. Shane whirled around.

"I'll do it later," Dylan snapped and stormed off. A moment later, his door crashed shut. Shane stared after him in stunned silence.

Whoa, what was that about?

Hunter's eyes widened and his lower lip trembled. "Daddy, why is Dylan mad?"

Shane rested a hand on his shoulder. "I don't know, buddy. But I promise it has nothing to do with you, okay?"

"He didn't want to help me." Hunter's voice quavered, and he seemed to be on the verge of tears. He idolized his older brother, and usually that was a good thing. Dylan was a pleasant, reliable kid. *Normally*. But something was going on with him at the moment, and Shane intended to get to the bottom of it.

8

FAITH ROLLED A SCOOP OF CARROT CAKE FLAVORED ICE cream—one of her personal favorites—into a cone and handed it to a pretty blonde with an English accent. "Here you go. I hope you enjoy it. Have a lovely day."

"I'm sure I will," she replied. "Thank you so much." Then she and her friend—who'd ordered chili chocolate and coconut—wandered out into the sun, and the next customer stepped forward.

"Hi, beautiful," Faith said to the little girl who had to stand on tiptoes to see into the freezer. "What can I get for you?"

"Ummm...." The girl scanned the options like it was the hardest decision she'd made in her life. A fact Faith adored. She loved to think her ice creams were so tempting that people struggled to choose between them. "Strawberry crumble, please."

Faith winked. "Good choice." She rolled the ice cream into a kid-size cone and offered it to her. "Come back later and you can try another."

She smiled shyly. "I will."

Behind the queue, the door opened, and Faith's heart

jumped for joy when Shane sauntered in with one hand stuffed in a pocket and the other rifling through his messy brown hair. He wore a vest over a pale-blue shirt, which meant he must have walked here during his lunch break. He met her gaze and she grinned, barely resisting the urge to lick her lips. He was easily as delicious as anything in the cabinet.

"Do you see what I see?" Megan murmured in her ear. Her business partner was manning the till while Faith dispersed ice cream like a champ. "Think he's here for you?"

"I'm not sure, but I'd like to find out."

Megan nodded. "Once we've finished with this lot, I can handle things while you talk to him."

"Thanks, sweetie." Faith held up two fingers to Shane, indicating she'd be with him soon, then returned to her customers and tried to pretend she wasn't wholly focused on his sexy presence lingering at the back of the shop. Once she'd worked through the backlog, she washed her hands and left Megan in charge.

"Hey, hot stuff." Taking Shane by the elbow, she led him outside, where she was less likely to be called on to help at the counter.

His cheeks pinkened, the way they always did when she used endearments. Her insides twisted in response. Did he have to be so dang adorable?

"Hi, Faith." He smiled, and she let herself enjoy a Shane Walker appreciation moment. "I wanted to check on you after yesterday and make sure you're okay."

Despite the reminder of Mason and memories she'd rather forget, his concern made her silly heart gallop. He'd been worried enough to come and see her? That meant something.

"It's sweet of you to drop by," she said. "I'm okay.

Cross my heart. I just wasn't feeling like myself yesterday."

"I could tell." His brows drew together. "I was concerned about you."

Aww.

"Thanks, but you don't need to be." She pointed to her smile. "See? Everything is good over here."

"I'm glad." His expression softened, and his eyes held hers. They were like pools of melted chocolate, and she could have stared into them forever. But then he brushed a loose hair from her forehead, his fingers caressing her skin, and a jolt passed through her. She yearned to rub her face into his palm like a cat. He curved his hand around her cheek and stepped closer. Her breath hitched. Was he actually going to do this? After years of crushing on him from a distance, was Shane Walker finally going to kiss her?

"Shane?"

"Shh," he murmured, smoothing his thumb beneath her bottom lip. He leaned forward, and her world imploded. His lips were soft on hers, and they moved slowly at first. When she didn't pull away, he bundled her closer, and his body felt wonderful. She grabbed his collar—something she'd always wanted to do—and touched her tongue to his lips. He shuddered. His lips parted and the kiss deepened. Oh Lord, the man could kiss. He might be out of practice, but she'd never know it from the way her legs liquefied, and she had to rely on him to hold her up. She opened her eyes, wanting to see him. His were closed, his dark lashes fanning out over his cheeks. So gorgeous.

Oh, man. She was in trouble.

Behind them, a throat cleared. She ignored it, clinging to him like the heroine of her favorite TV soap opera.

Alas, Shane did not seem willing to play into her fantasy. He drew back, wiped a smudge of lipstick from the side of his mouth, then looked over her shoulder.

"Uh, hi. Nice to see you."

"Well, I never."

Faith cringed. She recognized that voice too well. It was her mother's. Just when she was finally getting close to Shane. She turned and found herself the recipient of wide-eyed stares from her parents and Leon.

"Have you come for ice cream?" she asked, trying to cover the awkwardness. Meanwhile, her mind was racing. Was their presence a coincidence, or had Shane only kissed her to maintain their cover? Even though it would complicate things, she hoped for the former. The alternative was too mortifying, considering how she'd reacted.

Katherine cleared her throat again. "Actually, we came to see if you're free for lunch."

It was easier, she decided, to pretend she hadn't just mauled a man in front of them.

"Why don't you head around to the back, and I'll join you in a moment? Shane was just leaving."

"Superb idea." Darren took Katherine by the shoulder, prompting her to move. The three of them headed around the corner of the building.

Faith rested her head on Shane's chest and groaned. "Sorry about that."

"It's no problem at all." He wasn't touching her, but his breath was coming quickly, and regardless of his motivation for kissing her, it was clear it had affected him too. "That's what I'm here for, right?"

With that, he doused her ardor more effectively than if he'd pushed her off the pier. She was just another of his obligations, and he'd never truly want her. Why would a man who'd been with actress Diana Monroe ever want Faith from the ice cream parlor?

"Yeah, I guess so," she said, hoping he couldn't see her disappointment. "Thanks. I'll see you later."

Then she walked away from him and forced herself not to look back.

A COUPLE OF HOURS AFTER KISSING FAITH, THE GROUND still felt unsteady beneath Shane's feet. Their encounter had rocked him, and it had nothing to do with his long dry spell and everything to do with how compelling and addictive she tasted. He'd told himself it was okay to kiss her because he was playing a role, but in hindsight, he could admit to himself that the kiss had been more about staking his claim in front of the competition than keeping up the charade. Mr. Boy-Band Hair needed to know that Faith wasn't available for any shenanigans.

A shrill bell pierced the air and signaled the end of the school day. Shane's students started stuffing their things in backpacks and glancing at the clock, waiting for him to release them.

"Don't forget your homework," he said, standing to erase the notes from the whiteboard. "Now, be off with you."

They didn't need any more prompting. Thirty seconds later, his classroom was empty. He shrugged into his high-vis vest for traffic warden duty and was about to head to the gate when his phone rang. Fishing it out of his pocket, he saw his ex's name flash across the screen. Damn. He could have ignored nearly anyone else, but he and Diana rarely spoke, so if she was contacting him, it must be important. Knowing her, she'd waited until this exact time to call because she'd been stewing and wanted to talk the instant he was free.

He answered. "Hello, Diana."

"Shane." She sniffed, the sound disdainful enough to get on his nerves. Diana had a way of doing that, when it normally took a lot to bother him. Perhaps he was predisposed against her because of the fact she'd abandoned their marriage and sons to pursue fame and fortune in Los Angeles when she'd had no guarantee of success, and then had hidden from them so well it had taken him a year to track her down.

Yeah, that might have something to do with it.

"I'm at work. What do you want?"

"Haven't you finished?"

He sighed and willed himself to stay calm. "Just because class gets out at three doesn't mean I'm done for the day."

"Well, it ought to." She spoke with a slight American accent—something she'd picked up since leaving the bay. "I called to remind you that you shouldn't expose our sons to other women. Especially ones who aren't serious relationship material. If you want to fool around with some girl, kindly do it away from Dylan and Hunter."

Shane's jaw dropped. The nerve of her. As if she had any right to dictate what he could and couldn't do in his private life. She was in the magazines with a new man every other month. And besides, what was she talking about? He could only assume she was referring to Faith, and the boys hadn't been around when he'd kissed her earlier. They hadn't seen anything inappropriate.

"I have no idea what you mean," he said bluntly.

Diana tutted. "Dylan told me about your new girl-friend. Faith, is it? I remember her. Chubby redhead. She must be, what? Five years younger than you?"

He'd have to talk to Dylan about the situation with Faith. Clearly, his son had read everything wrong. Or perhaps he was a little closer to seeing the truth than Shane would like him to be. Regardless, he wasn't coming clean to Diana. For starters, it wasn't any of her business if he was dating. After the way she'd left, he had the right to see anyone he wanted. It had been three years since the divorce, for crying out loud. She'd shacked up with a famous director while they'd still technically been married.

"Diana, you don't have any say in who I date."

She scoffed. "I do if it affects our sons."

"The boys haven't stopped you from dating other men. Do you know how often Dylan sees photos of you with some strange guy and asks who he is?"

A beat of silence passed, and he thought he'd gotten through to her, but then she said, "They haven't had to face any of the men I've been with. Your girlfriend will become part of their daily lives. It's entirely different."

He resisted the urge to throw the phone across the room. "They haven't had to face any of the men you date because you made the choice to fly halfway around the world and leave them behind!"

She gasped, and he could picture her expression— equal parts hurt and shock. But as far as he was concerned, she deserved it. People couldn't make decisions like that and expect not to be called out on them.

"I needed to spread my wings." Her tone was defensive. "Explore my options and see whether my career could go anywhere. A few soap episodes in New Zealand are one thing, but I wanted to make it big. Besides, my relationships are different because I'm expected to flirt and be seen with high profile men as part of my job. I don't see you complaining when I send birthday presents you couldn't afford."

"Then you haven't been listening." He checked the clock. "Look, I need to go. You're being a hypocrite, and I can make my own choices about who I do and don't see in my spare time. If you wanted to have more say, you shouldn't have run away. Goodbye."

Hanging up, he gave in to the impulse to stamp his foot just once, then headed out for duty.

9

AFTER LOCKING THE SHOP ON FRIDAY EVENING, FAITH drove to Shane's place. It was her first time watching the boys since Dylan's outburst, and nerves gnawed at the lining of her stomach. Did he still resent her, or had he come around? She supposed she'd find out soon enough.

She parked, and headed inside, the box of pizza she'd purchased from Cafe Oasis tucked beneath her arm, because she wasn't above bribery. She knocked once and waited on the doorstep. When Shane appeared, his tie askew and his shirt partially unbuttoned, she suppressed a sigh. It was a shame he had a T-shirt on beneath his button-up. She wouldn't have minded seeing a flash of his chest. Would it be hairy or smooth? She liked to think he'd have a light dusting of hair. He was a manly kind of guy, but not over-the-top.

"Hey," he said, cracking a grin when he saw her. "What have you got there?"

"Pizza. Is that all right?"

"All right?" he echoed. "It's great. Dylan has been in a funk ever since we got home, and I can't seem to shake him out of it. I think it's something to do with his mum.

They've been talking a lot lately, but when I tried to get him to talk to me, he immediately shut down. Maybe pizza will brighten him up."

"Maybe." But she didn't think so. If Dylan hadn't spoken to Shane about his worries, then she doubted her presence would help. It was probably just salt in the wound. She stepped inside, past Shane, and turned to face him. "Anything I need to know?"

He continued unbuttoning his shirt, then shrugged out of it. "Dylan needs to finish his homework, and I asked him to load the dishwasher before he goes to bed."

"Okay, good to know." She carried on through the living area and dropped the pizza off in the kitchen, then checked the time. "Go. Have fun. The guys must be ready to start playing by now."

"Probably." He grabbed a jacket that was slung over the back of a chair, slipped his arms into the sleeves, then ran a hand through his hair, unintentionally spiking it up. "The cat needs to be fed in half an hour. Hunter wants to do it, but make sure you supervise him, or he'll end up feeding her the entire bag of kibble."

"Homework, dishwasher, cat," Faith repeated. "Got it. Now get out of here." She waved her hand at him in a shooing motion.

He cast a glance around as though making sure everything was in its rightful place, then looked back at her. "Thanks a million. I'll see you later."

"Bye now."

He left, and she went to check on the boys. Hunter was crashed in front of the TV, watching a cartoon show with robots. Meanwhile, Dylan was in his room with the door shut.

She knocked and called out, "Hey, Dylan, your dad

has gone now. I brought pizza if you want to take a break for dinner."

"I'll do my homework first," he yelled without opening the door. It seemed he wasn't going to make the night easy on her.

"Okay, we'll reheat it when you're ready." Returning to the living area, she dropped to the floor beside Hunter and sat cross-legged. "What are you watching?"

"Transformers." He wriggled closer and rested his head in her lap.

Faith smoothed a hand over his soft hair. "When this finishes, do you want to have pizza and watch a movie?"

He beamed and scrunched his eyes up. "Can I choose the movie?"

"Absolutely, you can."

They watched the rest of the episode together, although Faith paid scant attention to the TV, focused instead on the insanely cute boy dozing on her knee. Eventually, she roused him and popped the pizza into the microwave. Once they had food, they sat side by side on the sofa, and she scrolled through Netflix movies until Hunter found one he liked.

Five minutes in, Dylan emerged from his bedroom and padded down the hall.

"Hey there." Faith smiled at him. "Pizza is in the box on the counter. Do you want to join us? It isn't very far through."

His shoulders hunched. "I need to write a speech for school."

"But it's past seven on a Friday night. Wouldn't you rather do it over the weekend?"

"No." He glared so fiercely that she took a mental step back. "I'd rather get it all done now. That's what responsible people do, and I have enough going on without having to worry about it later."

Okay, low blow. He was right, of course. Dylan was a responsible kid. He got good grades and played on a number of sports teams, but she got the impression he was trying to tell her to get lost, and it wasn't only about his homework.

"Eat out here, though. You know your dad doesn't like it when you eat in your room."

"I know that. I know my dad better than anyone else because I'm his number two."

Well, that answered that. He was still laboring under the false impression she and Shane were more than friends, and he didn't like it. She deflated. Even though their relationship was just for show, it hurt that he wasn't open to viewing her as more than the babysitter. She'd always thought they got along well. She liked him, and she'd believed he liked her too. Apparently, he had a limit.

"Dad says he's canky," Hunter murmured, blinking up at her.

"I think you mean 'cranky,'" Faith corrected, melting in the face of his adorableness.

"Yeah. So don't take it wrong."

"Thank you, honey. I'll try not to."

Dylan didn't join them while he ate, opting to scoff his pizza in the kitchen before going straight back to his room. He came out a while later, seemingly in a better mood, and played hallway cricket with Hunter for a while. Eventually, they swapped to video games, and Hunter fell asleep. Faith carried him to bed and returned to find that Dylan had vanished into his room. She hovered outside his door, wondering whether to try talking to him, but in the end, she chickened out. Instead, she sprawled on the sofa, pulled a blanket over herself, and called Megan. She needed to hear a friendly voice, even if they'd spent all day together.

"Hi, gorgeous."

"Hey, Faith. How are you?"

Faith groaned. "Confused. I'm so confused."

"Oh?" Megan perked up. "Why is that?"

"It's all the Walker family's fault," she grumbled, snuggling deeper beneath the blanket. "Hunter is the only uncomplicated one."

Megan laughed. "Well, he is four. Give him sweets and a toy and he's happy."

"I wish all men were so easily pleased." Faith sighed. "Dylan still hates me. He hasn't outright said it, but he holed up in his room all night and wouldn't even sit with us for dinner."

"Sorry." Megan's voice was soft, and Faith held the phone closer to her ear. This was why she loved her friend. Megan was twice as empathetic as anyone else. "That must be hard."

"It is," she admitted. "This is going to sound stupid, but the worst part is that I keep thinking... why would it be so bad if I were dating Shane? This whole wedding date thing is fake, but he's a great guy. It hurts that Dylan is so anti us because I'd always thought that if something happened between Shane and me, at least I'd already know his sons love me. But Dylan couldn't make it clearer that he doesn't want me anywhere near his dad."

"Hmm." Megan seemed to be mulling it over, and Faith waited, knowing she'd say something eventually. "From what you've said, Dylan is close to his mum, right?"

"Yeah, I think so. They talk on the phone most weeks."

"So perhaps he holds out hope that she'll come back. Maybe she doesn't seem as distant to him as she does to everyone else because they keep in touch." Something rustled, and Faith heard barking in the background. "Shh, Pix," Megan ordered. "Anyway, what I'm saying is, he might think she's going to turn up and that it's his job to protect her place in the family."

"Huh." Faith could see the sense in that. Especially when she kept in mind that Dylan was still a kid, even if he seemed older at times. And that comment he'd made about his friend's parents who'd reunited…. Perhaps he hoped the same thing would happen with his own parents. "I can see that. Thanks, Meg."

"No problem. Just give him time. He'll come around. Don't try to force him."

At this, Faith smiled wryly. It wasn't in her nature to let a problem simmer on the back burner. "I'll try."

"Keep in mind that it could also be something else. Maybe he's used to having his dad to himself and doesn't want to share. Maybe he's worried Shane won't have time for him anymore."

"Hmm. Maybe," Faith mused. "Anyway, I'd better let you go. Kiss that sexy beast of yours for me."

"Oh, I will. Don't you worry."

POKER NIGHT WAS THE CLOSEST SHANE EVER CAME TO feeling like a real person rather than just a dad. No one needed his attention, there were no messes to clean up, and he could drink a few beers, safe in the knowledge that his boys would be taken care of. For the first year after Diana had left him, he'd stopped spending Friday evenings with his friends, certain that he'd be an irresponsible father if he did. But by now he'd come to realize that, much as he loved his sons, he needed to get away sometimes, and he could trust Faith or Bex to keep them in one piece.

Logan Pride hosted the game in his apartment above The Den—the local pub. Usually Shane was reluctant to leave at the end of the evening, but this time, he was eager to get home and see Faith. He walked back with his hands in his pockets to protect them from the chilly air. The stroll home was a great way to sober up, but his state of moderate sobriety didn't stop his heart from stuttering when he stepped into the living room and found Faith asleep on his sofa. She was cuddled beneath a blanket with only her head sticking out the top. Her face was slack, and she must have scrubbed it clean at some point because he could see a few of the freckles she typically hid beneath makeup.

Crossing to her side, he touched her shoulder. "Faith, wake up."

She murmured something and rolled over, burying her face in the cushions. A curtain of red hair fell over the edge of the sofa, brushing the floor. His heart constricted. It felt so right to come home to her.

"Faith," he repeated, shaking her shoulder more firmly. "It's me."

She moaned, and a bolt of desire shot straight to his groin. Dear God. He willed his body to calm down. She rolled over and blinked up at him, eyes slumberous. "Shane."

Inhaling slowly, he tried not to be turned on by the breathy quality of her voice. "How are the boys?"

She sat up and flipped her hair over her shoulder. "Both in bed. Hunter fell asleep early. Dylan tried to stay awake, but he got too tired."

"I'm glad you convinced him to go to bed." Shane perched on the other end of the couch. "I know he likes staying up to make sure I come home. I think it's a hangover from when his mother left. He's scared I'll leave and not come back. But I hate to think of him getting anxious over it every Friday."

Her face crinkled with sympathy, and she reached for his hand. "I'm sorry. That must be difficult."

"It is." But he didn't want to get all maudlin. "How did the night go? No problems?"

"Nope." She released him, apparently getting the message that he wanted to keep the tone light. She tilted her head and pursed her lips. His gaze became glued to that pink curve. She was so beautiful. Even now, with no makeup on and sleepy eyes. Hell, especially now. "Well, except that Hunter got a boo-boo. He and Dylan decided to play cricket in the hall and Hunter tripped over and got carpet burn on his knee. We gave it a wash and put on one of those Band-Aids with the Transformers on them. Bam." She made a 'Voila' gesture with her hands. "All better."

He shook his head, taken aback by the love he saw shining in her eyes. Love and affection for his sons. She was so sweet. And damn if he couldn't see her fitting into their lives perfectly.

"No tears?"

"None after that. It helped that Dylan played video games with him afterward." She laughed, and it lit her face. God, he wished he could come home to this every day. "You should have seen them. They were like Big Me and Little Me. So cute. Not that I told Dylan that."

"Of course not." He shook his head again, admiring her. Against his better judgment, words spilled from him, unfiltered. "You're so beautiful."

She stared at him in shock. For a long moment, he wondered if he'd crossed a line, but then her lips twitched and she laughed, husky from sleep. "Sure I am, with my hair standing up like a troll doll's and goobers in my eyes from napping." She touched the corner of her mouth. "Please tell me I didn't drool."

She wasn't taking him seriously, and for some reason, that didn't sit well. He stood, then offered a hand, and when she slipped hers into it, he tugged her upright.

"I'm serious, Faith. You're beautiful, and if the circumstances were different, fake is the last thing I'd want our relationship to be."

Pursing her lips, she eyed him warily. "Are you drunk?"

"Do I seem drunk? I know exactly what I'm saying."

What he didn't know was why he was choosing now to say it. He'd been attracted to her for years without acting. Why now? Was it because he'd discovered she tasted sweeter than ice cream and more addictive? Looping his arms around her waist, he pulled her close and rested his chin on the top of her shoulder.

"You're gorgeous, smart, and vivacious. I know you'd never be interested in someone like me, but I'd like to pretend, just for a moment. Can I pretend, Faith?"

"Shane," she said softly. "A man like you has a lot to offer. You're sexy, intelligent, and a great dad. Your wife was a fool to leave you."

That was more sweetness than he could withstand. He kissed her. To his complete and utter surprise, she kissed him back. Their tongues tangled, and he hoped he didn't taste like beer and pretzels. God knew that wasn't sexy. Her tongue stroked his, and without conscious thought, his hand curved around her breast and cupped it, testing its weight. She gasped, and he took that as a sign he was doing something right. Running this thumb over the outside of her dress where her nipple would be, he used his other hand to scoot her hips closer. The sensation of her body against his drove him out of his mind. It was too much. He couldn't think of anything other than her. The small sighs she made, the way her hands fisted in his jacket, the way her thighs perfectly cradled his growing erection.

Shit.

He was hard. He needed to stop.

Abort mission.

Grasping at the thinnest thread of his self-control, he reined himself in and peeled his body from hers. His breath came in pants, and he rested his forehead against hers while he returned to his senses.

"Wow," she murmured, her lips dangerously close to his. "That might have been the hottest kiss of my life."

Hell, yes.

Was it wrong that her comment made him feel like a gladiator who'd just felled his opponent?

"No one is around," he rasped once he could speak. "That kiss was for you and only you."

Her eyelashes fluttered, but not in a calculated way. More like he'd caught her off guard. Her forehead crinkled, and she looked unsure of herself and so much younger and more vulnerable than usual. He wished he could recapture her lips and keep on kissing her, but he didn't want to push too far. Whatever was growing between them, he didn't understand it, and he could tell she didn't either. They shouldn't rush into anything. Especially not in his living room where the boys could walk in at any moment.

"Thanks for watching the kids." Letting her go, he

stepped away far enough that he couldn't touch her even if he wanted to. "I'll see you at the wedding tomorrow."

Appearing to shore up her defenses, she nodded and gave him a lopsided grin. "Wear your most James Bond suit. I can't wait."

With that, she winked, grabbed her purse, and made for the door. He stared after her, wondering whether he was mad to consider that maybe—just maybe—this attraction between them could continue beyond tomorrow.

10

FAITH GRABBED A COOKIE FROM THE STASH BETWEEN THE passenger's seat and driver's seat and popped it into her mouth. "Oh my God. So good."

"That one is cherry chocolate," Megan said from the other side of the car. It was early morning on the day of Erica's wedding and they were on their way to the nearest mall, which was a reasonable drive from the bay.

"This is why it's dangerous to be best friends with an incredible baker." Faith switched on the indicator and turned a corner. "I've put on five pounds since you moved to town."

"And it's all gone to your boobs and butt," Megan replied smartly. "You know you suit your curves."

Faith shrugged. Most of the time, she liked her curves just fine, but every now and then an old insecurity filtered back in. Usually in the form of a memory she'd rather forget. She shook off the impending doubt. They were on their way to buy her a dress, and not just any dress, but one that would make Shane want to drag her into the nearest bedroom while simultaneously showing Mason exactly what he'd missed out on.

"What style are you looking for?" Megan asked as though reading her mind.

"Something that will blow Shane's socks off. I'll know it when I see it."

"Hmm." Megan nibbled on her own cookie. "How are things going with him?"

"He kissed me again." She couldn't keep the words inside. She'd never been any good at that. "It was quite a kiss, even though he might have been tipsy." Remembering the moment, she had to fan herself. "Actually, maybe he kissed me *because* he was tipsy."

Megan glanced over. "How do you figure?"

Faith stole another cookie. "I have a hypothesis." She took a bite. "I hypothesize that he likes me, but for some stupid reason he's decided he can't have me, so he exercises his amazing self-restraint to keep away."

"Interesting theory." Megan nodded. "Maybe he thinks he needs to dedicate all of his time to Dylan and Hunter, and that it would be selfish to date."

"I'm not sure I want to date him anyway."

Megan's brows drew together. "Why not?"

Ugh, of all the conversations she didn't want to have.

"Let's just say that I'm not sure I'm relationship material." She waggled her brows. "But Shane is a great guy, and I enjoy it when he kisses me."

"Of course you're relationship material," Megan countered because she was the world's sweetest person and couldn't let a slight against her friend go unchallenged. "Why would you think otherwise?"

Maybe because a string of boyfriends had told her so. She'd heard every variation of "You're too much" imaginable. But she didn't want to go down that road, so she changed the subject.

"I bet Tee is great in bed. Have you gone there yet?"

Megan's jaw dropped and her face flushed violent red. But then she straightened and folded her arms primly. "He is pretty amazing."

Envy lanced through Faith, swift and hot, but she slammed a lid on it. The last thing she needed was to be jealous of her best friend's sex life. Megan had been through hell and deserved every bit of happiness she had.

"*You're* amazing," Faith said back.

They both laughed, and the tension evaporated. A while later, they arrived at the outskirts of Auckland. Megan directed Faith to the mall, and she cruised the parking building until she found a spot. They strode inside together, on a mission. Faith did most of her shopping online because that was the best place—other than thrift stores—to find retro outfits. But today, she wanted something different. Rather than being quirky, eye-catching, or any of the other adjectives people usually applied to her, she wanted to be beautiful.

Taking her arm, Megan steered her into the kind of boutique that screamed expensive. Normally Faith would run screaming at the first sign of anything with a designer label, but she had enough money in the bank to splurge this once. Maybe she'd get a purse too. Oooh, and a new lipstick. Because nothing said sexy like a brand-new shade of red, or maybe bright pink. She started for a rack, ready to flick through the options, but Megan stopped her and summoned a retail assistant with a wave of her hand.

"Can I help you?" the well-coiffed assistant asked.

"Yes," Megan said. "We're looking for an outfit for my friend. She has a wedding this evening and wants something sexy enough to outshine everyone but the bride."

"No, I—"

Megan hushed her with a look. "Yes, you do."

Faith's eyebrows shot up. She'd never seen this side of her friend. Bossy. Confident. In charge. She liked it.

The assistant, who's name, according to her tag, was Becky, eyed her critically. "What do you have in mind?"

Faith let Megan answer. This was her show.

"Whatever you think is most appropriate."

Becky's eyes flashed with excitement. "Okay. Wait over by the changing room. I have some ideas." She bustled off, and the girls headed for the area she'd indicated.

"What was that?" Faith asked.

Megan ducked her head. "Charles was very image-conscious." Charles, her abusive ex, was currently incarcerated and awaiting trial. "Being with him meant always looking my best. I picked up a thing or two."

"Huh." Faith looked her up and down. "But you're always so...."

"Casual?" Megan supplied, her smile wry. "He's the reason for that."

"Well, good for you, sugar."

"In this case, my knowledge is good for you too."

Becky returned, weighed down by a number of dresses. She beelined for one of the changing cubicles and hung them inside, then turned to Faith. "Try each one on, no exceptions, and come out here so we can see." She sat, and Megan did the same.

Intrigued, Faith entered the cubicle and scanned the selection. There were at least half a dozen dresses ranging in length from mid-thigh to ankle and encompassing all colors except orange and yellow—a good call because they washed her out.

She opted for the red first to get it out of the way. She was well-versed in which shades of red she could pull off, and this wasn't one of them, but other than that, she did like the dress. It had a swishy skirt and low-cut bodice, displaying her best features to great advantage. Stepping back into her black heels, she marched out to show the others.

Becky cringed at the color. "Well, it was worth a shot."

Next, she tried a purple dress that she was inclined to like because the long skirt made her appear taller. Alas, Megan rejected it, saying it wouldn't wow anyone. The brown was elegant, but no one could call it sexy. The blue felt more like something she'd usually wear, and she pirouetted in front of the mirror, pleased when the skirt flared up.

"It's a lovely dress," Megan said. "Definitely eye-catching."

"You think it's the one?" she asked.

Becky held up a finger. "No one is commenting on what is or isn't 'the one' until you've tried them all. Let's see the black."

Faith changed, and then strutted out like a model on the catwalk, chuckling at the notion. Certainly no models had hips or an ass like hers.

Megan nodded approvingly. "Very sexy."

"But is it too sexy for a wedding?" Becky asked, tapping her chin in thought.

The fact they had to think about it was enough for Faith to add it to the rejects pile. She didn't want to look like she was trying too hard. That left one dress, which she'd been saving for last. It was emerald green with a plunging neckline and a fitted skirt. While she loved the color, she didn't think she could pull off something so formfitting. Nevertheless, she dropped it over her head and wriggled in, then turned to face herself in the mirror. She froze. The dress caressed her every curve without being tight and it flattered her complexion perfectly. She looked like a seductress. Toying with her hair, she imagined how she'd look once it was done.

Brilliant. This was the dress.

"Uh, Faith, are you coming out?" Megan asked.

She stepped out and twirled. "What do you think?"

Megan clapped her hand to her mouth, eyes wide. "You look amazing!" She turned to Becky. "Doesn't she?"

Faith grinned. "Tell me this is not the dress. I dare you."

"That's definitely the dress," Becky agreed. "Your boyfriend isn't going to know what hit him."

Faith and Megan exchanged a glance but neither corrected her.

"Now you need shoes."

"Oh, I have the perfect shoes for this dress already," Faith said. One of the perks of her shoe obsession was that she had enough pairs to match nearly every outfit. "High black sandals with a narrow heel."

Becky gave her a once-over. "Yes, that ought to do it. But are you sure I can't entice you to look?"

"Not today, sorry. I have a salon appointment to get to."

———

SHANE HAD NEVER UNDERSTOOD THE EXPRESSION "swallowed my tongue" until he got a look at Faith upon picking her up for the wedding. His eyes bugged out, and he only just managed to snap his mouth shut before drooling. If he thought she'd been attractive before, she was absolutely stunning in a sleek green dress with her hair pinned up in a knot on the back of her head. He was accustomed to seeing her in makeup, but tonight, her usual retro flair was absent, Faith having opted for classic and elegant. She could have been a different person, and that unsettled him. He knew who she was, didn't he? Then why did he have the creeping sensation there was a side of her he'd never seen?

"Hi, handsome."

At least her smile was familiar. But damn, he felt out of his element. Earlier, Bex had told him he looked smart after she'd trimmed his hair and he'd changed into his newly pressed suit, but those things seemed inconsequential compared to how glorious Faith was. She was so far out of his league, it was ridiculous.

"Wow," he breathed. "Just wow. You're stunning."

She brightened. "I am, aren't I? It's all because of the dress. It's magical."

"It's not the dress." It was her. As soon as she stepped foot outside, she'd be the center of attention. Suddenly, he wanted to forbid her to leave the house. It was a miracle she'd remained single for as long as she had. When men saw her as she was now, they'd be tripping over themselves to have her.

"You're so sweet." She kissed his cheek. *Not* where he wanted to be kissed. He wanted to strip off everything except her shoes and have his way with her until she never looked at another man again.

"I'm not being sweet," he argued, annoyed she'd believe that. Surely after the way he'd kissed her, and held her, and spoken to her last night, she should know better. "You're the most beautiful woman I know."

For a moment, her expression seemed to soften, but then something dark flitted through her gaze and she swatted his arm. "You smooth talker. Come on, let's get to the ceremony. They'll be starting soon, and I promised to meet Charity outside and walk in together."

Charity.

Her sister. The one he'd never met but had certainly heard of. He tried to help Faith into the car, but she brushed him off and got into the passenger seat, drawing her skirt tighter across her thighs. As he buckled up, he glanced down at her creamy skin and nearly groaned. She was going to be the death of him, and she seemed completely oblivious to it. He needed to adjust himself before his condition worsened, but he didn't want to be obvious about it, so he waited until they were driving to do so under the guise of untwisting the leg of his suit.

The ceremony was being hosted at the town hall, and when they arrived, Faith leapt out and scanned the vehicles that lined the street. She beelined for a faded red hatchback that looked like it dated back to the eighties. Whoever was inside wound the window down, and Faith leaned in. Meanwhile, he had to readjust himself again as her skirt clung to her round bottom. When everything was in place, he joined her, and smiled down at the petite strawberry blonde behind the steering wheel. He could see a resemblance to Faith in the shade of her hazel eyes and the shape of her mouth and assumed this was Charity. She was slightly younger than her sister, but the vast quantity of foundation plastered on her face couldn't conceal the dark circles beneath her eyes. Her knee jostled restlessly, and she was dressed to blend into the background, which was unusual considering she looked like a woman who ought to stand out in a crowd.

"Charity, this is Shane, my fake date," Faith said.

Shane frowned. "She knows?"

"Yeah." Faith shrugged. "There's not much I don't tell her."

He wondered whether Charity knew they'd kissed last night.

Charity's gaze settled on him, unnerving in its intensity. "He's not your usual type." Damn if that comment didn't sting. But then she added, "Maybe there's hope for you yet." She opened the door and glided out, as graceful as a ballerina. Stopping in front of him, she offered her hand. "I'm very protective of my sister." Her grip was disconcertingly firm, and her eyes narrowed with an unspoken threat. "You hurt her, and I'll hurt you."

"Char!" Faith draped an arm around Charity's shoulder and grimaced apologetically. "Sorry, she doesn't get out much."

"I approve." Anyone who wanted to protect Faith had his support.

"See?" Charity shrugged. "I didn't scare him off. I couldn't anyway, because this is just pretend, right?" The way she stared at him like she could see straight through him made him wonder if she'd noticed how preoccupied he'd been with her sister's ass a few moments earlier.

"Right," Faith agreed. "Shall we head in so we can get a good seat?"

Charity glanced around and ducked her head, looking as though she wished she could become invisible. "I'd actually prefer to stay out here for as long as possible. You know, avoid giving the gossips a chance to spread rumors before the ceremony begins."

Spread rumors? Scanning the area, Shane noticed what he hadn't before. A number of locals were casting glances in their direction, seeming fascinated by Charity —and not in a nice way. More in that fashion people had when they were waiting for disaster to strike.

"Char, you can't hide forever."

"Oh, yeah?" Charity's eyes flashed. "Just watch me. I'll stay for the ceremony, and then I'm out of here."

When the limo carrying the bridal party arrived, Shane and the girls hustled inside and claimed seats in the back row. For the entirety of the ceremony, he paid scant attention to the goings on at the front of the hall, too focused on Faith and the play of emotions over her face. She was an open book, and he admired that about her.

She was also gorgeous.

Reaching between them, he entwined his fingers with hers. He heard her breath catch, but she didn't look away from the bride and groom. She seemed entranced—and was that a hint of longing in her expression? He shifted closer to her. God, he'd never expected to have the chance to feel her like this, and without the boys around, he didn't have to worry about being too affectionate. If he wanted to touch her, he could. In fact, he should. It would play right into their ruse.

Dipping his head closer to hers, he murmured, "You deserve a day like this." She turned ever so slightly, and their eyes caught. "You deserve everything," he whispered, "And I wish I could be the one to give it to you."

11

FAITH SHIVERED. SHE DIDN'T KNOW WHAT TO MAKE OF Shane's sudden attentiveness. She clapped when the happy couple were announced man and wife, then whooped as they kissed, and exited down the center aisle. The reception would be held at a restaurant just out of town, surrounded by a lush garden where photos had already been taken earlier in the day. She and Shane farewelled Charity, who'd decided not to stay, and drove over together. They were early, so they walked through the gardens while they waited for things to kick off. He couldn't seem to keep his hands to himself, and she loved it. First, he rested a hand in the small of her back, then slid it over her hip, around the curve around her butt, and repeated the motion. She wasn't even sure he knew he was doing it. Around them, the flowerbeds burst with color, and their light perfume permeated the air.

Shane took her hand and drew her around a corner so they were separated from the other wedding guests by shrubbery. As soon as they were out of sight, he grabbed her by the hips and drew her to him.

"Can I kiss you?" he asked.

Her heart hammered in her throat. No one could see them, which meant he wasn't playing a role. He truly wanted to kiss her. She should refuse, but he was too tempting. Instead of replying, she took the initiative and pressed her lips to his. He pulled her closer, returning the kiss. She swayed into him, breathing him in, loving the way he tasted and smelled. Better than ice cream. So much better. Their tongues touched, and he groaned. Lust speared downward. Holy moly, she'd love to hear that groan every day. Preferably when they were both naked and he was sliding inside her.

He drew back, panting, and touched his forehead to hers. "God, Faith."

She angled her head, reclaiming his mouth. She hadn't had enough of him yet.

"Whoa, sorry!" The exclamation made them leap apart. "We'll just, um...."

Faith righted herself and turned. Brooke and Jack were standing at the end of their private grotto, their cheeks flushed as they held hands.

"We were looking for a private spot," Jack said wryly. "Guess we need to find one that's not already taken."

Brooke giggled, and her hand flew to her mouth. She looked mortified. "We're so sorry. I guess the wedding got us all excited, what with being so recently engaged ourselves."

"No problem," Faith said breezily, as though people walked in on her making out with the guy of her fantasies all the time. "We've had our turn. We'd better get back to the party now." She drew Shane away, noticing the way Brooke's eyes widened and turned speculative. Everyone in town knew she and Shane were only dating for appearances, but now people might begin wondering if there was more to the story. Not that she expected Brooke to gossip, but these things tended to find their way into the world.

"Well, that was awkward," Shane said as they returned to the group. "I'm sorry. I just couldn't seem to stop myself."

"There's nothing to apologize for," she assured him. "Let's see who we're sitting with."

It turned out they'd been seated at a table with her parents, Leon's parents, and Leon. Way to make things awkward. Since they were the first to go inside, Faith rearranged the name tags so she wasn't sandwiched between Shane and Leon because that wasn't a situation she wanted to be in. Before long, other people filtered in and joined them.

Dinner was buffet-style, and when they finished eating, they made conversation around the table. It was then that she noticed Shane's arm creeping along the back of her chair. When Leon asked her what it was like living in the bay, his hand dipped down and stroked the side of her neck. She shivered and leaned into the caress. His touch ignited all of her senses, and she couldn't help but hope that maybe it wasn't all acting. As he removed his arm and rested his hand on her thigh beneath the table where no one could see, she wanted it to be for no other reason than that he liked to touch her.

They sat through speeches and toasts, and with each one that passed, Shane grew bolder, caressing the inside of her thigh with his thumb, working higher, danger-ously near to the place where all her body heat had centered. If only he'd close the final distance. But he didn't. Probably just as well because she doubted she'd be able to hold herself together if he did. She wanted him too much.

When the music started, she shot to her feet. "Want to dance?"

Shane's brow furrowed. "I'm not what you'd call a great dancer. Or even a passable one."

She smiled. "As long as you're an enthusiastic one, I don't care."

Grabbing his hand, she drew him onto the dance floor. A slow song played, and she looped her hands behind his neck and swayed from side to side, pleased when he began moving with her. He'd been right—he was a terrible dancer, but each time their bodies brushed, awareness flared between them, and based on the darkening of his eyes, she wasn't the only one who felt it.

If she'd ever seen him this way before, she'd have been a goner. The absentminded professor was a distant memory. The man in his place resembled The Incredible Hulk far more than Dr. Bruce Banner. His gaze was intense, his jaw tight, and he looked like the slightest provocation could send him up in flames. She wanted to provoke him. She'd always been the type to poke a sleeping beast.

Swaying closer, her mouth near his ear, and she murmured, "I think you should kiss me."

She drew back just in time to see his Adam's apple bob. "For the ruse?"

She shook her head. "Because you want to."

One brow cocked up. "I do?"

She nodded. "Yes, you do."

She half expected him to laugh it off, but the dimness of the dance floor and the romance of the wedding must have worked their magic because he released her hips, cupped her face between his palms, and kissed her full on the mouth. Desire exploded like starbursts behind her eyelids. Pressing closer, she tangled her tongue with his, tasting wine and cheesecake on his breath. She gave up on any semblance of dancing and put everything she had into the kiss, hoping he could tell how much it meant to her and how much she wanted him.

They broke apart, both breathing heavily, and he searched her eyes—for what, she didn't know—then he wiped his mouth on his sleeve. She ran a finger around her lips in case her lipstick had smudged, and they took up where they'd left off—with the dancing, not the kissing.

A couple of songs—and another stolen kiss—later, a voice called her name. She turned and found herself facing Mason Delphine. He was resplendent in a white tuxedo and black shirt, but she didn't give a glowworm's ass.

"Can I cut in?" he asked, addressing her rather than Shane, no doubt recalling their run-in at the mini-mart when Shane had called him on his crap. She fanned herself. It made her hot even thinking about it.

"No," she said pertly. "You may not."

Mason's hand wrapped around her upper arm, and she remembered the way his calloused palms used to drive her nuts. "Come on, Faith. I know I screwed up, but it was years ago. I want a chance to make it up to you."

Okay, she was not letting this asshole from her past mess up the best night she'd had in forever. She shrugged his hand off and stared him down. She might have cowered last time she saw him, but in this dress, she felt like the boss bitch she knew she was, and she wouldn't shrink from anyone.

"Why would I give you a second chance when I already have a perfect man?"

With that, she hauled Shane into her arms and swept him into the dance.

SHANE WAS TRYING TO GET HIS HEAD AROUND THE unexpected turn the evening had taken when a shrill ringing from his jacket pocket interrupted their dance.

"Sorry, I need to check this," he said, knowing it could be about the kids. His stomach sank when he saw that it was Bex. "Is everything okay?" he asked as the call connected.

"I hate to interrupt your night, but Dylan isn't feeling well, and I'm not sure what's wrong."

His good mood evaporated, and with a hand gesture, he excused himself from the dance floor to somewhere quieter. "Is he vomiting?"

"No, but he's clutching his stomach and moaning. He says his head hurts too. I thought you'd want to know."

"I do, thank you." Even if his date was about to go up in flames. "I'll be over soon. We need to make sure it's not his appendix, although if his head hurts too, that would be unlikely."

She sighed. "I'm sorry, Shane. I know how much you were looking forward to tonight."

"It's okay. The boys come first." They always would. That's what being a father meant. "See you in five." Hanging up, he turned to find Faith at his side.

"What's wrong?" she asked.

Running a hand through his hair, he wished—for the first time he could remember—that he could have a night off from daddy duties. "Dylan is sick, and Bex doesn't know what it is. She's worried. I'm really sorry to do this to you, but I need to go home."

She nodded. "Of course you do. I'll come with you."

Disappointment settled in his gut. He didn't want to ruin her fun. She'd been having a great time, and he had no doubt someone else would happily partner her once he'd gone. Perhaps that Mason guy. Yeah, okay, so maybe he wouldn't mind if she left with him.

"That would be great, thanks. I might need someone to watch Hunter if Dylan needs to go to hospital."

She paled. "You think it's that bad?"

"I'm not sure. Let's go and find out." Together, they gathered their things and headed out to the car. Faith shivered, and Shane cranked the heater up to keep her warm. He stopped at Bex's place, and she greeted him out front with the boys and bundled them into the vehicle.

"How are you doing, buddy?" Shane asked as he drove home.

Dylan moaned. "I don't feel good."

"Is it your stomach?"

"Yeah, but not like pukey sick. It just hurts."

Uh oh. That could be appendicitis. Or potentially some kind of indigestion or cramp.

"When we stop, I want you to show me exactly where it hurts." He pulled up the drive and put the car into park. "Faith, can you take Hunter inside, please?" He handed her a key.

"Come on, cutie pie." Faith roused Hunter, who'd been napping, and he looped his arms around her neck so she could carry him in. Meanwhile, Shane unbuckled and checked on Dylan.

"It hurts here," Dylan said, gesturing broadly to his upper abdomen.

Shane frowned. Now he could understand Bex's confusion. That wasn't where you'd find an appendix. Perhaps indigestion was the more likely option. "What did you have for dinner?"

"Chicken and veggie stir-fry."

"Come on. Let's get you inside, and we can figure out whether we need to go to the hospital."

Dylan's eyes widened. "It's not that bad." He poked his stomach. "Really. I don't know why Bex made such a big deal of it."

Suspicion gripped Shane. His son had never been a good liar, and right now, something was up. He stepped out of the car and strode around to the other door. "Do you need me to help you inside?"

His suspicion increased when Dylan scuttled out of the back. "I think I'm starting to feel better."

If he'd felt anything other than peachy the entire evening, Shane would eat his hat. He was getting the impression his son had faked an illness. The question was why.

"Did Bex give you anything for the pain?" he asked as they walked inside. "Panadol?"

"Yeeeah." He drew the word out, reluctant to answer.

"Did it help?"

"Not back then, but maybe it's kicking in now."

"Uh-huh." In the lounge, Shane instructed Dylan to wait on the couch while he went to get a thermometer. Faith had wrapped Hunter in a blanket on the armchair and vanished into the kitchen. When Shane returned, thermometer in hand, Dylan squirmed. "Open up." As he'd expected, his son's body temperature was perfectly normal.

Faith came around the corner, bringing a tray laden with mugs. She set it on the coffee table. "Hot chocolates for everyone. Proper ones, made with Belgian chocolate."

"Marshmallows?" Hunter asked.

She winked at him. "And marshmallows."

What a sweetheart. He'd cut her night short, and rather than ditch him, she was helping them out.

"Oops." They all turned just in time to see Hunter slosh brown liquid down his chin and onto his lap.

Faith bolted upright. "Don't move, honey. I'll grab a towel."

The minute she left the room, Dylan narrowed his eyes at Shane. "Why'd you have to bring *her* home with you?"

Shane's jaw dropped. "Excuse me?"

Dylan stood, shoulders back, pain apparently forgotten. "I don't know why you think she's so special. Her hair is a weird color and she dresses like she's from the past."

A whimper in the doorway made them both turn. Shane's heart plummeted to his shoes when he saw Faith standing there, no doubt having heard every word. But before he could insist his son apologize, she pasted a smile on and breezed into the room, towel in hand. She dabbed Hunter dry while tension crackled around her, then lifted him out of the chair.

"Why don't you and I go read a story?" she suggested, and when he nodded, she carried him from the room.

Shane paced over and closed the door behind her, then he whirled on Dylan. "I hope you're pleased with yourself. You hurt Faith's feelings, and she's never been anything but nice to you."

To Dylan's credit, he looked pained, but still defiant.

"Are you even sick?" Shane asked.

"No," he admitted, downcast. "But I don't want Faith to take Mum's place. We don't need anyone else. We're fine just like we are."

"Oh." Deflated, Shane sank into a chair. "Is that what you think she's trying to do?"

"Well, yeah. I mean, everyone around town says you're together, and her parents think you are, and then you went to the wedding. That's the sort of stuff you do with a girl you like. The kind of thing you used to do with Mum."

Shane sighed. It seemed he had some explaining to do and an apology to make. "Look, I need to tell you something, but first, you have to understand that nothing excuses your behavior tonight. You worried Bex and me, and Faith had to leave her cousin's wedding early because of you. That's not acceptable."

Dylan ducked his head and mumbled something.

Shane powered on. "That said, Faith and I are not dating. Hey, look at me."

Dylan raised his eyes, glowering.

"Buddy, I'd tell you if I was dating someone. Hunter is too young to understand, but you deserve to know if there's a woman in my life." Crossing the room, he knelt beside his son. "What I'm about to say is a secret. Do you promise not to repeat it to anyone else?"

Dylan nodded.

"I need the words."

"I promise," he muttered.

"Good. Faith's parents wanted to match her up with that guy, Leon, but she wasn't interested, so I helped her out by pretending to be her boyfriend. That's what friends do. They help each other."

A frown marred Dylan's forehead. "You were faking it?"

"Yes."

"You and Faith aren't really dating?"

"No, we're not." Although he couldn't help wondering whether it would be so bad if they were. Technically, their reason to pretend had passed, but he liked to think the kisses and touches between them had been more than just keeping up appearances. For his

103

part, they certainly had been. "I think you owe Faith an apology."

Dylan had the decency to look ashamed of himself. "Yeah, I know."

That might be the best Shane was going to get. "I expect you to make it right."

Dylan's shoulders straightened. "I will."

For the sake of curiosity, Shane asked, "If I were dating Faith, why would that make you so angry?"

Dylan shrugged, expression turning sullen—his default as of late. "She's nice, but I like us the way we are. If Mum came back, that would be one thing, but this is different."

Shane frowned. "What would make you think there's any chance of your mother coming back? She's been gone for years."

Dylan's shoulders hunched. "She says she might come back when she gets too old to be a movie star."

She does?

It was the first he'd heard of it, and he was going to have to have words with Diana. She couldn't go putting ideas like that in her son's head.

"That won't be for a long time yet, Dyl. Maybe never. Actresses can have long careers these days. Besides, even if she did come back, we wouldn't get back together."

"You don't know that." The words were defensive. "Caleb's parents just got back together, and they said it would never happen."

Ah, now things made more sense. Damn Caleb's parents for planting ideas in Dylan's head. He needed to accept that Diana was never coming back.

"Yes, I do know." But he wasn't going to push the matter. Dylan was worked up enough as it was. They'd talk about it when he was calmer.

12

OUCH. NOTHING STUNG LIKE THE HONESTY OF A CHILD. Especially one in a particularly vicious mood. They seemed to have a sixth sense for which nerves to poke, and while Faith knew her relationship with Shane wasn't real, so she wouldn't have to reconcile Dylan to the idea of her as a stepmother, his rejection hurt. How many evenings had they played video games together, or taken turns putting Hunter to bed because Dylan liked to do that sometimes too?

She understood his not wanting things to change. Most kids from broken homes wanted to see their parents get back together, or at the very least, avoid a stepparent who might ruin the family dynamic, but that didn't stop her eyes from flooding with tears the moment she was out of sight. Hunter, being the absolute darling he was, grabbed her hand and tried to pull her into bed for cuddles. With one arm around his narrow shoulders and the other holding the book, she read him a story about a dog who'd lost his bum. It was his favorite, and she could recite the text by heart. Before she reached the end, he'd fallen asleep.

Easing from the bed, she pulled the blankets up to his chin, then switched on his night-light and turned off the overhead lights. She sank to the floor and drew her knees to her chest. She didn't want to return to the lounge. She'd rather not know whether Shane and Dylan had discussed her. She'd rather slink out the back door and walk the short journey home. Unfortunately, she'd left her coat and purse in the other room.

Climbing to her feet, she hauled in a lungful of air and put her game face on. In her experience, it was best not to let people see they'd gotten to you. She lifted the corners of her mouth, put a bounce in her step, and headed down the hall. At the end, she hesitated, listening until she could be sure she wasn't interrupting something, and then entered the living room with her chin held high.

"Dylan has something to say to you," Shane said as she closed the door.

She resisted the urge to cross her arms and turned to Dylan. "Oh, yeah? What's that?"

Confusion flicked across his features, along with shame and a heavy dose of reluctance. "I'm sorry."

She nodded, steeling herself so she didn't betray the extent of her hurt. "Apology accepted. Perhaps next time you ought to make sure someone isn't within earshot before saying anything negative about them."

"Yeah." A flush crept up his cheeks. "I will."

"Great." She retrieved her jacket from the back of the sofa, slipped it on, buttoned it up, and then grabbed her purse and shoved it into one of the pockets. "I'd best be off. You two have a nice night."

She strode to the exit, but Shane rushed to her side and stopped her as she reached it.

"Wait, don't leave angry. We should talk about this."

"I'm not angry," she lied. "Life's too short to waste being upset about what people say." Aware that Dylan was watching, she didn't kiss Shane's cheek as she'd have liked to. "Dylan needs you," she added. "Honestly, I'm fine. Thanks for tonight. I enjoyed having you there."

"You're welcome." He looked baffled. "I'll always be there for you. Surely you know that."

She nodded. "I do. Bye, now."

"I'll give you a ride home."

"I'd prefer to walk, thanks."

She left before he could change her mind and strolled down the sidewalk, her path lit by streetlamps. Cold air swirled around her neck, and she pulled her jacket up around her ears to keep warm. As her heels clacked along the asphalt, she couldn't help but wonder whether the chemistry growing between her and Shane was worth pursuing. How much was she prepared to sacrifice to have him? Could she handle being cast in the role of evil stepmother?

No, she didn't think so. She enjoyed her uniqueness and didn't generally care if people disapproved of her clothing or the things she said, but when it came to Shane's family, she did care. She couldn't turn it off. And having someone who didn't want her there would be a nightmare. Sighing, she resolved not to think about men of any age for the remainder of the night. Her parents and Leon would be leaving tomorrow, so she'd focus on getting a decent sleep and then enjoying her morning with them.

IT TURNED OUT THAT AFTER AN EVENING WITH THE MOST beautiful woman Shane knew, spending two days without her was like trying to quit sugar cold turkey. He craved her. And yeah, they'd talked on the phone, during which he'd apologized for Dylan again, but everything was different now. Their fake relationship had ended, and it seemed that anything between them had also gone up in smoke.

He stood at the kitchen counter, slicing vegetables and adding them to pots. They were ready to go on the stove when someone knocked on the door.

"Dylan, can you get that?" he called out.

"It's probably Faith," Dylan muttered, not having recovered from being grounded for a week following his fake illness.

For several seconds, Shane heard nothing, but then a thud echoed through the house, followed by the sound of something being dragged. Intrigued, and slightly concerned, he dried his hands and followed the noise. Just inside the door, he found Dylan and a tall, slim woman with pale blonde hair. The floor fell away beneath him. He knew who she was before she turned, but he prayed he'd gotten it wrong. Brilliant blue eyes speared him as her plump pink lips stretched into a million-dollar smile, and her nose was tipped with red because of the cold.

Diana.

She beamed at him. "Well, aren't you a sight for sore eyes?"

He couldn't manage to respond. He hadn't seen her in person since he'd kissed her goodbye four years ago and came home to find her gone. She hadn't returned to the bay, and he'd never visited her in Los Angeles after he hunted her down. Why would he? She'd abandoned him.

"What are you doing here, Diana?"

"She's back," Dylan proclaimed, grinning even more broadly than his actress mother.

Meanwhile, Shane fumed. He knew Diana, and whatever their son might wish, she wasn't back for good. She had a life of stardom in California, and she wouldn't leave it willingly. She'd come back for a very specific reason—with a goal in mind—and he wanted to know what it was.

"Why?" he demanded.

"Dad!" Dylan stepped in front of her, shielding her from him. As if Diana had ever been the one who needed protecting. She always had every situation under control. Dylan eyed him meaningfully. "She's here to see us."

"Daddy?" A high-pitched voice had them turning around. Hunter stood in the hall with his thumb in his mouth and a toy dinosaur tucked under his arm. "Who's the strange lady?"

They all froze. Then Diana's eyes narrowed. "Don't you recognize me, darling?"

Hunter backed up, shaking his head.

She knelt and opened her arms. "I'm your mummy. Come give me a hug."

If she was expecting a tearful reunion with her younger son, she was in for a shocking disappointment. Hunter was shy at the best of times, and considering the tension in the house for the past couple of days, he was even more reserved than usual. He stumbled backward, and then spun and raced around the corner to hide inside his bedroom. Diana's jaw dropped. She didn't seem to know how to react. He supposed she was used to people throwing themselves at her. She was beautiful, talented, and successful.

Fucking heartless.

"You poisoned him against me," she accused, rising to her feet, her pale eyes flashing. "My own baby doesn't know who I am."

"Don't be ridiculous," he said, refusing to participate in her theatrics. "I didn't need to poison him against you. You left when he was three months old, and you haven't been back. Why on earth would he know you? You're a stranger to him, and he's a shy kid. That's all there is to it."

Diana looked at Dylan, seeking confirmation. Dylan nodded, his gaze whizzing back and forth between them. "Yeah, Hunter takes a while to warm up to people."

Shane crossed his arms, pleased that Dylan had backed him up. With the hero worship written across his face, he'd half expected the kid to toss him under the nearest bus if it meant keeping Diana happy. As it was, she couldn't say a thing, and it was priceless because the only person Diana had to blame for Hunter's reaction was herself. Shane and Diana stood there in the entrance, at an impasse.

"Aren't you going to invite me in?" she asked eventually.

"No." Not in his lifetime. "How long has this trip been in the works? Why didn't you tell anyone you were coming?"

She shrugged one slender shoulder, and for the first time, he noticed that her formfitting jersey had a low V-neck that displayed the tops of her breasts. Breasts he recalled having been considerably smaller. He frowned. Was she intending to seduce him into letting her stay until she'd had enough of playing house? Because she *would* grow weary of it. That was inevitable. Whatever she was doing here, it was all a game to her. To him, it was their lives.

"I decided to visit after Dylan called on Saturday. He sounded upset, and I wanted to make sure everything was all right."

Shane glanced at Dylan, who hung his head, cheeks flaming. While the situation frustrated Shane, he didn't blame his son. None of them had handled things well, and he should have taken the time to explain everything earlier. But he also didn't buy Diana's explanation. Dylan had cried and begged and pleaded with her to come back dozens of times over the years, and she'd never set foot on New Zealand soil. Why now?

The voice in the back of his head told him that this was about Faith. Diana had a competitive streak, and he doubted she liked the thought of someone taking her place—even though she'd given it up a long time ago. If Diana had spoken to Dylan on Saturday evening, it had probably been before he pretended to be sick and before Shane had told him the arrangement he'd made with Faith, which meant Diana would have no idea they weren't actually dating.

He wouldn't enlighten her. Partly because it was hypocritical of her to think she had any right to weigh in on who he dated, and partly because, if she intended to stay in town for a while, it would be nice to have a shield between them.

"How can you afford to be away from filming?" he asked, still not stepping aside to allow her further into the house. She'd never lived here—he'd bought it after she'd gone—and she wasn't welcome now.

Waving a hand in a typically flippant move, she crossed to Dylan's side and rested a hand on his shoulder. He tilted his head up, practically glowing. Shane wanted to wrench her away. Did she even care that she was toying with their children's emotions?

"Filming has ended for the season. I have six entire weeks of vacation before I'm due back." She smiled cattishly. "Isn't that wonderful?"

Diana was in her third season of filming a popular television series about three women battling their way to success on Wall Street. If they had six weeks off at the end of filming, that meant she'd had two such holidays previously and made no attempt to return to Haven Bay.

"Good for you," he said tightly. "But you can't stay here."

"Please, Dad," Dylan said, turning wide eyes on him. "Please, please, please."

Shane shook his head. Diana had chosen fame and fortune over family, and they all had to deal with the consequences of that choice. "No."

"There's nowhere I'd rather be." This time it was Diana's eyes that were big and pleading. Bitterness curdled his stomach. Did she really think she could manipulate him the same way she used to?

He jerked his head toward the door. "Can I talk to you outside for a moment?"

Her lips curled, and he knew what was coming the moment they stepped outside. She pressed herself to him and batted her eyelashes. Once upon a time, his body would have reacted hotly, but no longer.

"I know you missed me," she murmured, swaying closer.

He moved away. "Maybe for a couple of weeks. But then I realized what a selfish person you must be to leave your family with nothing more than a note." His fists tightened. "Your three-month-old baby, Diana. You didn't even care about him enough to stay. Do you know how much he cried when you abandoned him?"

She rolled her eyes. "You're being melodramatic, and it doesn't become you."

"You can't stay." On this, he wouldn't budge. "You forfeited any right to call us your family when you boarded a plane to Hollywood with no intention of coming back."

Reaching out, she trailed a finger down his chest. "But I did come back."

"I wish you hadn't."

Her expression didn't waver, but the shock in her eyes told him he'd struck a direct hit. "Is this because of your little tramp?" she demanded, her claws coming out. "Dylan told me about her, you know. He doesn't like her."

Just like that, she evened the playing field. He'd forgotten how spiteful she could be.

"This has nothing to do with her. I don't want you manipulating Dylan, getting his hopes up, and leaving again. On that topic, why have you been telling him you might move back to New Zealand one day?"

She shrugged. "I might. For all you know, I could be here to stay now. What makes you think I intend to leave?"

"Experience." He didn't like the way she was studying him as though she had the upper hand. "Commitment isn't in your DNA."

"Why don't you give me a chance and see?"

"I said no."

She scowled. "You're being ridiculous."

"You're the one who's ridiculous." Their volume was escalating, but he couldn't seem to stop it. "Now I'm asking you nicely to please leave. Find a hotel room, have dinner, catch up on sleep, and come back tomorrow. We can talk then." Opening the door, he reached inside for her suitcase and deposited it at her feet, ignoring Dylan, who'd clearly been eavesdropping.

Diana poked Shane in the chest with a perfectly manicured nail. "This isn't going to end the way you want it to." Then, nose in the air, she huffed and stalked away, dragging her suitcase with her.

13

FAITH AND MEGAN WERE CLOSING UP FOR THE EVENING when a woman appeared in the entrance of The Shack. She had unnaturally blonde hair, a gorgeous complexion, and a body that was literally the fantasy of hundreds of thousands of men across the world.

Diana Monroe.

Faith would recognize her anywhere, and not only because she was Shane's ex. She was a star. Movies, TV, music videos, advertisements—you name it, she'd done it. While she may not be an A-list celebrity, she was firmly in the B-list. Diana hadn't seen her yet, so Faith dropped behind the ice cream cabinet, pretending to pick something off the floor. The other woman hadn't been to Haven Bay since she'd hightailed it out of town four years ago, and her return couldn't mean anything good. At least, not for Faith. She might be here to win Shane back and reclaim her family.

"What are you doing?" Megan hissed, joining her on the floor.

"That's Diana Monroe," she replied, scooting closer as the doorbell sounded.

"So?" Megan asked, raising a brow. "You're Faith St. John. Badass boss babe. Entrepreneur. Scared of no one. Get back up and face her before she sees you being silly."

Faith straightened. Megan was right. She didn't roll over and play dead for mean girls. Not these days. She'd done it once, pulled herself up by her bootstraps, and made the decision never to do it again. Over the counter, she gave Diana Monroe her widest smile. "Can I help you?"

Instead of addressing Faith, Diana looked at Megan. "Will you excuse us for a moment?"

Megan thrust her slender shoulders back. "I'm afraid not. We're about to close, and I have work to do. You won't even notice I'm here."

Faith sent her a grateful smile. At least she wouldn't have to face the wicked witch alone.

"Okay, if that's how you want it to be," Diana continued, unconcerned. "I'd rather do this without an audience, but needs must." She looked down her nose at Faith, which to be honest, wasn't a great feat as Diana was a good few inches taller and also wearing heels. "Faith, is it?" She didn't wait for a reply. "I'm back to remind my family who they belong to." She swept a lock of hair behind her ear, exposing a long, elegant neck. The kind of neck Faith would never have. "Shane is mine, and so are the boys, whether they know it or not. So you can take your chunky ass and stay far away from my husband."

"Excuse me?" Faith demanded, flabbergasted. Was a film star actually in her ice cream parlor, telling her to stay away from a man because she saw her as a threat? On what planet did that make sense? And why would any man want her when they could have Diana? The woman

116

was nuttier than a fruit cake if she didn't see that there was clearly no contest.

"You heard me," Diana snapped. "You're a nobody. Who do you really think he wants?"

Faith leaned over the counter. "You want to know what I think?" she asked, pleased when her voice didn't waver.

"I don't care what you think."

Faith ignored her. "I think that you can't handle the fact Shane divorced you and now he and the boys have their own lives." She rested on her elbows because otherwise she might reach into the chiller and fling a scoop of chocolate mint at the hateful woman. "You ran away from everything and expected it to all be waiting when you were ready to take it back. Guess what, girlfriend? Life doesn't work that way, and you have no ground to stand on. Unless you plan to buy something, I'd appreciate it if you'd get the hell out of my shop."

Diana whirled, her blonde hair forming a halo as a ray of sunshine struck it. She glided out, holding her head high like a goddamned queen.

Megan scoffed. "Is she serious? Something is crammed way too far up her ass."

Faith dropped the ice cream scooper, which she only just noticed she'd been clutching. "I have to say, that wasn't on my list of things I thought I'd be doing today." She looked at Megan. "Do you think she's been in town long?"

"There were a ton of suitcases in the taxi outside, so I'd say she just arrived."

"This can't have been her first stop." Something about that didn't add up to Faith. "Where do you suppose she's staying?"

"Well...." Megan drew the word out hesitantly. "Based on the way she came at you, it seems like she's planning to spend time with Shane and his family."

An icy tentacle wrapped around Faith's heart and squeezed. She'd had the same thought but hoped she'd been mistaken. "I need to ring Shane and make sure he knows she's coming." She didn't want him to be blindsided. Having his starlet ex turn up on your doorstep would be hard enough with forewarning. She paused. Had he known she was coming? He hadn't mentioned it. Shaking off her uncertainty, she dialed his number.

"Faith?" He sounded stressed, and she hoped she hadn't been too slow.

"Diana is in town, and I thought you should know, if you didn't already."

"Shit," he said, then muttered something worse under his breath. "Yes, I've had the pleasure of seeing her. She turned up half an hour ago and I sent her away, but I never dreamed she'd hunt you down. I'm so sorry. Are you okay?"

"I will be." Once her heart rate returned to usual. "I think the bigger question is: are you?"

He sighed, the sound so weary that she wanted to wrap him in a hug and never let go. "I haven't seen her since she signed the divorce papers."

She leaned against the counter. "I thought as much. Any idea why she's back?"

"To mess with me," he suggested, and she suspected he was only half joking. "Why does Diana do anything? Because she wants to. It was probably a whim. She spoke to Dylan on Saturday night and must have hopped on a plane straight after, because it would have taken her a while to get here. I'm hoping she'll regret the impulse once she's had some rest, and she'll turn around and go home."

Faith doubted that would happen, but she let him hold out hope. "Perhaps she will." Megan appeared in front of her and indicated she was leaving. Faith nodded and blew her a kiss. "Are you all right?"

He hesitated for a long beat. "I know this is a lot to ask, but would you mind extending our pretend relationship until she leaves? I need as many barriers between us as I can get."

Faith closed her eyes and hauled in a breath. Honestly, she hated the thought of exposing herself to that dreadful woman again, but if Diana had come all the way here because Dylan ran his mouth about her, then she was partially to blame for the current situation and should own her part in it. Besides, this was Shane. He needed her. When had she ever been able to say no to him?

"Sure thing. I'll be your bodyguard. Your woman-repellent. Would you prefer I take the clingy route or the ice bitch route? Believe me, I can do either."

At this, he laughed, and she loved the sound of it so much that she'd have swooned if not for the counter holding her up. "Just be yourself. Thank you, Faith. And again, I'm incredibly sorry."

She smiled, feeling a little saucy. "You'll make it up to me, gorgeous."

She hung up before he could respond.

SHANE'S TEETH GROUND TOGETHER. THE NERVE OF THE woman. She must have looked Faith up as soon as she'd left his place, which made him feel both wary and guilty. Clearly, Dylan had told her Faith's full name and God only knew what else. While Faith hadn't said anything about their exchange, he could imagine how it had gone. Diana wasn't the type to take any perceived threat lying down—something he'd once loved about her. She'd probably warned Faith off and called her a few choice names while she was at it. His ex-wife could be malicious.

A smoke alarm went off, jolting him from his reverie, and he raced to the kitchen in time to see smoke billowing from the oven. *Damn.* The garlic bread was toast. Blackened and charred. He opened a window and tried to wave the smoke outside, his eyes stinging. Everything else was salvageable.

"Great," Dylan complained, having finally emerged from his bedroom after shutting himself away when Diana left. "Burnt bread on top of everything else."

"Can you make sure Hunter is okay?" Shane gritted out, grasping the frayed ends of his temper.

Dylan shrugged. "Already done. He's fine."

"Thank you."

Jerking his chin in acknowledgment, Dylan spun around and left. Shane sighed, rubbing his eyelids. He didn't know anything about parenting a tween, and he was lucky Dylan was such a responsible kid, because he was pretty sure he was messing it up.

Tossing the remains of the bread out the window, he gulped the fresh air, then checked the vegetables and chicken, which needed to cook for a while longer. The kitchen situation under control, he grabbed his cell phone and flicked through his contact list until he reached Diana's number. He'd used it maybe half a dozen times since he'd programmed it in, and each time he wished he didn't have to. Now was no different. But she needed to be told that he wouldn't tolerate her antics. The call rang once, and then went to voicemail.

"I can't believe you went after Faith," he said following the beep. "That's not okay. It's none of your business who I date, or sleep with, or decide to have a relationship with. You and I haven't been together for a long time, and you can't suddenly choose to take an interest in my life. Mine, or the boys. If you get them used to seeing you and then take off, you'll break their hearts. Have some common decency and just get the hell out of here before you do any more damage."

That done, he plucked up his courage and went in search of the boys. They were together in Dylan's room. Shane sat on the bed with Hunter while Dylan slouched on the floor.

"We need to talk about your mother," he said. Turning to Hunter, he continued, "Do you remember the woman you talk to on the phone sometimes? That's who you met tonight."

"Oh." Hunter's voice was small, and he shrunk in on himself. "She was angry with me."

Dylan scoffed.

"No, Hunter, she was angry with me," Shane corrected. "And confused because you didn't know who she was."

Hunter studied his feet. "I don't 'member seeing her before."

His heart ached for the little guy. "That's okay. You were really young when you saw her last. But Dylan is old enough to remember her better, aren't you, bud?"

Dylan nodded, staring at Hunter as though willing him to remember. "She used to take me out of school, and we'd go to the city to watch a play or see a movie. It was the best."

Shane cringed inwardly. He'd been the one who'd had to explain the numerous sick days to the school administrators when he hadn't even realized they were happening. Dylan and Diana had been very close-lipped. But that's how it always had been. Diana was the fun parent, and he was the reliable one.

"Did you know she was coming?" Shane asked, the possibility only now occurring to him.

"No," Dylan said. "But it's the best surprise. Ever since Caleb's parents remarried, I hoped she'd come back so we could be a family again."

Shane's heart sank. Dylan was going to be crushed when he learned the truth, because there was no doubt in Shane's mind that Diana wouldn't be here for more than a couple of weeks.

"She's only visiting," he said gently. "We all need to remember that, okay? I know it's tempting to get excited because it's been so long since you saw her, but she won't be staying. She needs to be back on set in six weeks."

Dylan deflated. "Yeah." But then he perked up again. "Maybe she doesn't want to be on TV anymore. Maybe she's sick of it."

And maybe the moon would stop orbiting the earth, but Shane didn't think so. Diana was the way she was. Self-centered and addicted to attention. That had never changed.

"Just don't get your hopes up."

Dylan glared at him. "You should have let her stay. She's our mum."

"You may be her family, but I'm not. That ended when we signed the divorce papers. This is our home. Hers is in Los Angeles." In a mansion. While they lived in a villa that badly needed repairs. But she hadn't challenged him for custody during the split, so in return, he hadn't requested any form of financial assistance. He'd just been relieved she hadn't gotten it into her head to take the boys overseas because custody cases rarely favored the father, although he liked to think in these particular circumstances, they might have.

He tugged a hand through his hair, grounding himself in the present. "She can't stay here," he told them. "But if she wants to spend time with you, I won't stop her. I just need you both to be honest if she calls you or drops by, okay? I won't be mad. I just need to know."

"Okay, Daddy," Hunter agreed.

Dylan didn't respond, and Shane didn't force the matter because doing so wouldn't end well. Instead, he excused himself to make some more calls. The first was to Logan, who, as the owner of the local pub, was well connected to the town's gossip tree.

"Diana is in town," he said by way of greeting.

"No shit?"

"She's already been here and down to The Shack to talk to Faith. If she comes sniffing around, I'd really appreciate it if you could stonewall her." Diana knew Logan and Shane were friends and that Logan was a single, good-looking guy who'd be vulnerable to her brand of charm. As such, he imagined Logan was reasonably high on her hit list. "I know she's a celebrity and all—"

"She's a stone-cold bitch, and if she comes by, I'll make it known she's not welcome."

Shane's shoulders dropped in relief. "Thanks, man."

"No worries. I've got your back."

Next, he called Bex. She reacted more violently than Logan had. As a fellow single parent, she knew how horrible it had been for him when Diana ran off and left him with a seven-year-old and a baby.

"If I see that awful woman, I'll ruin her nose job," she promised.

Shane wished he could laugh, but his mood was too grim. "Actually, the nose is natural. The breasts, though…. Pretty sure they're not."

She snorted. "Figures. Is there anything I can do to help?"

"Actually… this is completely unrelated, but I was wondering if you'd be able to watch the kids one evening. I, uh"—he took the plunge—"I'd like to ask Faith out on a real date."

"Yes!" she exclaimed. "I'd be thrilled to keep an eye on them if it means you finally get the chance to live your own life." He could hear the smile in her voice. "What prompted this? Please say it wasn't Diana."

"It wasn't." That, he knew for sure. "I've enjoyed spending time with her, and I'm not ready for it to end yet."

"Smart man. Jewels like Faith don't come along often."

"I know. I just hope I'm not setting my sights too high." Aside from the boys being hurt, that was his biggest fear.

Bex laughed incredulously. "You were married to a film star. All the mothers at school drool over you. You could have any woman you want, and I'm not saying that because I'm your friend."

Shane rolled his eyes. "I was dumped by a film star. The mothers like flirting with me because it's harmless fun." Harmless for them. He felt cornered every time he got caught in their sights.

"If you say so. Oh, crap. I have to go. Izzy just exploded a bag of flour over the kitchen."

"Good luck with that."

Shane's final phone call was to Hugh MacAllister, a

retired lawyer who now served as the town's representative on the local council. Hugh had been Shane's divorce attorney, and although he didn't practice law anymore, he kept up to date with the legal legislation.

"Hi, Hugh," he said when the man answered. "It's Shane Walker here. Do you have a moment to talk?"

"That I do." Hugh was one of those men who spoke slowly and clearly, with a deep voice that always sounded sincere. The kind of guy people instinctively trusted. "What can I help you with?"

"I need your advice. Diana is in town."

Hugh hummed in the back of his throat. "That must be difficult for you. Is she staying long?"

"I don't think so, but you know Diana. Being honest isn't her strong suit. Anyway, I was wondering if I have any options to keep her away from the boys. At the moment, I don't mind her seeing them, but if she starts playing games, I want to know what my options are."

Hugh thought for a moment. "You could request to change the custody arrangement so she has no visitation rights, but that would be a slow process, and considering her visibility on the global stage, I wouldn't recommend it. She could afford a squadron of attorneys if she wanted."

Shane nodded. He'd feared as much. "I know I'm required to go to reasonable lengths to ensure she can visit with them. It's just that she's just never wanted to before."

"I'm afraid there isn't much you can do legally unless she endangers them or tries to break the terms of the custody arrangement."

On that note.... "If she did want to challenge me for custody, do you think she'd have a chance of success?"

Hugh sighed. "In a fair and equal world, she wouldn't

have a hope. The courts frown on child abandonment. But with her status and wealth, it's possible. Not likely, but possible."

Shane slumped into a chair. Goddamn. He hoped it wouldn't come to that.

14

WHEN SHANE WOKE, HE HELD OUT HOPE FOR A BRIEF moment that the previous night had been a bad dream. But then he realized what had woken him. His phone. He reached for it and saw Diana's name flash across the screen. His optimism disintegrated.

"Hello," he said, raising it to his ear.

"It's the morning," Diana said, sounding cross. "Am I allowed to talk to you now?"

Ugh, she was worse than a petulant child. "It's before seven."

"I want to take the boys out for the day," she announced. "I was worried I'd miss them before they left for school."

"Hunter goes to kindergarten, not school."

She tsked. "There's no need to be judgmental. I forgot they're separate here. They're usually grouped together in L.A. So, what do you say?"

He stared at the roof, wishing he didn't have to have this conversation. "No. It would be irresponsible of me to let Dylan miss school."

If eye-rolls made a noise, he'd just heard it.

"It's one day, Shane, and it's a special occasion because I'm in town. Don't be such a killjoy."

His teeth ground together. "How sad is it that the boys seeing their mother is a special occasion? Don't push me on this, Diana. You're not the one who has to explain why they never see you or why you suddenly disappeared from their lives."

"You've never understood—"

"No," he interrupted. "*You* don't understand. Those kids are precious to me, and I'm not going to let you fuck them up any more than you already have." He steamrolled on. "As a matter of fact, I've spoken with my lawyer because that's how much I don't trust you. If you're serious about wanting to see them, you can come by after school tonight."

"Okay, I can work with that. I'll come over and make dinner."

"No." He bit out the word. If she turned up and made a show of being a domestic goddess—which she would— the boys might get the wrong idea. He didn't want them to see their mother in the kitchen and start believing she was back long-term or that she was part of the family. As far as he was concerned, she'd given up that right. He also just plain didn't trust her not to manipulate him. "You can visit, but you're not cooking here. If you want to share a meal with them, you can go out for dinner."

She scoffed. "Do you enjoy making this difficult? Are you trying to rub my face in the fact you have access to my sons and I don't?"

"That's not what this is about. I'm protecting them." God, it was too early in the day to have this conversation. His brain wasn't operating at full capacity yet.

"From me?" she asked, incredulous.

"Yes, from you."

She huffed. "Fine. I'll book a table at Sailor's Retreat, but I expect you to be there too."

"Make a reservation for five people," he said. "Text me the time."

Hanging up, he flicked through his contacts until he found Faith and typed out a message.

Shane: *Is there any chance you'd consider coming to dinner as my plus-one? Diana wants to take the boys to Sailor's Retreat. I promise to make it up to you. How does dinner on Thursday sound? Just the two of us.*

Faith: *Won't I be intruding? That sounds like a family thing.*

Shane: *Not at all. You might be the only reason I cling to my sanity. Please say yes.*

Faith: *I suppose your sanity is worth preserving. But only if you're sure you want me there. Dylan won't like it.*

Shane: *I've explained the real situation to Dylan, and I'll give him a heads up before we arrive. He might not love it because I think he secretly hopes Diana and I will get back together, but I promise he won't say anything disrespectful.*

Faith: *Okay, let me know when. I'll meet you there.*

Shane: *Thanks. You're incredible.*

Smiling, he set his phone aside and hauled himself out of bed. It was going to be a long day, but at least he could look forward to seeing Faith.

FAITH ADJUSTED HER NECKLACE—A VINTAGE LOCKET—AND fortified herself prior to entering Sailor's Retreat. This was not her idea of a fun evening, but Shane had sounded desperate, and there wasn't much she wouldn't do for him. She'd chosen her classiest dress, certain that Diana would bring her A-game, and spent extra time on makeup, taking care to get it just right. Her outfit would be her only armor against a Hollywood diva with her claws out.

Making her way inside, she spotted the group at a table in the corner. Finding them wasn't difficult. Not when everyone in the place was sneaking glances at Diana, no doubt trying to figure out whether she was actually who they thought. Diana never publicly discussed her past—no surprise there because it wasn't exactly flattering—and though the locals knew what had happened, few others did. The paparazzi didn't bother extending their reach to New Zealand.

As Faith approached, Shane glanced up and caught her eye, smiling warmly. The smile turned her inside out and almost made her forget the hell that was sure to come. "Hi, Faith."

"Hi, you handsome bunch."

Diana looked over her shoulder, coolly appraised Faith, and arched a brow. "I don't recall inviting you."

"No," she agreed, "but Shane did." Rounding the table, she slipped into the empty seat between him and Hunter, who reached over and gripped her hand. The little boy looked enormously uncomfortable. She could relate.

Shane shrugged. "I thought that if this is a family dinner, then all of the family should be here." He was baiting his ex, and Faith wished she knew why. She adored him, but she had the unpleasant feeling of being wielded as a weapon in the war between them. This table was a battlefield, beyond a shadow of a doubt.

Faith forced a smile. In her experience, it helped to keep a cheerful face through adversity. "Have you already ordered?"

"No." Beneath the table, Shane's hand slid onto her knee and squeezed. She melted in her seat. While he didn't say anything, his eyes screamed of gratitude, and in that moment, she didn't care whether half the people there wanted her gone. He needed her support, which was all that mattered. "We only arrived a few minutes ago."

"Great." To Diana, she said, "I'd recommend the crayfish. It's delicious."

"I know," Diana replied, all sweetness. "If you recall, I used to live here too."

"Yes," Faith agreed, "but it was a long time ago, and things tend to change."

Shots fired. Take that, you scheming bitch.

"They do." Diana's lips firmed. "Weren't you in high school back then?"

Shane stiffened, but she smoothed a hand over his. She could take care of herself.

"Actually, I'd just purchased my business." She'd had a crystal clear vision of what she wanted from life, so she'd gone to college right out of high school, completed her study in three years, and owned the deed to The Shack by the time she was twenty-three. In contrast, Diana hadn't encountered any success until she was around the same age Faith was now.

Diana sneered. "Oh, yes. The ice cream parlor. How quaint."

"It keeps me in food and shoes, so I'm happy." She loved her job, but she wasn't about to expound on the glories of ice cream and the joy it brought only to have Diana shoot her down.

"I can see that." Diana gave her a once-over. The kind that said she saw every bit of extra flesh Faith had. Diana was Hollywood slender, except for those boobs.

"Diana," Shane warned. "Don't."

A waiter approached, and they ordered. Faith got the crayfish. Diana did not.

Faith gave Hunter her attention. "How was kindergarten today, honey?"

"We built stuff out of boxes. Mine was best, 'cause Daddy teached me how."

Her heart softened. Aww. Wasn't he just the cutest? She knew that Shane took Hunter to Sanctuary most weekends to practice their DIY skills, and it seemed like he might have a future in building or carpentry. "Did you bring it home? I'd love to see."

He nodded. "Yep."

"We'll show you later," Shane said.

Not to be outdone, Diana addressed Hunter. "Did you tell them your mummy has come to stay?"

He shrank into his chair and glanced at Faith with big round eyes, as though seeking her support. Reaching over, she took his hand to reassure him, and he shook his head, staring down, almost as though he were afraid of Diana. But then, he was shy, and Faith supposed his mother was a virtual stranger. She felt a pang of sympathy for the other woman. Whether or not she deserved it, that had to hurt.

"I told my friends you're here," Dylan said proudly. "They've all seen you on TV, and my teacher asked if you could talk to the class about how to have a career as an actress."

Diana beamed, and her eldest son basked in the approval. "I'd love to. Feel free to give your teacher my number so we can discuss it. Perhaps your friends would like to meet me too?"

He nodded. "Yeah, they've never met someone who's been in movies before."

"That settles it then. I simply must come to your school."

Dylan grinned, and for his sake, Faith hoped Diana kept her word. It was obvious how much he adored her.

Diana turned to Shane. "I suppose I could visit your school too, if the students would like that."

Shane's expression soured. Everyone at the table knew they absolutely would. "Unfortunately, I doubt the principal would allow it."

"Pish, I'm sure I could talk him around."

At this, Faith hid a smile. The principal, Michael Briggston, was a close friend of Shane's, and he was involved with their mutual friend, Bex. Michael would refuse Diana on principle because he cared about Shane, and he wasn't the kind of man who could be cajoled into anything.

Their dinner arrived, and they started eating. Faith noted that Diana only picked at the edges of her food. That annoying sympathy reared its head again. While Shane's ex was a talented actress—Faith had seen her films—a lot of her success was down to her beautiful face and figure. As a result, she supposed the other woman could scarcely afford to eat anything other than vegetables lest she put on weight. Then Diana spoke again, and her sympathy evaporated.

"Dylan, darling, how is rugby going this year?"

The tips of Dylan's ears reddened. "Rugby season is over," he mumbled, hunching his shoulders. "It's cricket season at the moment."

Something his mother ought to know.

"Right," she said, smiling and nodding as though she hadn't unwittingly inflicted an emotional wound upon her vulnerable son. "And how is it? Is your team doing well?"

He shrugged. "We mostly win."

She flashed teeth that had been chemically whitened. "That's my boy."

"Remember, it's not all about winning, though," Shane said. "It's about having fun."

Diana rolled her eyes. "All of life is a competition, and pretending otherwise doesn't help anybody." She turned to Hunter. "Do you play any sports?"

"He's four," Shane exclaimed, setting his cutlery down with a clang. "So no, he doesn't, and if you'd been paying attention, you'd know he prefers creative outlets."

"An artist, eh?" Diana watched Hunter with interest. The little boy squirmed in his seat. "There are a lot of options for people like you in Hollywood."

Shane's scowl was thunderous, and Faith imagined she could hear his teeth grinding from two feet away. "He's four, Diana. Let him be four."

Diana cut a minuscule piece of salmon and raised it to her lips. "They're never too young to start thinking about the future."

"You don't know Hunter, so don't pretend you do."

For a prolonged moment, the only sounds were cutting and chewing. Diana seemed to have taken his rebuke to heart. But then she leveled her gaze on Faith.

"I've finally figured out who you remind me of," she said, as though it was a mystery she'd been pondering for days. "When I worked with the Hemsworth brothers, they had a personal assistant. Same orange hair and strange fashion sense."

It didn't escape Faith's notice how casually she'd name-dropped the Hemsworth brothers, probably for the combined purpose of belittling her and reminding her of how superior Diana's connections were.

"You'll have to introduce me," Faith replied. "I bet she has some great stories to tell."

Diana waved a hand dismissively. "Oh, I don't know her name." She laughed. "Why would I?" Pushing back her chair, she stood. "If you'll excuse me, I'll be back soon."

As she headed to the restroom, Faith leaned close to Shane and spoke quietly. "On our date, I expect dessert and plenty of wine."

"Done," he replied grimly. "I appreciate you being here."

Faith nodded, but she couldn't help wondering exactly what purpose she was supposed to serve. Diana had to know that there could be no competition between the women. Diana was glitz, glamor, and self-assurance. Faith was retro outfits, excessive volume, and plentiful curves. Pretending there was any question who a man would prefer made her feel like a fraud, but then Shane smiled, and her heart sang bow-chicka-wow-wow. There was no question of her leaving. She wouldn't abandon him with the woman who'd broken his heart. So she ran through a few self-affirming mantras in her mind, bolstered her self-confidence, and somehow made it to the end of the evening.

"I'll drive you home," Shane said after he paid the bill. He'd insisted on covering her meal since she'd done him a favor.

"I brought my car," she said. "But thanks for the offer."

They walked outside, and Shane drew Faith aside as Dylan hugged his mother goodbye.

He didn't touch her, but his gaze was like a caress. "I wish I could kiss you right now."

Faith moistened her lips. "So do I. But you'd better not in front of Dylan and Hunter."

He sighed, raking a hand through his hair. "One day, I will."

Flutters erupted in her stomach. With that simple statement, he'd made his intentions clear, and she liked it. A lot. Shane wanted to do the naked tango with her, and she couldn't wait for that time to come. "Bye, gorgeous," she said, sashaying away. "Dream of me."

15

D<small>URING THE TWO DAYS BETWEEN THE WORLD'S TENSEST</small> family meal and Shane's date with Faith, he had plenty of time to think about how to make things up to her. She'd handled dinner with grace, as well as a heavy dose of sassiness. Hunter had sought comfort from her, and based on the way Diana tracked every interaction between her son and Faith, she'd been well aware of it. Strange, when she'd never cared before, but having another woman usurp her place seemed to have set off the part of her DNA that wanted to be the queen of any domain in which she found herself. During their years of marriage, Shane had become well acquainted with that aspect of her personality, and at times, even admired it. But not anymore. Now he saw her behavior as the self-centered attention-grabbing ploy it was.

But tonight was all about Faith. At six, he dropped the boys off with Bex and Michael. An hour later, he'd primped himself to within an inch of his life—or as far as he could go without wearing a suit and being laughed out of Sailor's Retreat—and drove to her place to pick her up. He'd volunteered to be the sober driver since she well and truly deserved a few glasses of wine after what she'd endured for his sake. When she was nowhere to be seen, he climbed out of the car and strode to her door, then knocked firmly.

"Just a minute!" she yelled from somewhere within the house. "Please come in."

He did, and then perused the colorful artwork on the walls. Strolling further inside, he noted the quirky furniture, which included an ornate bookshelf in the hall and one of those old-fashioned stools people sat on while they played piano. He wondered whether she'd ever learned to play. For some reason, she didn't strike him as the musical sort.

Walking further into the house, he came to the bedroom door and hurried past to avoid catching sight of her in a state of undress. If he saw any part of Faith's divine body, they'd never leave the house. Especially not when Bex had okayed a sleepover and advised him to make the most of it. And yes, he wanted to make love to Faith—he suspected the desire was mutual—but before that, he needed to come clean about his feelings for her. Feelings that grew each time he saw her and went well beyond attraction or friendship.

"I'm coming, I promise," she called, her footsteps thudding across the floor behind him.

He turned, a smile at the ready, but the sight of her made his brain stop functioning. She'd dressed simply in high-waisted pants and a purple blouse. Her hair was loose over her shoulders and looked so silky he longed to wrap his hands in it. When she kissed his cheek, he noted that her silver heels were several inches tall.

"Gah." He shook himself. "You look amazing,"

Her answering grin flooded him with warmth. "You're pretty decent too, hot professor."

He glanced down at himself. "I was going more for 'single father who has it together, actually had time to shave for once, and isn't a complete loser with women.'"

Slowly, her smile stretched wider. "I think you hit the nail on the head, but there's no reason why you can't be those things and also a hot professor." Her smile turned naughty, and his jeans tightened inconveniently in response. "I always wondered what it would be like to be one of those students who got extra 'tutoring.'" She made air quotes with her fingers. "They always seem to score higher."

Shane's tongue tied itself in a knot. She was a vixen, and he had to get her out of this house right now or they'd never get anywhere. He craved her too badly.

Taking her by the elbow, he escorted her to the front door. "I have a booking at Sailor's Retreat. I know it's not particularly exciting since we were there just the other day, but I wanted to be nearby in case something goes wrong with the boys. I'm not used to being apart from them."

"Shane." Faith placed her hand on his. "Sailor's Retreat is lovely. I'm more interested in the company than the food."

"Good." Now, if only someone could jump-start his heart, because he was certain she'd stopped it. God, how was he going to make it through the night?

He led her to the car and drove the short distance to the restaurant, where he parked near the pavilion so she wouldn't have to walk far in pumps. A waitress met them inside the entrance and led them to a small table in the corner.

"I'll be back to take your order soon," she said, passing Shane a bottle of water.

Faith opened the menu. Shane didn't touch his, determined to get the hard part of the evening out of the way first. He sipped water to wet the inside of his mouth.

"Thanks for coming tonight and for helping with Diana. I know that goes above and beyond what we initially agreed to, but you should know that it means a lot to me."

"You're welcome." She cocked her head. "Why do I get the feeling you're gearing up for a speech that you've practiced in the mirror?"

The question shocked a laugh from him. "Maybe because I am."

"Okay." She waved a hand graciously. "By all means, continue."

He sighed. "You don't make this easy."

Her expression softened. "Sorry. I wasn't trying to be awkward. I tend to make light of things to mask my real thoughts and feelings. It's a character flaw."

One he could relate to, indirectly. He'd had to mask the extent of his personal struggles when Diana first left because otherwise he might not have been able to hold onto the boys. Besides, people didn't want to hear "No, I'm not okay. I lie awake in bed every night wondering what I did wrong and how I misjudged somebody so completely."

"You don't have to protect yourself from me," he said softly. "I promise."

Her throat rippled as she swallowed. "I know. It's a habit."

He wondered what had forced her to adopt it. She came across as carefree and self-assured, but maybe it was an act. Had someone hurt her? Anger heated his gut. If so, he wanted to know who and how, but that would come later, when she trusted him fully.

He bolstered himself. "I like you, Faith. You're

passionate about everything you do, and a lot of fun to be around. I—"

"Shane and Faith? For the second time in a week?" Dougal, the owner of Sailor's Retreat, interrupted Shane mid proclamation. "*Sans* family this time." A bead of sweat trickled down the shiny dome of his head. "I hope you're spoiling this lovely lady after what she had to deal with the other day."

"I'm hoping to," Shane said levelly. "If she'll let me."

"Oh, I fully intend to." Faith winked at Dougal in a way that left no doubt what was on her mind, and that lightened Shane's heart. He already knew she liked him as a friend, and if she wanted more, it was only a short stretch from there to returning his feelings, right? "How are you doing, Big D? Keeping well?"

Dougal shrugged. "Sylvia is happy, and you know what they say—happy wife, happy life. Anyway, I won't hold you up any longer. Enjoy your evening, folks."

As he left, Faith reached across the table and took Shane's hand. That simple gesture said a lot because they both knew that news of their solo date would be around town by noon tomorrow. "Where were we?"

"I believe I was halfway through my speech," he said. "I'd reached the part where I was listing the many ways in which you're a great woman."

She nodded, ticking them off on her fingers. "Passionate, fun—anything else?"

"Really damn beautiful."

Her cheeks reddened, filling him with delight.

"Let me get to the point. I like you, and I want to have the right to kiss you whenever I feel like it. I want to know, with one-hundred-percent certainty, that when we kiss, nothing about it is pretend."

Her fingers tightened around his and her pupils

expanded, darkening her eyes. Internally, he celebrated. It may have been a long, *long* time since he'd been intimate with someone, but he recognized the symptoms of arousal. Now for the hard part.

"I can understand if you don't feel the same way, given my messy past and the fact that every unattached man who comes through town seems to vie for your attention. I'm just a worn-out divorcé with very little free time, an interfering ex, and a ready-made family. But I'm tired of putting my hopes and dreams last, so I decided to take a chance and see how you felt." His lips pressed together, and when she didn't respond, he said, "I'm finished now."

AM I HEARING THIS RIGHT?

Faith could scarcely credit Shane's words. He'd blown her away. How on earth could he think she'd see him as anything less than the sexy, intelligent, caring man he was? Diana must have done a real number on him.

He cleared his throat. "You can say something now."

"Oh." She jerked back to the present, having been caught up in the emotion of the moment. The poor guy. She'd left him hanging. "I feel the same way, and you shouldn't sell yourself short. You're an amazing man, and easy on the eyes too. As far as the boys go, they're not a downside to me. I adore them, but if we want to try seeing each other for real, we have a long way to go to get Dylan on board."

He nodded, and she appreciated that he didn't try to bullshit or bluff his way out of acknowledging the problem. "We do. But don't take his rejection personally. I think he's gotten the idea that Diana and I will get back together—especially now that she's here. But that's never going to happen. Dylan likes you." He squeezed her hand, and his lips curved up. "He's just a bit messed up over the divorce. Once Diana goes home and he realizes there won't be a grand reunion like with his friend Caleb's parents, he'll warm up to the idea of us."

His statement niggled at a raw patch of insecurity in the back of Faith's mind, and she couldn't help but wonder: was Dylan the only one in the family who would choose Diana if given the chance? Shane's ex was successful, rich, and insanely beautiful—at least on the outside.

Faith wasn't the type of woman to sit on a question like that, so she came straight out and asked. "If Diana were to move to Haven Bay permanently, would you take her back?"

He blanched and stared at her like she'd slapped him. "Hell, no. Any woman who abandons her children is not the kind of woman I'd choose to have in my life. End of story."

Okay, so that made her feel better.

"She's beautiful."

"So is a leopard right before it strikes." He shook his head. "Beauty isn't everything, and it's not like there aren't other beautiful women around here." His smile softened, and his eyes darkened. "Like you."

She laughed. "Smooth, Walker, but there's a difference between Diana and me."

Reclaiming his hand, he rested his chin on it. "And what's that?"

She scoffed. "As if it's not obvious."

"Explain it to me," he said. "Because I don't see it."

She sighed. Was he really going to play dumb? "For starters, she's basically every man's living fantasy. Like a twenty-first-century Marilyn Monroe, only thinner." In fact, she'd seen that exact comparison in a women's magazine a few weeks back.

"What can I say?" He shrugged. "I prefer my women with their souls intact."

Her hand flew to her mouth, and her eyes boggled. She'd never heard him say anything so blunt or insulting about another person. Usually, he was nice. Almost too nice.

"Honestly, Faith," he continued, as though she weren't having a conniption, "You're every bit as gorgeous as she is—and younger, which I'm certain annoys her to no end—but this isn't about looks, and I hope you realize that. You're infinitely more likable than Diana. Besides, it isn't a competition. She's in my past, and I'd very much like you to be my future."

Faith melted faster than an ice cream in the midsummer heat, realizing how silly she'd been to indulge her insecurities. Normally, she was better than that, and if the circumstances were different, Diana's appearance wouldn't matter to her in the least. But because of her celebrity status and the fact she'd left Shane rather than the other way around, Faith had let herself travel down a path she wouldn't usually.

"It means a lot to hear that, and I'm sorry for asking. I just needed to be sure of your feelings where she's concerned."

"My feelings for her are nonexistent, except when it comes to the boys. On that front, I'm frustrated because she stirs everything up and then doesn't deal with the fallout. I'm also furious because whether it's intentional or not, she's toying with their emotions."

"Okay." Faith swallowed. "I appreciate the clarification. Now, shall we talk about something more pleasant?"

His shoulders sagged with relief, and it struck her that this was probably the first time he'd had to have this conversation since he'd gotten divorced. As far as she knew, he hadn't dated, and people around town made a point not to mention his ex-wife to him—or to anyone, as a matter of fact. There was a determined wall of silence as far as Diana Monroe was concerned.

"Such as?" he asked.

She allowed her lips to curve into a seductive smile. "What about how hot you looked in a suit last weekend?"

"Me?" He ran a hand through his hair and gave her an aw-shucks look. "You were the one who stole the show. That dress?" He closed his eyes, and his jaw tightened. "I wanted to rip it off you all night."

She shivered. "You did?"

"Yeah." He leaned across the table. "None of that touching was pretend. Those kisses were me trying to tell you how I felt. I just wasn't brave enough to say it yet. I mean, what would a woman like you want with me?"

Seriously, she was done for. "I'm getting the impression we've both wanted this for a long time and have been afraid the attraction was one-sided. What a shame, when we could have been enacting babysitter/single dad role-play fantasies."

He snorted. "That's a thing?"

God, he was clueless. Totally adorable.

"Yes, and for good reason. Surely you know by now that there's nothing sexier to many women than a man who's good with kids."

"Huh." He frowned. "Who knew?"

At that moment, the waitress interrupted. They each ordered, and Faith requested a fruity cocktail. When they were alone again, some of the tension from their previous conversation had dissipated.

"Tell me more about your family," he said. "There are your parents and Charity. Anyone else?"

"No, just us. There's not a lot to say, really. Dad's a minister. Mum's a busybody, but she means well."

"And Charity? What does she do?"

"She's a barista in Auckland."

He nodded, his expression thoughtful. "She's younger than you, right?"

Faith twisted her hair around her finger, wondering where this was going. "Yep, she's the baby of the family."

"She struck me as being an old soul."

Faith stopped twisting her hair and studied him warily. "She is. Not surprising considering what happened with her ex." The waitress returned with the cocktail, and Faith took a healthy drink from it. "How much do you know about the Hagley Investment scandal?"

"I remember that Samuel Hagley's investment firm defrauded a lot of people, and when it went south, he took their money and ran."

Faith took a deep breath. She always felt bad sharing Charity's history with anyone, even though it was hardly a secret. "The first Charity knew anything was amiss was when they arrested her."

"Oh." The word was full of meaning, but then his brows knotted together. "That poor girl. She must have been young at the time."

"Early twenties. Samuel was nearly twice her age, but she was in love with him, and nothing could change her mind. Mum and Dad tried to talk her out of marrying him, but there's no telling a girl that age anything when it comes to the man she's crazy about. She was legally old enough to marry him, so she did. Then everything fell apart."

"Wow."

Faith winced. "Yeah, she was totally alone. Our relationship had been damaged prior to that, so I didn't have much to do with her until a while after."

He poured himself a glass of water, and she waited, sensing that he had something on his mind. "You're sure she didn't know about the investments?"

"I'm certain. You can't fake that level of heartbreak."

"That bastard." His lips pressed into a firm line. "He let her take the fall?"

"He sure did. She might have served time if she hadn't agreed to testify for the prosecution when they finally tracked him down and took the case to trial. The problem is, no one around here remembers her role in putting him away. A lot of locals lost money, and since Hagley is in prison and not around to face them, they take out their anger on Charity, his young trophy wife. She left town immediately, and this was the first time she's been back."

"Understandable," he remarked. "It's too bad, but I can see why she stays away."

"Even if no one blamed her, I think she still would," Faith confessed, unsure why she was being so open. She hadn't even expressed these thoughts to her parents. "She wraps herself up in a layer of cynicism and snark, but she holds herself accountable more than anyone else ever has. She thinks she should have known something was amiss. She's too hard on herself. At the time, she was barely an adult and very inexperienced."

"Perhaps, but no one likes to have the wool pulled over their eyes. When it comes to poor choice of spouse, I can relate."

She smiled. "But you're making up for that now."

The look he gave her made her want to squeal or swoon. "I certainly hope so."

While they ate, they talked more. Faith told him what it was like to grow up in the bay and her memories of summers at the beach. She confessed how lonely she'd been as a teen because the other kids at school had thought her strange, but she didn't share what had happened when she was eighteen. She liked him thinking well of her and wanted that to continue. If he found out how stupid she'd been, she may as well flush his good opinion down the toilet.

In return, Shane regaled her with the trials and tribulations of life as a single father, making her laugh more than she had in ages. When she asked where he'd grown up, he told her about being raised in Wellington by a loving middle-class family. He had a sister, no brothers, and the family members took turns hosting Christmas. This year, the Walkers would be spending their festive season at Haven Bay.

"The boys are excited for it," he said, polishing off his dessert. "My parents spoil them rotten. They'll be here for Dylan's birthday too. That's not far off."

Faith's stomach knotted. She hadn't met his family before, and much as she looked forward to it, she couldn't help but fear that they'd be suspicious of the new woman in his life after the way Diana had hurt him. She couldn't blame them if they were because she'd be the same way toward any new man Charity started dating.

He held her gaze, and she got lost in his deep brown eyes.

Nerves? What nerves?

He glanced away, ending the moment, and she

stabbed a fork into her cake, then shoved a hunk into her mouth. She never ordered ice cream when she ate out because it inevitably didn't live up to her standards. But then, Dougal had been asking her to sell to him in bulk for years, and she hadn't, primarily because she didn't know where she'd find the time to make large batches. The only way would be to hire another person. Since taking on Megan as her business partner, profit had increased, but she wanted to be in a more financially secure position before having anyone else rely on her. She and Megan paid the business's bills out of their gross profit and split whatever was left. An employee would want a regular wage or salary, and she wasn't sure she could promise that.

When she couldn't eat another bite, she pushed her plate away and wiped her mouth on a napkin. It was time to be brave. Shane had made the first step by asking her out. If she wanted this date to go further, it was her turn to take the initiative. Resting her chin on her palm, she studied him through her glasses.

"So, Shane, how would you like to start this relationship off the right way?"

He stared back, one side of his mouth hitching up. "What's 'the right way'?"

She leaned closer and lowered her voice. "With the naked tango."

His lips parted. "As it happens, Bex has the boys all night."

"You don't say?" Things just kept looking up. "What do you reckon we go back to your place?"

He shot to his feet, his chair scraping back over the wooden floor. "Let's get out of here."

16

SHANE WHITE-KNUCKLED THE STEERING WHEEL AS HE
turned onto his street. Faith's hand rested on his thigh so
close to his crotch that if she shifted an inch, she'd find
out exactly how excited he was to get her alone. It had
been years since anyone touched him sexually—except
for himself, of course. Her fingers stroked along the
inseam of his jeans and he gulped, trying desperately to
keep his mind on the road. Finally, they reached his
house, and he swerved into the drive and slammed on
the brakes. They both jolted forward.

"Sorry," he muttered. "Having a hard time concen-
trating."

Faith's teeth sank into her lower lip, and she settled
her torturous hand over his erection. "Hard, huh?"

"Oh, damn." He flung the door open and climbed out
as gracefully as possible while sporting a massive erection and aching balls, then he strode around the car and
hauled her from the passenger seat. He backed her
against the vehicle, caging her between his arms. In this
position, they were much the same height, and he angled
his mouth over hers, plying her lips open while his hands

frantically touched every part of her they could find. She tasted of cake, and she was curved generously in all the right places. He slid his hand into her hair, and the strands slipped over his fingers like red silk. He tugged, drawing her head back so he could drop kisses along her neck. She sucked in a shaky breath.

Fuck, what was he doing? They were in his driveway where anyone could see. Not to mention, he'd pressed her up against the cold metal of his car. Guilt pricked at him.

He pulled back. "Sorry. Would you like to come in? I'll try to be more civilized. I don't usually maul my dates on the front lawn."

Her eyebrows shot up. "Don't usually, huh? So, only forty percent of the time?"

He shook his head and backed away, because the only other choice would be to latch onto the pulse point fluttering at the base of her throat. "I misspoke. I haven't dated since Diana left. You're the first. I just meant that I'm not in the habit of disrespecting women."

"Oh." At this, she seemed thoughtful. Then she winked. "I don't mind." She brushed past him and sashayed toward the house. When she reached the porch, she glanced over her shoulder. "Are you coming?"

He hurried to catch up. Life with Faith would certainly never be boring.

As he fumbled with the keys, he faced up to the truth. "Uh, Faith. I don't know if you've realized this, but I haven't had sex in years.

"I thought that was probably the case."

The key slotted into the lock and he stepped back to let her in. She headed straight for the bedroom, and he followed, watching the swing of her ass and promising himself he'd fill his hands with it before long.

"I'm concerned I'm going to lose my cool and embarrass myself." Being unable to see her face made the admission easier.

But then she swung around. "Shane, we've got all night. If round one ends too quickly, there's always round two. Or were you planning to have your way with me, then kick me to the curb?"

He rolled his eyes. She was teasing, trying to take his mind off things, and he appreciated it. "I'm up for as many rounds between now and dawn as you can handle."

"Good." He loved that self-satisfied smile on her lips. He'd keep it there forever if he could. "In fact," she added thoughtfully, trailing a finger down his chest, "Why don't we take the edge off for you, so it isn't a mad sprint to the finish later?"

He swallowed. "What do you mean, 'take the edge off'?"

She sunk to her knees, giving him a spectacular view of her cleavage, and reached for the button of his jeans. His back hit the wall. "If you come now, you'll have more stamina the second time around." She eyed his fly. "And personally, I've always wondered what you're hiding behind here." Her deft fingers had the zip open in seconds, and she peeled his waistband down.

Summoning more self-control than he'd ever thought possible, he stilled her with a hand on her shoulder. "Whoa, hold on. If your mouth touches me anywhere below the waist, I'm a goner."

"That's kind of the point." She slid her hand inside his jeans and palmed his bulge.

"Doesn't seem fair," he panted as she cupped him and squeezed. "What about you?"

She sat back on her heels and released him. "I'm sure

152

you'll make it up to me. But if you don't want this, we can—"

"No, I do." His dick strained toward her as though it sensed how close it had been to getting relief. "Don't stop."

Grinning wickedly, she ran a hand over him, and then pulled his underwear down, freeing him. He was painfully hard, and she licked her lips.

Touch it. Please. Stop the torture.

Considering this was the closest he'd come to sex in forever, his patience was rapidly waning.

"I love it," she announced. He laughed raggedly. He'd done a little personal grooming earlier in case they got to this point. He hadn't expected it, but he'd wanted to be prepared, just in case. That was the same reason he'd purchased a new box of condoms. He was a planner.

She wrapped her palm around his length and pumped once. His hips jerked, and he fought to stay upright. Then her mouth closed over him, and he groaned. Warm, wet, soft.... Heaven.

And it had been *so long*.

Her tongue glided along the shaft, then flicked over the head, and his hands fisted at his sides. She worked him with her mouth, and he fought to keep his eyes open, not wanting to miss a second of it. Her lipstick had rubbed off, and her lips were pale pink against him. She gazed up at him through her glasses, her hazel eyes alight with mischief, looking like every naughty fantasy he'd ever had. Somehow, this was the most connected he'd felt to another person in years. Since long before Diana left. Their marriage hadn't been perfect by any stretch. In hindsight, it hadn't even been good. But Faith.... With her, he could have something amazing.

Don't be that guy who gets mushy during a blow job.

It was difficult, but he managed to bite his tongue. When he talked to her about his emotions, she deserved to know it wasn't because he was on the verge of the best orgasm ever.

She sucked harder.

"Holy crap." His hands twisted in her hair, and the last of his conscious thoughts fled. He became a mindless, needy mass of man. Thighs trembling. Chest heaving. Hands grasping. She stroked his balls so fucking gently, and he couldn't take any more. "Faith, I'm gonna—"

She released him with a pop. His hips thrust uselessly forward, finding nothing but air, and he teetered on the edge of bliss. Meanwhile, she stripped her blouse off, and her bra followed. He gulped. He'd never seen breasts so lush and perfect. Pale, luminous skin. Pink aureoles. A deep space between them.

"Sorry about that," she said, taking him in her hand and stroking. He groaned, and his head hit the wall. "I know how much you like these, and I didn't want to waste an opportunity."

An opportunity for what?

He didn't have to wonder long because she gathered her breasts together and positioned his dick between them.

"Oh, God." He groaned. "Are you.... Can I...?"

Jesus, he couldn't even get the words out.

"Yes." She winked, and he just about came right then. She slid him up and down in her cleavage, and all it took was for her to lick her lips to send him hurtling into oblivion. His vision faded to black, and he bent forward, catching himself on her shoulders.

When he regained control of his mental faculties, he opened his eyes and found her grinning up at him, the result of years of pent-up lust forming a sticky coating over her chest.

"Ugh," he grunted, righting himself. "Sorry, I...." He trailed off, unable to explain why he'd thought it would be a good idea to spill himself all over her like that.

"Relax, Shane," she said, getting to her feet. "That's exactly what I wanted, and I think you needed it. Now I'm going to shower and clean off. Join me?"

"How stupid would I be to say no to that?" He followed her to the bathroom, his heart thudding rapidly in his chest. He could scarcely believe what they'd just done. It was hands down the single hottest experience of his life, and he had a feeling they were only getting started. How had he gotten so damn lucky?

In the bathroom, she started the shower and shimmied out of her pants, revealing herself to him fully for the first time. She was all porcelain skin and mouthwatering curves. He couldn't choose which part of her he wanted to touch first.

"You're beautiful," he rasped. A natural redhead too. He'd never been sure because it was difficult to believe that anyone had such glorious auburn hair without the aid of a bottle.

She discarded her glasses, stepped beneath the stream of water, and gestured at his body. "Your turn, and make it nice and slow."

Oh, he could do that. He could play this game with her. She'd been right: now that he'd had his own release, taking his time would be much easier. One by one, he undid the buttons on his shirt, maintaining eye contact with Faith the entire time. When he reached the last one, he paused, drawing it out. Her eyes narrowed, but she didn't urge him on. He parted the shirt, pleased when her eyes darkened with desire. He'd worried he wouldn't live up to the younger, fitter men who flirted with her at the ice cream parlor, but her expression told him she liked what she saw.

Her hands journeyed downward over her breasts and the swell of her hips and into the slickness at the top of her thighs. His jeans came off with a whole lot less finesse. He tossed his socks away and joined her.

"Do you have any idea how sexy you are?" he demanded, grabbing her hips and yanking her closer.

Water sparkled on the tips of her lashes. "Why don't you show me?"

Good suggestion. He backed her into the wall, sank to his knees, and proceeded to do just that.

———

FAITH WOKE HOURS LATER WITH SHANE WRAPPED AROUND her body. She smiled into the dark. Considering how she usually slept—starfished across the bed—it was a miracle he'd managed to find room and hadn't ended up on the floor. She burrowed closer. He smelled of soap, with a hint of old books—his usual scent, and she utterly adored it.

The *things* he'd done to her last night. The man possessed a spectacularly skilled tongue. He'd licked her like she was the tastiest treat he'd ever tried, and it hadn't taken long before she'd been quivering in his arms. Then they'd collapsed into bed and promptly fallen asleep. They hadn't gotten around to actually making love, but there was no time like the present. She rolled over to face him and pressed a kiss to his mouth.

"Shane?"

He mumbled something.

"Want to pick up where we left off earlier?"

At this, his eyes snapped open. "Yeah." His voice was rough from sleep and sent shivers down her spine. She kissed him again, and this time, he returned it, drawing her into the warmth of his body. Something hard poked her belly, and she grinned. Not all of him was sleepy. She snaked her hand between them and wrapped her fingers around him, pumping gently.

He rocked into her hand. "You can wake me like this any time."

Oh, yeah. She was getting lucky.

"I'll remember that." She continued caressing him, enjoying the way his breath became shallow and soft sounds emerged from his throat. He slid his fingers between her legs and teased her. Then, when her breaths matched his, he slipped one finger inside her and stroked her channel.

She trembled. "You really know what you're doing."

He dropped kisses along the curve of her shoulder. "I've had a lot of time to think about what I'd do if I ever got you naked."

She gulped. Here she'd thought her crush on him had been unrequited. "What else did you think about?"

"Being inside you. Making you scream. I have this theory—" He paused to nibble on her ear lobe, and her grip around him tightened reflexively. "—that you'll be loud in bed."

She tried to chuckle, but she was too turned on to do anything more than sigh. "I'm loud everywhere, so it's probably a safe bet."

He rose on his elbows above her, his eyes glittering in the dark. "I don't want to guess. I want to know."

Yeah, she was on board with that. She stretched up, trying to kiss him, but he reared back, dodging her mouth, his gaze locked on her face while he tormented her.

"You're only teasing yourself too," she told him.

His jaw clenched. "I want to make it good."

"It is," she assured him. "It will be. Because it's you."

He gave her the kiss she'd been craving, then pulled away. "I want the light on."

She stiffened. She had nothing against making love in the light, but generally, she didn't know her lovers' dating history. Shane had been with an absolute goddess of a woman. How could she compare? And yes, she knew he'd already seen everything, but only after she'd driven him mindless with desire. This felt different.

Sensing her hesitation, he got off and gathered her close. "I can leave it off if you'd prefer, but I love your body, and I want to watch you while I'm inside you."

She silently chastised herself. It wasn't like her to be shy. She'd never been that way, and she shouldn't start just because the situation had stirred up some old memories and insecurities.

"Turn it on," she said, deciding to be brave. "I want to see you too."

He laughed. "Let's hope you don't get buyer's remorse when you see what you're in bed with."

His words eased her nerves. He was as unbalanced as she. They were both muddling their way through this.

"As if. You're the hottest daddy in town, Mr. Walker."

He dropped his mouth close to her ear. "Make me believe it."

A moment later, he reached for the lamp and switched it on, illuminating them both in a soft orange glow. He scanned her body—or what was visible of it—and his lips curved appreciatively. "Beautiful."

Through his eyes, she felt like she was. Returning the

favor, she studied his lean, compact body, gazing from his broad chest to his flat stomach with a happy trail that made her very happy indeed, and lastly, the eager erection that she knew would fulfill all of her sensual cravings.

"Sexy as hell," she proclaimed, pleased when his eyes crinkled at the corners and he kissed her. She loved his mouth on hers. Loved falling into a whirlpool of sensation as their bodies moved together. He grabbed a condom and rolled it on, then he was pushing inside her, filling her like they were made for each other.

"You feel amazing," she whispered, holding his gaze as he began to thrust. They moved rhythmically. Faith, not content to be a passive party, wrapped her legs around him and urged him on. She kissed, sucked, and licked along his throat and whimpered when he shoved harder and deeper in response.

"You like that?" He did it again, grunting with the effort.

"More," she demanded, grabbing his butt and grinding on him.

"Oh, shit." He raised his hips and slammed into her, his balls slapping against her ass. "This is my new favorite place."

"Good." Her head fell back, and she writhed beneath him, fighting desperately against the climax building within her. She wanted to draw this out for longer. To find pleasure with him. But he had other plans, and with a single flick of his finger, she came apart, crying out his name.

"That's it," he murmured. "That's it, beautiful girl."

She squeezed her eyes shut so that the pleasure—combined with his endearment—didn't make her cry. Not in a bad way, but in a "Holy shit, I'm falling in love with this guy" kind of way. She wasn't ready for that, so she just clasped him tighter and clenched around him, not letting up until he groaned long and low and jerked as he found his own release.

Faith buried her face in his shoulder, hoping to share all of the emotions she was feeling without having to say a word. He held her just as desperately, and their heartbeats synced, beating as one.

She didn't sleep again after that. Her heart was in too much trouble.

17

THE DAY AFTER THE BEST NIGHT IN RECORDED HISTORY, Shane's sky was bluer, his sun was brighter, and the most frustrating students couldn't bring him down. He walked with a spring in his step, and when approached by one of the mothers who seemed to enjoy backing him into a corner, he managed to escape with everything intact—including his mood. All of that lasted until an expensive rental car pulled up at school while he was on traffic duty, and Diana stepped out.

Immediately, his back teeth clamped together and his spine stiffened. He hadn't seen her since dinner on Tuesday, but he'd known she wouldn't have slunk away. She'd have made a scene. Quietly leaving wasn't her thing. Designer sunglasses hid her eyes, but he felt them laser-beaming into him. Before she could take a step toward him, a pair of parents seemed to recognize her and rushed over, speaking excitedly. She smiled. She'd always loved being the center of attention. While she was talking to them, the bus from the middle school came around the corner. The one Dylan was on. Her head snapped up as though she was a predator that had sighted prey.

"Can we cross now?"

Shane jerked in surprise. While he'd been staring at Diana, a group of children had assembled, ready for him to help them across the street. "Oh yeah, sure thing."

He waved for the next car to stop and stepped into the center of the road, holding the orange flag while the kids hurried over to their parents. By the time he got back to the sidewalk, Diana had parted from the couple she'd been with. Scanning the area, he spotted her beside the bus.

What's she doing?

Whatever it was, it couldn't be good. One of the older students came through the gate, and Shane held up a hand to stop her. "Milly, do you mind being traffic warden for five minutes? I need to take care of something."

"Yep, I can do that."

"Great." He handed her the flag and high-vis vest, then hurried to the bus Dylan was disembarking from. "What are you doing?" he asked Diana.

She ran a hand through the length of her blonde hair. "What does it look like? I'm picking up Dylan. We're going to the beach."

Dylan joined them, and Shane turned to him. "Did you know about this?"

He shrugged, his expression sullen. "Yeah. I didn't think it was a big deal."

"Well, it is."

Diana waved dismissively. "It's a harmless visit. What's the problem with that? He's my son too."

"Yes, but I have sole custody. That means you have to clear things like this with me first."

She slipped her sunglasses off and tucked them into her purse. "For now."

Wait—what's that supposed to mean?

"Excuse me?"

She lifted one delicate shoulder. "You heard me. I was merely agreeing that for now, you have sole custody of the boys."

Shane's stomach bottomed out. Was that a hint she planned to challenge him for custody? Or was this a ploy to unsettle him and win Dylan's favor? Speaking of, Dylan was watching their back-and-forth like it was a tennis match. Guilt weighed heavily on Shane. They shouldn't be having this discussion in front of him.

"Away you go," he said gently. "Just be home before eight."

Finally, the tension seemed to ease from Dylan. "Thanks, Dad."

"Eight," he said to Diana, pointedly.

She rolled her eyes. "I hear you. Come along, Dylan."

WHEN THE SHOP QUIETENED FOR THE AFTERNOON, FAITH decided to get a head start on cleaning. She was sweeping the floor when she glanced up and spotted a scene outside the window that made her freeze. There, on the pavilion, was Diana Monroe, holding court for a cluster of tourists. Off to the side, with his hands in his pockets, stood Dylan. Another pair of tourists joined the group, jostling him further away from Diana. He backed off, putting space between himself and her posse, his shoulders hunched.

Faith's heart squeezed. Poor Dylan. It was obvious he wanted to spend time with his mother. Meanwhile, she was busy lapping up attention from everyone in a hundred-foot radius. Returning behind the counter, Faith grabbed her phone and texted him.

Faith: *Want a free ice cream? Come on in.*

She watched him check his phone and look in the window. Then he turned back to Diana, trying—and failing—to talk to her. Finally, head low, he shuffled over to The Shack.

"Hey there," Faith called. "You look like you need ice cream. What flavor?"

He didn't meet her eyes, and from the way he scowled, she wondered if he was still mad at her. Never mind. She wasn't one to hold a grudge against a preteen. While he perused the options, she washed her hands. She was alone in the store because Megan had headed away early to spend the weekend with her family in Auckland.

"Russian fudge, please," Dylan said.

"No problem. Coming right up." She scooped the caramel-colored ice cream into a cone. "With chocolate dip?"

"Yes, please."

She dunked the ice cream into her vat of chocolate and made sure it had dried before popping it into the stand atop the display case. "Here you go."

He took it and glanced over his shoulder, as though debating whether to go back outside.

"Must be hard having a famous mum," she said as she started wiping down the counters, not wanting to put him on guard.

"It's cool," he replied in a tone that said otherwise. "No one else at school has a mum who's been in the movies."

"I bet. She's pretty unique." Faith didn't mean that in a good way.

Dylan eyeballed her, clearly trying to tell if she was being sarcastic. "She calls me sometimes when she's not at filming. Dad knows, but we don't talk about it."

"Uh-huh." If he was about to get something off his chest, she didn't want to say anything to stop him.

"He just doesn't understand. But—"

The door swung open, interrupting whatever he'd been about to say. Diana stood in the entrance, glaring at Faith in a way that brought back memories of Mason's ex-girlfriend, Gigi, and the other mean girls from high school.

"What do you think you're doing with my son?"

"Serving him ice cream." She refused to be cowed. "He was going out of his mind with boredom waiting for you to finish with your adoring fans."

Diana sniffed. "Dealing with fans is just part of being related to a celebrity. Come, Dylan. We've got better places to be."

Shaking her head, Faith watched them go. What Shane had seen in that woman—besides the obvious— she didn't know.

"Thanks for the ice cream," Dylan called as they exited, earning him an evil eye from his mother.

Faith chuckled. Some parental instincts appeared to be universal.

———

At five past eight, Diana dropped Dylan at home. Shane knew she'd timed it purposefully to rile him. She wanted to send a message that he wasn't in control of the situation, but she also wouldn't push things far enough that he could accuse her of ignoring him. This was a familiar tactic. One he'd largely forgotten until now and didn't miss in the slightest.

"Thanks for bringing him back," he said begrudgingly.

"No problem." She cocked her head and studied him thoughtfully. "After we ran into your girlfriend, we bought dinner and ate it at the beach. This town really needs to invest in a greater diversity of dining options."

Shane didn't disagree, but he wasn't about to admit that. "You saw Faith?"

She rolled her eyes. "Like you didn't already know that."

"I didn't."

"Huh. I thought she'd have run to you the moment we left. Isn't she keeping tabs on us for you?"

"No, why? Wait." He held up a hand to stop her. "Dylan, why don't you make a start on your homework?"

"Okay." He seemed relieved to have the opportunity to escape. Backpack hanging from one hand, he headed to his room.

"What happened with Faith?" he asked once Dylan was out of hearing range.

"Oh, nothing much." The cameras loved that catlike smile of hers, but he hated it. "While I was talking with some fans, she lured Dylan into her quaint little shop for ice cream. I figured you'd asked her to spy on us, but the ice cream surprised me. Have you given up your health food obsession?"

"Just relaxed it." He'd certainly had no idea about the ice cream, but he didn't care about it at the moment. He was more concerned with whether Diana had left Faith unscathed. "What did you do?"

Her eyes widened, all innocence. "What makes you think I'd be anything other than perfectly cordial?"

He shook his head, disgusted with her and with

166

himself. He hated these conversations that were effectively tennis matches with parried questions and evasive answers. Give him good old-fashioned bluntness any day.

"Just go."

She frowned. "Aren't you going to thank me?"

Shane clutched the fraying ends of his patience. "For what?"

She seemed surprised by his confusion. "For taking Dylan out and spending time with him."

That cemented it. She was a terrible mother.

"No, I'm not going to thank you for doing something any mother should do. You're lucky to get the chance to be around him, not the other way around."

With a huff, she swung around, and the moment her feet passed over the threshold, he shut the door behind her and locked it. Then he ran a hand through his hair, wondering whether he needed to call Faith to apologize —again—or if it was more urgent to check in with Dylan and make sure Diana hadn't gotten into his head, as she was so talented at doing. Deciding Dylan was more vulnerable than Faith, he went to his son's room and knocked.

"Yeah?" Dylan called.

Shane cracked the door open. "Can I come in?"

"If you want."

He opened it further. Dylan sat on the edge of his bed with his arms crossed, scowling. Shane joined him, leaving enough space between them so that Dylan wouldn't feel crowded.

"How was dinner with your mum?"

"Fine."

Ah, so that's how this was going to go. "I heard you got ice cream too."

Dylan still didn't look at him. "Yeah, and?"

"Was it good?"

This seemed to catch him off guard. "Yeah. The Shack makes the best ice cream." He meant that Faith makes the best ice cream, but he didn't want to use her name. Sighing, Shane wondered whether Diana had tried to poison Dylan against her, or if this was all coming from him.

Dylan scuffed his foot on the floor. "Mum says she might come back permanently if she was allowed to move home."

A sharp pain stabbed Shane in the chest. How dare she get their son's hopes up like that? She was manipulating him to get what she wanted. Diana would never live here full-time. She loved stardom too much. But she had no problem toying with Dylan's emotions in order to screw with Shane. Hesitantly, he rested a hand on his son's skinny knee.

"She's welcome to move back to the bay," he said, hoping he wasn't about to screw up monumentally. No one had ever prepared him for the myriad ways he could mess up his children. "I hope she does because you deserve to have her around, but there's something you need to understand. Your mother and I are never getting back together. No ifs, buts, or maybes. We're just not."

Dylan yanked his leg from beneath Shane's hand and stood, then marched to the other side of the room and sunk to the floor, where he drew his knees to his chest.

"Is it because of Faith?"

Ugh. Shane winced. Dylan really had a hang-up where she was concerned. Was it resolvable?

"No, buddy, it's not. Even before Faith and I started spending time together, I wouldn't have invited Diana back into our house. It's not where she belongs."

"But she's our family," he insisted. "Caleb's parents got

back together after his dad's girlfriend left, so why can't Mum come back if Faith leaves?"

"Family wouldn't run away to America and leave us behind," Shane reminded him softly. "That's something your mother did before I even knew Faith. I'm sorry, but just because Caleb's parents worked it out doesn't mean we can. It's a completely different situation."

Dylan's eyes welled with tears, but whether they were of sadness or frustration, he couldn't tell. "Why does it have to be?" he demanded. "She came back."

For now.

"You're not making things easy," Dylan continued. "Why won't you give her a chance?"

Shane leaned forward. "If you took a flight to Los Angeles without clearing it with me first and hid for a whole year while I tried to find you, would you expect me to forgive you straight away?"

"No." His voice was small.

"Exactly."

But Dylan wasn't done yet. Chin on the top of one knee, he studied Shane, his hair flopping in his eyes. "Is Faith your girlfriend for real now?"

Shane decided to shoot straight with him. "Not officially, but I'd like her to be."

"Hmph."

Wanting to be on a more even level, Shane sank to the ground opposite Dylan. It was time to show his hand. "Faith makes me happy. She's funny, and a bit crazy, and she loves you guys."

At this, Dylan rolled his eyes.

"Dyl, let's talk about this, man to man. Whether you like it or not, your mother and I are divorced, and I'm going to want to date again at some point. It might not be now, but it'll happen. If it can't be your mum, wouldn't you rather the woman in our lives be someone you like?"

"But why do you have to date? I don't want things to change. I don't want you to get too busy with her and not have time for us."

"Oh, buddy." Shane sighed. "I will always have time for you. You and Hunter are the most important people in my life."

Dylan peered across at him. "You promise?"

"I promise," Shane said solemnly.

"Okay." Dylan raised his chin. "I guess Faith is all right."

It was a small concession, but to Shane, it seemed momentous.

18

SHANE DRAGGED HIMSELF AND THE BOYS DOWN TO SCHOOL at the ass crack of dawn, after checking and rechecking Dylan's bag to make sure he had everything he needed so he could be shipped off to camp for the night. He'd offered to be a parent volunteer and join the excursion, but Dylan had begged him not to. Apparently, he'd reached the age when his dad was no longer "cool", so Shane clapped him on the shoulder and waved goodbye as the bus took off. Then he and Hunter returned home to eat yogurt with fruit for breakfast.

"Would you like to do a sleepover with Izzy tonight?" he asked as they sat at the table.

Hunter's brows knitted together. "On a kindy day?"

"That's right, bud. It's a special occasion. Dylan gets to go on camp, so why shouldn't you get to do something too?" He crossed his fingers, hoping Hunter would go for the idea. Even though Bex's daughter, Izzy, was a couple of years older, she and Hunter got along well.

"Yeah!" Hunter exclaimed. "Can we camp on the floor?"

"You'll have to ask Miss Cane about that. Why don't

you pack a bag, and she can pick you up after kindergarten?"

Hunter started to stand, but Shane stopped him. "Hold up. Finish your breakfast first."

Hunter grumbled but complied, shoveling yogurt into his mouth until it was gone, then he raced away to pack. Shane grinned and sent Faith a text.

Shane: *We're on for tonight. Come over for dinner at 7pm.*

If his sons both got to spend time with friends, it was only fair he did too, right?

How many candles is too many?

The day had flown by, and Shane found himself setting the dinner table in a frantic rush, walking a fine line between romantic and over the top. He wanted to woo Faith, but not set the house on fire. Deciding three candles was enough, he lit them, then packed the rest away and dimmed the lights. He'd already laid out cutlery and napkins, so he hurried back to the kitchen to stir the pot of spaghetti bolognese that was a few minutes from being done.

In his past life, Shane hadn't been much of a cook, but he'd learned quickly after Diana left because taking care of himself had been the only way to stop the Bridge Club from turning up with casseroles every other night. Much as he'd appreciated their support, he hadn't wanted their pity. Especially in the early days when he insisted Diana would return as soon as she realized her mistake.

He poured two glasses of red wine and carried them to the table, then sliced French bread to accompany the spaghetti and grabbed the salad he'd prepared earlier. The rap of knuckles on wood caught his attention, and he glanced at the clock. Right on time. Then why did he feel so flustered and caught off guard?

He scanned his button-down shirt for sauce stains as he hurried to the front door. He yanked it open and stopped abruptly to stare. Faith wore a yellow cocktail dress and funky retro heels that must have been four inches high.

His gaze drifted down her amazing legs. "Wow."

She grinned, drawing his attention to her bold red lips. "You look pretty wow yourself." She handed him a small cardboard box that he hadn't even noticed she'd been holding. "Dessert, courtesy of Megan."

He lifted the lid. Nestled inside were two cupcakes topped with a thin layer of pink frosting and fresh strawberries.

"Strawberry and champagne," she explained. "She wanted to go with chocolate-covered strawberries, but I thought that might be a little on the nose."

"They look great." He tucked the box under his arm and offered her his hand. She interlocked her fingers with his and followed him into the house.

"Should I take my shoes off?"

"God, no." He glanced down at her calves again. "Do you have any idea how sexy they are? I want to be the one to take them off, but not until after dinner."

Her grin turned naughty. "Well, if you insist." She sniffed the air. "Something smells delicious."

"Spaghetti bolognese," he said, "With homemade pasta."

He showed her into the dining area, and her eyes widened. "If you're trying to impress me, it's working."

"Good." He escorted her to the table and pulled out a chair. "Tonight, you get the full date experience because

I've been a bit remiss up until now. Give me two minutes, and I'll be out with dinner."

He set the cupcakes on the counter and checked the selection of food to make sure everything was in order. He dished up two plates of spaghetti, added a few slices of bread, and arranged the side salads in white bowls. It looked as good as it was going to get. He brought the salads out first, placing one in front of Faith and the other where he would sit. On his second trip, he watched Faith for her reaction, and he wasn't disappointed.

She perked up and waved a hand to waft the scent toward herself. "That smells scrumptious."

"Thank you. It's my signature dish."

She flashed her teeth. One of the things he loved about Faith was how wholeheartedly she did things. She fully committed, even when it backfired on her, and that was exactly the kind of woman he wanted in his life.

"Is this how you woo all the ladies?"

He claimed his seat and raised a wine glass to clink against hers. "There's only one lady I'm interested in wooing."

Her grin faded but not in a bad way. More like he'd taken her by surprise. He didn't know why that would be the case. "I'm serious," he continued as she tucked into her meal, humming in pleasure when she got her first taste. "I know it's corny, but I mean every word. I haven't dated since the divorce went through because I don't care about dating just for the sake of it. I'm spending time with you because I see you as someone I might want to share my life with. And to that end—" He sipped his wine and forced himself to swallow. "—I'd like us to be official."

"Official," she mused, holding his gaze, the flecks of green in her eyes brightening. "As in...?"

"As in, tell the boys, tell the whole town, official." Thank God he hadn't eaten anything yet. His gut wouldn't be handling this so well. "As in, you and I don't date anyone else, and perhaps one day we move in together and get married. That kind of official." When her lips parted and her nostrils flared, he hurried on. "Not immediately. I'm not trying to force you into anything you're not ready for. I just want you to know I'm thinking long-term."

Slowly, her lips curved up. "Have I told you that you're adorable when you're flustered?"

"Uh, no." He ran a hand through his hair. "So, what do you say?" He cringed internally. *What do you say?* Talk about unromantic.

She rested her elbows on the table and leaned closer. "I say, hell yes."

His racing heart began to calm, forcing him to admit he'd half expected her to reject him. Any sane woman would. He came with a ton of baggage. But for some reason, she wanted him.

"Great, then it's official." He smiled. "You're all mine."

"Same goes for you, buster. Every member of the mum brigade is going to know you're off the market before the week is over."

He laughed. "Feel free to take out an ad in the school newsletter if it makes you happy."

"I just might." She scooped spaghetti onto a piece of French bread and bit into it. "Seriously, this is good. Be honest with me: how nervous were you before popping your question?"

"Maybe a one out of ten."

She rolled her eyes. "Liar. But I'm glad you did. I, uh." She looked down, her expression uncharacteristically vulnerable. "I haven't had much luck in relationships, and it means a lot to me to know that we're on the same page and that I'm not hanging out on a ledge by myself."

His gut tightened. "Sweetheart, you'll never be alone on that ledge. I'll be right there with you"

How had he not noticed that she was feeling her way along as much as he was? And what was the poor dating history she'd mentioned? He'd never given it a lot of thought, but now that he did, she hadn't had a boyfriend for as long as they'd been friends. She'd had flings with tourists from time to time, and flirted her heart out with The Shack's patrons, but never anything more. She was a vivacious woman with no shortage of options, so why had she chosen to stay single?

Perhaps he wasn't the only one who'd been scarred by the past. But one thing was for sure. Whatever damage Diana had done, he was on his way to falling in love with Faith St. John, and he just had to cross his fingers and pray she wouldn't wreck him.

FAITH'S LIMBS TANGLED WITH SHANE'S, AND SHE USED HIS chest as a pillow. She should have drifted into a blissful sleep considering how well he'd worn her out, but something niggled at the back of her mind. A dark, insidious doubt that wouldn't seem to quiet. She couldn't recall feeling this strongly about a man before. Not even during her intense relationship with Mason. She saw Shane, and wanted to touch him. She touched him, and wanted to hold him. Then every time she held him, she feared that she was tumbling into love.

None of which would be a problem, except for a couple of teeny-weeny little hitches. The obvious one was Dylan, but Shane also didn't know about her past.

176

Tonight would have been the perfect opportunity to tell him. He'd set the tone by making himself vulnerable. Once or twice, she'd opened her mouth to come clean, but she just hadn't been able to. She feared it would make him look at her differently. But then, he was bound to find out at some point, and it would be best if he heard it from her. She just needed to get the timing right.

19

SHANE WAS HUNCHED OPPOSITE DYLAN AT THE DINNER table while they worked through his math homework together. "If x plus five is seven, and $2x$ is four, then what's x?"

"Two."

"Correct." He moved on to the next question. "What is the square root of sixty-four?"

Dylan's eyebrows pinched together in concentration. "Eight?"

"You got it. This one is a bit harder. If—" The doorbell cut him off. It took him a moment to place the sound because no one ever used it. Most people in these parts knocked. "Keep going, buddy. I'll be back in a minute."

Hunter tried to follow him, but Shane pointed at his drawing of Tinkerbell and indicated he should keep coloring. The cat loved having Hunter's undivided attention while he sketched her. Not that it was much of a likeness. When he opened the door to reveal their visitor, he immediately wished he'd pretended not to hear the bell. Diana stood on the threshold, pouting with pink lips and dressed in designer slacks and a blouse that hid nothing at all.

"We need to talk," she said.

A shiver of premonition slid down his spine. Whatever this was, it couldn't be good.

"Come in. Dylan will be pleased to see you."

She didn't smile. He'd known she wouldn't, because in saying so, he'd inadvertently reminded her that her other son couldn't care less. "Actually, I'm here to see you."

"I'm busy."

Her eyes narrowed. "Make time."

Sighing, he stepped aside to let her in. "Fine, but only if you say hi to Dylan first."

"I'd be happy to." She stalked through the house as though she owned it, heading straight to the living area, where they'd been working on their homework together. "Hi, boys," she said, with the graciousness of a returning queen.

"Mum!" Dylan shot to his feet, beaming. "Are you here for dinner?"

"I'm afraid not," Shane broke in before she had the chance to accept the invitation.

"This is just a flying visit," Diana agreed, catching him by surprise. "I need to have a word with your dad." She turned to him and arched a brow. "How about in your bedroom?"

He winced, not wanting the boys to get the wrong idea. "I'd prefer the lounge."

"Trust me," she murmured. "You want to do this in private."

Her tone made him nervous, and he acquiesced, taking her to his room and circling the bed so it was between them. She shook her head as though he were being childish, then unzipped her purse, extracted her phone, and handed it to him wordlessly. Shane glanced down and everything inside him froze. It was a photo of Faith. Much younger—perhaps eighteen or nineteen—completely naked and sprawled on a bed with a come-hither gaze. He shoved the phone back into Diana's hand as though it had burned him.

"What the fuck is this, and how did you get it?"

She laughed. "It's nothing half her graduating class hasn't already seen."

"Excuse me?" She was playing games, and he hated it.

"You'd better sit down. You're not going to like this."

He sat. "Explain. Fast."

Diana tucked her flirty skirt beneath her legs and perched on the edge of the bed. "Let me tell you a story. One about a chubby teenage girl—"

"She's fucking gorgeous," he interrupted, "Exactly how she is. You know it, and I know it, so don't make a fool of yourself by pretending otherwise."

She rolled her eyes. "Whatever the case, she was so desperate for attention that she sent unsolicited pictures of herself to the most popular boy in school. One who already had a girlfriend."

"I don't believe you." Faith wasn't like that. He could imagine her agreeing to a naked photoshoot because she wasn't shy about her sexuality, but sending the results to someone who was in a relationship? No, he couldn't see that at all.

"Well, you'd better believe it." She swiped the phone and offered it to him again. He kept his hands firmly on his lap. "There are more," she said. "I have this from a source very close to the situation—the guy's girlfriend. She did what any woman would do and made sure her friends knew what Faith was."

Nausea threatened to overwhelm him. "You're telling me these photographs were shared around among the girls in her year while Faith was still in high school?" What kind of person would do such a thing to a vulnerable teenage girl? "That's disgusting."

"Yes, I know," Diana said with a sneer. "Mason Delphine thought so too. That's why he confessed everything when his girlfriend found the picture."

Mason. As in, the ex from the wedding? The one who'd been trying to get her alone and had cornered her in the mini-mart? No wonder she was so uncomfortable with him. All of a sudden, Shane wished he'd tried to beat the crap out of the asshole. Most probably, he'd have failed, but he'd have felt better about it in the present moment. Something else occurred to him. Why would Faith introduce him as an ex if, as Diana was saying, they'd never been together? The story didn't add up.

"Your new lover is inappropriate and a bad influence on my sons. If you stay with her, I'll have to sue for custody." She shrugged lightly. "I'll have no choice."

Goddamn. He'd never been so tempted to wring her neck. Not even when he'd finally tracked her down after she'd hidden from him for a year.

"Are you seriously going to use a young girl's trauma against her?"

Diana scoffed. "Trauma? The only one traumatized in this story was my new friend when she found the photos in her boyfriend's phone."

Shane rubbed his temples. "If that's what you think, then you're even more ruthless than I believed. You're being petty, vindictive, and mean. You go ahead and file for custody. I've already spoken to my lawyer, and we don't believe there's a court in the country that would grant custody to a woman who abandoned her children for years and hasn't paid a cent of child support when she clearly earns enough to go around."

Diana had the nerve to be outraged. "I paid for Dylan's phone."

"Yes, without discussing it with me first."

"I wanted him to be able to contact me."

Shane leapt to his feet and smashed his fist on top of the dresser. "You weren't worried about that when you left a seven-year-old boy to wonder where his mother had gone. Do you know how hard it was to explain that Mummy left him behind? I had to report you missing. As far as we knew, you might have been abducted and forced to leave a note. But you were selfish then, and you're selfish now. Any judge will see that."

Mouth agape, she crossed her arms defensively. "I have a prominent stature, and I can afford the best legal team."

"None of that will do you any good around here. Not when I have the entire community, including the police, prepared to testify on my behalf." His gaze fell to the phone in her hand. God only knew why anyone had kept that photograph all these years, but it wouldn't be beyond Diana to spread it around, along with a spiteful rumor, just to get back at him. "If you show that to anyone, or hurt Faith in any way, I'll do everything in my power to make life difficult for you." He held out a hand. "Give me the phone. I'm deleting them."

She raised her chin. "No."

"Do it," he ground out. "Or I'll forbid you from seeing Dylan, and I'll make sure he knows you had a choice about it."

Reluctantly, she passed him the phone. "It doesn't matter, anyway. Gigi forwarded them from her email archive, so they'll still be out there on the internet somewhere."

He deleted the picture and thumbed through, deleting two more, then gave it back. "At least you won't have them. Now get out of my house."

"But what about—?"

"Out."

Grumbling, Diana turned on her heel and left. He followed her to the front door and closed it behind her. Then he made a call. He needed to warn Faith.

AFTER SPENDING ALL DAY AT THE SHACK, FAITH RETURNED home to a mountain of housework. Her chores had been sorely neglected, and she still needed to tidy up after her guests. She was hanging laundry when her phone rang. Seeing it was Shane, she smiled, and her heart sped up.

"Hey, handsome. Or should I say, hi, boyfriend?"

He didn't laugh. "Faith." His voice was strained. "There's something you need to know." Uh-oh. She didn't like the sound of that. "You should sit down."

She *really* didn't like the sound of that. Was he planning to break up with her after only one full day as a couple? That had to be the shortest relationship in the history of the bay.

She hung the last towel over the drying rack. "Hang on a sec." She headed for the sofa. "I'm sitting. What's up? Are you and the boys okay?"

"We're fine." He sounded stilted. Awkward. "Diana came by."

She stiffened. "Oh?"

"She brought a picture with her on her phone. A photograph."

The bottom dropped out of her stomach. She knew what was coming next. She pressed her lips together and blinked back the tears welling in her eyes. Her past had caught up with her. If he'd seen the photographs, he must have heard the story. She felt sick.

"Faith?"

Could she hang up now? Did she have to sit here and listen to him break her heart apart all over again?

"I'm here."

"The photos were from when you were a teenager. You were naked. She said half your graduating class had seen them."

Faith squeezed her eyes shut. This couldn't be happening. "That's a fairly accurate guess."

"She also said that you sent them to a boy who had a girlfriend because you wanted his attention."

She tried to swallow, but her throat was dry. "That's how the story goes."

He sighed, and she could hear his frustration, but deflecting questions like this had become second nature to her. She didn't know how to be open about it, if that's even what he wanted. Why didn't he just dump her already?

"What happened? I want the truth. I don't care what Diana heard. The person I've come to know so well wouldn't do that."

"You don't believe it?" Dare she hope?

"No." His tone gentled. "But I wanted to warn you in case she spreads it around."

She shook her head, forgetting he couldn't see. "I don't care about anyone else. All I care about is what you think and whether this changes anything between us."

"It doesn't change a thing," he promised. "I care about

you. I don't give a shit about your past unless it's hurting you in the present."

The pressure around her chest eased, and she exhaled slowly. "I'd understand if it did change things. I was an idiot back then, but it didn't go down the way those girls say."

"Of course not. Tell me. I want to be able to support you."

Well, when he put it like that, how could she resist?

"Mason and I used to date. That's part of the story no one ever heard. We were a couple long before he and Gigi Wagner were. We kept it secret because he told me his parents would throw a hissy fit if they found out. It turned out that wasn't true. He just didn't want his friends to know he was dating the chubby girl. He was the school's star athlete, and he was ashamed to be into curves because it made him different from his friends. You know how teenagers can be. While we were together, I let him take those photos for the nights when I couldn't be with him."

He hummed in thought. "That makes far more sense."

"Yeah." She continued before she lost her nerve. "Anyway, when Gigi moved to the area, he broke up with me, saying she was perfect for him. The prom queen to his king of the rugby field. I asked him to delete the photos, and I trusted he would, but apparently, he liked them too much. Gigi found them and demanded an explanation, so he threw me under the bus and told her that I'd been harassing him." Tears clogged her throat, even though she'd supposedly gotten over the awfulness of what had happened. "He made me out to be the desperate fat girl, and Gigi showed all her friends and taunted me mercilessly for the rest of the year."

"Mason let this happen?"

"Yeah." A bitter taste entered her mouth. "I tried to talk to him about it once, but he just laughed it off. I texted and called, but he never replied, and he never gave me the chance to be alone with him again. So no one ever knew the truth because it didn't matter what I said, it just made me look more pathetic and gave my classmates even more reason to laugh at me."

"Fuck. That bastard. I knew there had to be more to the story, but I'm so sorry you went through that. Teenagers are brutal. As far as I'm concerned, it all falls back on your ex's shoulders." She heard him haul in a breath, like he was trying to get a hold of himself. "God, I wish I'd known this when I met him."

"Why?" she asked, curiosity getting the better of her. "What would you have done?"

"Anything you wanted me to." She sensed he was barely keeping his temper in check. "You deserve someone willing to fight for your honor. You trusted him with intimate pictures, and he abused that trust. The asshole deserves to eat a fist."

Her heart filled to the brim, and she closed her eyes, tears squeezing out the corners. "Shane Walker, you are the sweetest man ever."

"I am?" He sounded baffled.

"Yes." Although she was glad he hadn't tried to punch Mason, who'd no doubt have flattened him in an instant, the fact that he wanted to was the nicest thing she'd heard in a long time. "You don't...." She hesitated, nibbling on her lip. "You don't judge me for what happened? I mean, I did let him take the photos."

"I don't judge you for it, Faith."

The tension in her shoulders eased. She hadn't even realized she'd been so wound up. Lifting her feet onto the sofa, she stretched out and rested her head on the cushion. "Thank you."

"Don't thank me. It's common human decency. Is this why you haven't had a serious relationship during the time I've known you?"

She winced. Trust a smart guy to get straight to the point. "Partially. I have a hard time trusting anyone after what Mason did, but that's not the only reason."

"Then what is?"

Gah, did she actually have to spell it out for him?

Trust, she reminded herself. *It's about trust. Something he never had with his ex.*

"I have dated a few men over the years. The relationships never progressed very far. I've been told I'm not 'long-term relationship material.' Apparently, I'm 'fun to be with' at the beginning, but after a while, I become 'too much.' Those are direct quotes."

"Bullshit," he snapped, and she couldn't help but feel a little gratified. "That's ridiculous. Any guy who said that doesn't deserve you and isn't man enough to handle you. While I'm on the topic, you said before that Mason made you out to be a desperate fat girl. I fucking love your body. You're sexy, and confident, and turn me on. Size doesn't play a part, and I'll gladly shout it from the rooftops."

Heat flashed downward, taking her by surprise. Could she adore this man any more than she did in this instant? "Thank you, and don't worry, I know that now. But try telling it to an eighteen-year-old with D-cups and a big ass who's being laughed at by everyone in the cool crowd."

"The things I'd like to do to that ass...." His voice was husky and low, sending a shiver up her spine, and her nipples tightened in response. He cleared his throat. "I don't care what a bunch of idiot kids said—or any of your brainless exes. I want you to be the woman in my life."

"That's lucky." She smiled, finally beginning to feel the first threads of hope. "Because I'm serious about you, and I trust you." She bit back the words *I love you*. It was too early for that, wasn't it? They may have known each other for years, but their relationship was very new. She'd hold onto that confession for another time.

20

As usual, Shane was the last to arrive at poker night because he'd had to wait for Faith to get to his place before he could leave the boys in her capable hands. Then, once she'd turned up, he'd been distracted by her kissable lips and drawn her into the laundry for a few stolen moments. Now that he'd finally made it, he dumped a bag of trail mix on the table and realized he'd left the vegetable sticks and hummus at home. Oh well. They'd make a nice snack for tomorrow.

"Good to see you, man." Logan gripped his hand and slapped him on the back. "How are you doing?"

"I'm all right." He'd be better if he'd stayed in the laundry with Faith all evening, but she'd insisted he spend time with his friends, knowing how much more human it made him feel.

"Just all right?" Jack asked. "I heard the local mums are up in arms because Faith had the audacity to steal you out from under them."

"Oh ha-ha, very funny."

"This time, he's actually right," Kyle said from his position at the end of the table. "The gossip at the library is that your ex turned up just as you're finally moving on." He grinned the dimpled smile that had women lining up for personal book recommendations in their lowest cut shirts. "According to the rumor mill, you're winning in the battle of the exes because your new girl-friend is younger and everyone loves her."

Shane groaned and dragged a hand through his hair. "Do people ever mind their own business?"

The Pride brothers exchanged glances.

"Nope," Logan replied. "Especially not since Diana Monroe herself showed up in The Den and made a scene."

Shane flopped into a chair and wasted no time accepting the beer Tione handed him. "I'm sorry."

Logan shrugged. "Don't be. It was actually good for business. The tourists loved her, and she was flaunting herself all over the place, if you know what I mean. There was no sneaking into the back corner to enjoy a wine in peace."

"Of course not." He scoffed at the thought. "She thrives in the spotlight."

"Don't worry. She didn't win any friends among the locals."

"Never thought she would." People around here were too loyal for their affection to be bought by money or fame. Eager to change the subject, he said, "Where's Ster-ling this week?"

"Out of town on business," Tione replied. "What about Michael?"

"Doing a movie night with Bex and Izzy." Shane grabbed a pretzel while Logan dealt cards. Bar snacks were another reason to love poker night. He didn't feel like he had to model good eating habits for the boys. That said, he always brought a healthy option anyway, to ease his conscience. Jack and Kyle played the big and little blinds, and the game began.

"So," Kyle said as they moved around the circle. "Faith."

"What about her?" Shane asked.

"Did you know she and I went to high school together?"

"I thought she was older than you."

Kyle nodded and adjusted his wire-framed glasses. "Only by a year. We didn't have much to do with each other, but neither of us fit in very well. She had a hard time, and I don't want to see her hurt."

"Amen to that," Logan added. "You're one of my best mates, but if you screw her over, you'd better find a new watering hole."

"Good thing I don't plan on hurting her." He glanced at his cards and pushed a chip forward. "Call. We still need to talk to the boys about our relationship, but provided we can pass that hurdle, I intend for this to be the last time I ever go through the whole dating thing."

Tione grunted. "Keep it that way. She's Megan's best friend, and if Faith is unhappy, then Megan is unhappy."

"No one is allowed to make Megan unhappy," Jack said *sotto voce*. Everyone laughed. Well, everyone except Tione.

Shane thought back to something Kyle had said earlier. "I didn't realize you didn't enjoy school, Kyle."

He shrugged. "It's a long story. Let's save it for another time."

Faith lay on the sofa, wearing a soft robe that concealed the surprise beneath. Both boys were in bed, and it wasn't unusual for her to make herself comfortable after they'd fallen asleep, so if they emerged, she doubted either of them would think anything of her attire. Their father, on the other hand....

Him, she had plans for.

When she heard the key in the lock, she glanced down to check everything was in order. Her feet were bare, and she'd done her lipstick and eyes in the mirror earlier. Bright red. She fluffed her hair, ensuring it fell over her shoulders the way she wanted it to, and held onto the robe's belt, which was tied in a bow above one hip. Footsteps sounded in the hall, and then he stepped into the lounge, and she promptly loosened the belt and let her robe fall open to reveal the corset, thigh-high stockings, and garters.

Shane's eyes nearly bugged out of his head. She grinned, satisfaction rising within her. Without saying a word, she pulled the gaping robe closed, turned, and strode toward his bedroom. Once inside, she dropped the robe to the floor and swung around to let him look his fill.

"Holy crap," he breathed, and then he was on her with his hands on her ass, hauling her against the front of his body. His kisses took her breath away. This was exactly the response she'd hoped for. He slipped his hand between her legs and his fingers through her wet heat. "You're not wearing underwear."

"Nope." She grinned like the cat who'd caught the canary. "Easier access."

"For this?" He shoved a finger inside her, and she gasped. That, she hadn't expected. He crooked it, and her knees gave way. She would have fallen back onto the bed, but he caught her and lowered her carefully, as though she were something precious. His finger still inside her, he cupped his palm over her sex, pressing on her clit. She moaned into her hand, trying to muffle the sound so they wouldn't disturb the boys. "Feels amazing."

"I can tell how much you want me." His voice was husky, his eyes black with lust. "Hell, Faith. Best welcome home ever." He knelt between her thighs and leaned close, blowing softly. She shivered. Then he stroked his tongue right along her center, lusciously and unhurried.

Her hands flew to his head, threading into his hair. "Do that again," she urged. "Please."

He did everything she asked and more, settling his mouth over her and licking her like she was the most delicious ice cream he'd ever tasted. The noises he made in the back of his throat drove her crazy. Little groans and sighs that told her he was enjoying this as much as she was. Finally, he reared up, his eyes as wild as she felt. "Need you now."

"Then take me." He stripped off his clothes and reached for a condom, but Faith stopped him. "I'm on birth control, and I trust you."

He froze. "Are you saying...?"

"I want you inside me with nothing between us." She'd thought about this, and she knew it was what she wanted. He meant more to her than anyone else, so it was fitting she share herself with him more intimately than she had any other man. "Do you trust me that much too?"

"Yes." He closed his eyes and rested his forehead on hers, slowly releasing a breath. When his eyes opened, they were even darker than before—if such a thing were possible. He rolled onto his side and pulled her into the curve of his body so they were spooning, then reached around and stroked her, sending flickers of fire scattering along her nerves. She parted her legs, and he thrust into her from behind in one smooth, perfect motion. They both sighed at the exquisite sensation. Then they began to move.

She bit her lip when he caressed her hip, over her belly, and dipped his hand into the V of her legs. Feeling him both behind and in front of her—being surrounded by him—was the hottest thing she'd ever experienced. Especially with the added thrill of knowing they needed to stay quiet. She tilted her head back and captured his mouth. Their kisses were wet, tongues stroking, gazes locked, and the intimacy of the moment sent her careening into bliss. A moment later, he buried his face in the back of her neck and jerked inside her, finding his own release.

They lay there for a few minutes until he withdrew and murmured that he'd be back in a moment. He returned with a towel and a damp cloth and cleaned them up.

"Thanks." She was debating whether to ask if she could stay when he climbed beneath the covers and patted the space beside him. "Are you sure?"

He smiled softly, and warmth unfurled within her. "One hundred percent. As long as you don't mind slipping out before the boys see you."

"I don't." After all, they'd arranged a dinner to talk to Hunter and Dylan about their relationship tomorrow, so hopefully, she'd never have to sneak out again.

She joined him in bed, and pure contentment washed over her when he drew her close. She'd never been brave enough to imagine having him all to herself like this, especially not with those photographs hanging over her head, but falling asleep to the sound of his breathing was absolute perfection.

21

HOW DID ONE DRESS FOR DINNER WITH THE FAMILY SHE hoped to eventually call her own? Faith scanned the options in her closet. Her work outfits were too stylish, and her other dresses were too formal. What about jeans? Or were they too casual? She wanted Hunter and Dylan to be comfortable with her but also to understand that they were having an important conversation.

Ugh, why is this so hard?

She snatched a pair of loose black pants from a hanger, held them against herself and looked in the mirror. Classier than jeans but more low-key than a dress. What should she pair them with? The canary-yellow blouse? Ick, no. She'd purchased the top on a whim, but yellow really wasn't her color. How about the pale pink one that tied around the waist? Holding the two items together, she nodded. With a camisole beneath the blouse, and her matching pink polka-dot pumps, it would do nicely.

Decision made, she donned the new outfit and slipped her phone into a matching purse. She headed to the kitchen to collect the box of cupcakes Megan had left and a small carton of her trial-run PB&J ice cream. She stacked the goodies in her passenger seat and drove to Shane's house. When she knocked, footsteps pounded on the other side of the door, and then Hunter pulled it open, grinning widely.

"Hi, Faith!" he exclaimed, spreading his arms wide.

Holding onto the cupcakes and ice cream with one arm, she bent and hugged him. "Hey, cutie pie. I brought treats."

"Is it ice cream?"

She winked. "Always. Where's your daddy?"

"In the kitchen." Taking her hand, he led her into the house. She couldn't help but notice that Dylan's door was closed and he wasn't in the living area. "We're making burgers."

"Oh, you're helping, are you?" He was too precious.

"I'm doing the lettuce."

Shane looked up as they entered, his gaze skimming her from head to toe so hotly she could have sworn her skin burned where it lingered. "You look nice."

She grinned and checked him out in return. Dark jeans, button-down shirt, tweed vest. What was it about those vests that made her want to lick him?

"Hunter tells me we're having burgers. I brought cupcakes and ice cream for dessert."

"Great." He flipped a burger patty in the frying pan. "There's plenty of room in the freezer for the ice cream."

She packed the ice cream away while Hunter resumed pulling apart lettuce leaves. "How can I help?"

"Actually, I think we're about done here. Or we will be as soon as these patties are cooked. Could you ask Dylan to wash his hands and come to the table?"

"Sure thing." This was something she'd done plenty of times before, so why was she so nervous?

Because Dylan has already told you he doesn't want you dating his dad.

Yeah, there was that.

Pausing outside his door, she knocked softly. When he didn't answer, she knocked again. "Dylan? Are you in there?"

"Yeah. Hang on," he called back. Thirty seconds later, he emerged. "What is it?"

She could tell a scowl wanted to break through his expression, but he was fighting it. She celebrated the progress, even though it hurt to know he instinctively wanted to push her away.

"Dinner will be ready in a couple of minutes. Can you clean up and come to the table?"

"Okay." He headed to the bathroom without a backward glance.

She sighed. They'd taken a baby step forward but needed to make more progress. What could she do to make him like her as much as his father's partner as he did as his babysitter? Because she had no doubt he knew that she and Shane were dating, and his behavior stemmed from either a resistance to change or wanting his parents to get back together. At some point, he'd come around, wouldn't he?

God, she hoped so.

When she returned to the dining area, Shane had arranged dinner plates on the table, with burger ingredients spread out in the center.

"Assemble your own," he said as he appeared from the kitchen with four glasses stacked together and a bottle of Coca-Cola under his arm.

"Great." She looked down at Hunter and smiled. "Do you need a hand, buddy?"

"Nope." He shook his head and puffed with pride. "I've made burgers before."

"Well, then you'll have to teach me." She watched him clamber onto a seat and then chose the one beside him.

"Is Dylan coming?" Shane asked.

"Yes. He's washing his hands."

They waited for Dylan to join them before beginning. Hunter insisted he and Faith do everything the same, so she copied his painstakingly careful movements as he piled his burger with condiments, an adorable furrow of concentration on his brow.

While they ate, they didn't talk, except to inquire after each other's days. When they were finished, Faith wiped sauce from Hunter's face with a napkin. Then she and Shane exchanged glances. He looked as nervous as she felt, but she let him take the lead because these were his sons, and it was up to him to deliver the news as he saw fit.

Before he could speak, Dylan made a big show of checking the time on his phone. "I promised to call Mum. I'll be in my room."

"Wait," Shane said as Dylan began to rise out of his seat. "Hold on a moment. There's something Faith and I need to tell you."

Sighing heavily, he lowered himself back into the chair. He clearly knew what was coming and didn't want to hear it. She felt a twinge of regret. She'd never wanted to give him reason to look at her the way he was doing now, as though she were an intruder. Hopefully, one day they could repair their relationship. She smiled at him tentatively, and he glanced down at the tabletop.

"Faith and I are dating," Shane said, and was met with silence—sullen, on Dylan's part, and confused on Hunter's. Shane met Hunter's baffled gaze. "That means

198

she's my girlfriend. She's going to be around here more often, and sometimes we might want to go out and do grownup things together."

Dylan snorted but didn't lift his attention from the tabletop.

Meanwhile, Hunter hummed in thought. "Do we get ice cream all the time now?"

The question shocked a laugh out of Faith. Trust a kid to get to the important stuff. "That's up to your dad, but between you and me, I think we can talk him into having it for dessert, at least."

Hunter nodded, his eyes shining with excitement. "Are you gonna live here now? 'Cause you can share my room."

Her heart threatened to implode from cuteness overload. "I'm not moving in just now, honey, but maybe you and me could do a sleepover sometime and build a blanket fort. What do you think?"

"Yes, please." He turned wide, pleading eyes on Shane, and Faith did the same. "Please, Daddy."

Shane ran a hand through his hair, looking from one of them to the other with a combination of affection and amusement. "I think that can be arranged."

"Yay!"

"What about you, Dyl?" Shane asked. "What do you think of this?"

Dylan shrugged. "It's okay." He glanced at her. "Faith's cool, I guess. And if she comes with ice cream...."

Shane pounced on the olive branch. "Do you want a special ice cream for your birthday next weekend?"

"I can make any flavor you like," she offered, grabbing hold of the lifeline Dylan had thrown. "Megan can make your dream cake too. My gift to you. Interested?"

This brought a smile to his face. "Can she make a caramel cake?"

"Too right, she can." Faith had never actually seen her do so, but she knew it was possible, and Megan was an absolute goddess when it came to whipping up batter. "She could even make you a cake where each layer is a different flavor if that's what you want."

His grin widened. "That might be fun."

Hallelujah. Had she found the secret to getting through to him? Cake did fix all, so why not their relationship?

"It's settled," she announced. "Tomorrow, let me know exactly what you want, and I'll make sure you get it."

"Okay." He nodded, and her heart lifted. "Thanks."

"Speaking of tomorrow," Shane said, "It's the Christmas parade. We should all go together."

Faith smiled. "That sounds perfect."

22

THE FOLLOWING MORNING, FAITH LEFT MEGAN AND HER sister, Mikayla, who was visiting from Auckland, in charge of The Shack so she could join the Walker family for their first official outing together. She met Shane and the boys in the town square where the Christmas parade would be centered.

She waved to Hugh MacAllister, the town council representative who was coordinating the event, and then hugged Shane in greeting. When he kissed her cheek, the touch sizzled all the way down to her toes, and she felt an answering blush rise on her cheeks. After keeping their feelings on the down low, it was strange to touch him in front of the boys. Dylan rolled his eyes at their display, but she didn't take it personally. Kids weren't known to enjoy the adults in their lives engaging in public shows of affection.

Stalls lined the square, set up by local craftspeople selling handmade Christmas cards, fudge, artwork, and a range of other wares.

"Have you guys had time to look around?" she asked.

"No, we just got here." Shane brushed hair off his

forehead, looking far too handsome in a T-shirt and scuffed jeans. "Where do you want to start?"

She scanned the options, seeing nothing that really called to her. "I don't mind. What would you boys like?"

Dylan shrugged, and Hunter pointed at a stall furnished with brightly colored children's toys across the square, near The Den. On their way over, they ran into Caleb, Dylan's friend from school, and the two boys dropped behind the rest of the family to talk between themselves. When they reached their destination, Hunter smiled shyly at the woman running the stall and walked alongside the edge of the table, checking out the options. Faith crouched beside him as he reached for a miniature toolkit and plastic hammer.

"Could I use this for DIY Saturday?" he asked.

"I bet you could," she replied, thinking that Kat would go out of her way to make sure there was something he could do with it. Behind her, Shane was speaking with the stall manager. At the sound of her name, Faith straightened. "You mentioned me?"

The lady smiled. "I was just saying how lucky you are to have snapped this guy up."

"I know, right?" She smiled back. "I don't think he realizes what a catch he is."

The woman shook her head. "He never has. I'm Lanie. Shane teaches my stepson. It's lovely to meet you."

"You too." Faith liked Lanie already. She felt a tug on her skirt and glanced down at Hunter. "What's up, cutie pie?"

He pressed his lips together and waved for her to come closer. Lowering herself down, she put her ear near his mouth.

"Can you ask Daddy about the tools?" he asked.

Faith exchanged a glance with Shane. "I think that's your job. He's not scary, is he?"

Hunter grabbed onto her hand and looked up at Shane. "Can I get the hammer and tools? Pretty please?"

"Let's see them."

Hunter released Faith's hand and grabbed the little hammer. Meanwhile, Lanie leaned across the table and gestured for Faith to do the same.

"It seems like he's taken a shine to you," Lanie murmured.

Faith cocked her head. "He's known me for most of his life. I babysit pretty often."

"Ah." Lanie gave a knowing smile. "Is that how you and Shane got together?"

"Kind of. It's a complicated story."

"The best kind." Lanie reached into her pocket and offered Faith a business card. "Some of the other mums will probably snub you because you snatched up their eye candy, but if you ever need a mum friend, give me a call. I live just out of town and run the toy shop in Te Awa Tui."

Faith beamed and slipped the card into her purse. "Thanks. That's so sweet of you."

Lanie winked. "We stepmothers need to stick together."

Shane paid for Hunter's new toys, and Faith looked around the square, feeling warm inside. A few yards away, Dylan and Caleb were chatting animatedly, and she could hear bagpipes in the distance, indicating the parade was about to begin. The local Highland Pipe Band always opened the action, and Hugh MacAllister, dressed as Santa Claus, closed it.

They filed over to the road and waited. The sound of the bagpipes grew louder. Shane hoisted Hunter onto his shoulders, and Faith's heart nearly overflowed. The two of them were so damned adorable together. Even Dylan pocketed his phone and joined them. A number of floats came trailing behind the Highland Pipe Band. From here, she could see Bex's daughter Izzy on the school float, dressed in a tutu and twirling happily. The Glamping Ground had decorated a float, as had the library, with Kyle Pride dressed as a reluctant sexy Jesus. More than one lady swooned as he passed. Then the swooning turned to shameless catcalls with the arrival of the surf life-saving club in red-and-green swimsuits.

Elliot, the police officer, drove his cruiser, its lights flashing, and children shrieked as he cranked the siren. The *kapa haka* group came next, swinging *pois*. A long train of bedazzled tractors drew up the rear, with the Santa Claus float at the end. Unlike the rest of the procession, which continued around a corner and onto Marine Parade, Santa stopped, and his elves hurried to lower a staircase for him to walk down into the square where he headed for an extravagantly decorated throne.

"Hunter, do you want to meet Santa?" Shane asked.

Hunter looked dubious. "Maybe."

"Well, I'll take you over there, and if you decide you don't want to, just tell me to giddy-up, okay?"

His son laughed. "Okay, Daddy."

"I'm going to buy some of that fudge," Faith declared.

To her surprise, Dylan offered to come along since his friend had left. The two of them made their way to the fudge stall, where she bought a piece of cookies-and-cream fudge for herself and one of Russian fudge for him.

"Thanks," he said as they ate. They started walking back toward Shane and Hunter, who'd lined up in the queue to meet Santa, but Dylan dawdled, so Faith slowed her pace. "I'm, um, sorry for being weird about the whole you-and-Dad thing."

Her heart stuttered, and she glanced over, but he was focused on his fudge with single-minded determination. "That's okay." She thought quickly, not wanting to ruin the moment. "I mean, I'd rather there be no weirdness, but I understand where you're coming from."

"So, we're all right?" he asked.

"Yeah." She smiled. "We're okay."

At least, they were until she looked up and saw Diana standing beside Shane. Eyes narrowing, Faith picked up her speed. She heard Dylan mutter, "Uh-oh." Diana wasn't alone. Her companion, a handsome guy in his forties, hung back while she spoke to Shane. All of a sudden, she spun around, her expression punched.

"Oh, hello, Fiona. I was just telling Shane that Timothy and I have been to visit Anderson Gray." She waited expectantly, as though they should be impressed by her hobnobbing with a former Hollywood celebrity.

Shane chuckled. "Did you even make it as far as the door to Gray's mansion?"

Diana's brows drew together, and if Faith wasn't mistaken, her cheeks flushed beneath a layer of makeup. "Excuse me?"

"Don't take it personally," Shane continued. "He doesn't talk to anyone if he can help it."

"I'll have you know that Anderson and I are old friends. We had a good catch-up." Behind her, the man Faith assumed to be Timothy snorted, and Diana cut him a furious glare. They all shifted uncomfortably. She had the feeling everyone present knew Diana was stretching the truth, but no one had any idea what to say about it.

But then Dylan did.

"Mr. Gray is a grumpy old man," he said.

Faith's jaw dropped and she barked a laugh of surprise. Diana's eyes snapped from Dylan to Faith and back, as though uncertain where to settle.

"I hate to correct you, dear," Diana said, "but Anderson is actually a handsome young man."

Okay, that cinched it. Diana had not spent any time with Anderson Gray recently. While the guy had been a heartthrob in his day, he'd become a mess. An agoraphobic, unshaven, unfriendly man with the mother of all chips on his shoulder.

Dylan shrugged. "Whatever. He doesn't let us play on his beach."

"It's not his beach," Faith reminded him. "He just acts as though it is."

Diana's smile grew strained. "I'd best be off. People to see, things to do. But Dylan, darling, do call me so we can plan your birthday next weekend."

With that, she gave a regal wave and left. Timothy trailed behind her like an obedient puppy.

―――――――

After Hunter had perched on Santa's knee, looking equal parts excited and terrified, and emerged unscathed, Shane guided his family around the stalls in the center of the square. Dylan dropped back to talk to another of his friends, and Shane kept an eye on him to make sure he didn't leave the area. Meanwhile, he, Faith and Hunter paused at a funky jewelry stand, which he had no interest in, but he noticed that Faith seemed quite taken by some of the pieces. In particular, she focused on a chunky necklace with shells fashioned into a series of blue flowers.

She oohed and aahed over it, bringing a flush of joy to

the jeweler's face when she asked who'd made it because the craftsmanship was exquisite. He could see she wanted it but could also sense her reluctance to buy it. Faith may have a vast collection of outfits, but he had a feeling she collected most of them through sales or by browsing thrift stores. She hadn't become a successful business owner in her twenties by being careless with money.

"We'll take it," he told the woman, fishing his card out of his wallet to pay.

She beamed. "Excellent."

"Oh, no," Faith protested, and the woman paused before scanning the card. "You can't buy it for me."

He raised a brow. "Why not?"

"Because it's too much. I can't let you do that."

"I want to." He really did. After all she'd done for him and the boys, he ached to express his affection for her in whatever way he could. He wished he could buy her all the vintage jewelry and dresses her heart desired, but he'd start small. And perhaps he had a little caveman in him because he wanted Faith wearing something he'd bought for her. He wanted to mark her as his.

"In my experience, if a man wants to buy you a gift, you should let him," the jeweler remarked with a smile.

Faith wavered.

"It's really pretty," Hunter said, and Shane wanted to high-five him. *That's my boy.*

Laughing, she threw her hands in the air. "Okay, then. Thank you."

She kissed him. In full view of everyone. And he loved it.

The woman wrapped the necklace in tissue paper and handed it to Faith in a paper bag. She tucked it carefully inside her purse. They continued around the stalls, and when they'd looked at everything and Hunter was worn out, they returned to The Shack, where Faith had to work for the afternoon. Shane kissed her goodbye, ignoring Dylan's groan of embarrassment, and left her with flushed cheeks and hazy eyes. Just the way he liked her.

FAITH ENTERED THE SHACK FEELING AS THOUGH SHE WAS walking on air.

"That was some kiss," Megan said from behind the counter. The place was devoid of customers since everyone was at the parade, but Faith had no doubt they'd start to filter in soon.

"I know," she sighed happily. "He's such a good kisser."

"Very handsome too," the third woman in the room said. She crossed to Faith and shook her hand surprisingly firmly for such a petite person. "Hi, I'm Mikayla. My friends call me Mik."

Faith appraised her, thinking hard. "Victoria Justice, but shorter."

"Excuse me?" Mikayla demanded, hands on her hips.

"Relax, Mik," Megan said. "Faith uses a mental trick where she associates people with celebrities so she can remember them."

"She called me short."

"You are short."

"Hmph." Mikayla huffed. "I'm five-two." She tucked a strand of dark-brown hair behind her ear. "I suppose I've been compared to worse though." She spun around, and together, she and Faith joined Megan behind the counter. Faith couldn't help but be impressed by the efficiency of

Mikayla's movements. She wasted no energy flouncing around, and in her black pencil skirt and form-fitting top, she looked sleek and aerodynamic. Strange descriptors, perhaps, but they fit her well.

"Is this your first time to the bay?" Faith asked.

"No. I visited when Megan first came here, and I've made a couple of weekend trips." At that moment, her phone rang. "Mikayla here," she said after lifting it to her ear. A moment later, she stepped away, carrying on a hushed discussion.

"It'll be work," Megan explained. "She's always on the clock. Her boss won't let her have a day to herself." She shook her head, frowning.

Her attitude surprised Faith since Megan rarely disliked anyone. "Is he too tough on her?"

"Too dependent," Megan said, then glanced over at Mikayla and lowered her voice. "She's been in love with him since she started the job. He'll never make a move because he can't afford to lose her, but that doesn't stop him from playing her like a violin when it suits."

Faith grimaced and sunk into a stool behind the counter. "That sounds rough. Poor Mik."

"Don't let on that you know."

"I won't," she promised. "Hey, can I ask a favor?"

"Of course." Megan swiveled her stool around as a couple entered the store.

When they didn't approach the counter, Faith continued. "We're celebrating Dylan's birthday next weekend, and I need to bring the best caramel cake he's ever had."

Megan laughed. "Are you trying to bribe your way into his good graces?"

"Shamelessly." They'd made progress today, but she suspected he was still a long way from welcoming her into the family with open arms. "So, can you do it?"

"Absolutely. When do you need it by?"

"Saturday, please." Faith scooted over and hugged her. "Thanks so much. I love you." The customers came over and Faith stood to address the woman. "What can I get you, sugar?"

"Feijoa and ginger, please," she said. "Two scoops."

"No problem. Coming right up." She rolled the ice cream into a cone and propped it in one of the holders before turning to the guy. "And how about you?"

"I'll just have hokey pokey."

"A classic." Faith prepared it and took their payment. By this time, Mikayla's phone call had ended, and the Talbot sisters left The Shack. Faith grabbed her phone and Googled children's birthday parties, interested to find out what she could expect come the following weekend. She was scrolling down the second page of search results when the door swung open and Betty and Mavis —two of her regulars—entered.

"Hi, hot stuff," Faith called, fanning herself. "Did it get warm in here, or is it just you?"

Betty preened, stroking her fluffy white hair, while Mavis just rolled her eyes. The old grump. Faith adored them.

"Faith-girl," Mavis said, as she tended to. Faith was pretty sure Mavis actually believed that to be her name. "Don't you worry—that child-abandoning charlatan, Diana Monroe, has nothing on you, and everyone worth anything sees through her." Trust Mavis to get straight to the point and to say exactly what Faith needed to hear.

"Thank you. That's very sweet of you."

"It's not sweet," she grumbled. "It's true."

"I know." Faith hopped off her stool and kissed Mavis's cheek, then Betty's.

"The Bridge Club have been discussing a campaign to

run her out of town," Betty said. "We've come up with several ideas, and all you need to do is say the word. We'll send her running back to L.A. like the coward she is."

Chewing on her lower lip, Faith considered their offer. It was tempting. Especially when she knew how effective the Bridge Club could be when they rallied for a cause. But while Diana leaving might be good for Faith, it may not be the best thing for Shane's family.

"Thanks for the offer." She sighed, scarcely able to believe what she was about to say. "You'd better not, though. It's good for the boys if she's nearby."

Mavis scoffed. "She'd gladly accept our help if the situations were reversed."

A fact that only made Faith more certain of her decision. She didn't want to stoop to Diana's level. "Thank you for thinking of me, but I have it under control."

Betty's eyes narrowed. "If you're sure...."

"I am."

The older woman's face fell. "And here I was, looking forward to giving that awful woman a piece of my mind." She looked so dejected that Faith had to laugh.

"By all means, do so. But don't do it on my account, and don't go starting any crusades."

Betty nodded. "If that's what you want."

"You're making a mistake," Mavis said, never one to beat around the bush. "That woman is a snake."

"Yes, but she's a snake who's the mother of my boyfriend's children. Now, can I get you ladies any ice cream?"

Betty requested a red velvet, and Mavis asked for mint chocolate. Faith served them, and then returned to studying her cell phone. Except this time, she turned her mind to Christmas. It wasn't far off now. What would she get for Shane as a gift?

Oooh, she had lots of ideas about that. She grinned to herself. Most of them involved tiny silk outfits and alone time.

23

On Tuesday, Shane collected Hunter from Bex's place and arrived home to find the lights on and music playing. Dylan was playing video games in the living room.

"How'd you get home?" Shane asked as they entered. His son had supposedly been at a friend's place. It had been a long day, and Shane ached to take a load off, get into something more comfortable, and crash on the sofa. Unfortunately, he still needed to cook dinner, do the chores, and make sure the boys had both completed their homework.

"Mum picked me up," Dylan said. "She said you okayed it."

"You didn't think to check with me?"

Pausing his game, Dylan turned to face him, grimacing. "I thought she was telling the truth." He shrugged. "She's my mum."

A mother who didn't have any custody rights and whom Shane hadn't spoken to since the Christmas parade. But he didn't growl at Dylan, because the kid had a point. Since when were children expected to question their parent's actions?

"Okay, buddy. She didn't talk to me, but it's not your fault. Is she still here?"

He nodded, his expression growing cautious. "In the kitchen. Don't kick her out. She wanted to surprise you."

"With what?" Having his ex turn up and let herself into his house unannounced was not his idea of a pleasant surprise.

"Dinner, I guess."

Shane nodded and looked down at Hunter, who stood near his feet. "Wait here with Dylan. I'll be back soon."

He found Diana standing at the stove, frying halloumi in a pan, with a couple of other pots simmering. The food smelled pretty good considering she'd never been much of a cook. Obviously being in L.A. had taught her a thing or two.

"Shane!" she exclaimed, beaming the smile that had enchanted men all around the world. "I'm so glad you're here. How was your day? Tell me all about it." Bustling over, she dropped a kiss on his cheek before he had the wherewithal to pull away.

His jaw clenched, and he wanted to yell at her to leave because she wasn't welcome here, but mindful of their sons in the other room, he kept his voice low as he asked, "What are you doing?"

"Making our dinner," she said in a tone that scolded him for asking such a silly question. "So we can discuss Dylan's birthday next weekend. I've been looking at local bands and there isn't much selection, but if we go wider, I can hire someone from Auckland. Do you have an event planner? The best ones book out months in advance."

"Whoa, slow down a minute." He shook his head, his brain still trying to process the fact that she was here, let alone anything else. "This isn't some big Hollywood party. We're having a barbecue, sending the kids out for a surf lesson, and then playing backyard cricket. Nothing fancy. That's what Dylan wants."

Diana flipped the halloumi and rolled her eyes. She checked a pot, and he smelled pumpkin. "That's before he knew we could afford options. I'm here now, and he can have anything he wants. Cost is no barrier."

A thought occurred to him. "Did you even remember it was his birthday before we ran into each other at the Christmas parade? Because this is the first you've mentioned it, and considering it's your first time home in years, I'd have thought you'd be all over the celebration from the start."

Her eyes narrowed, and her nostrils flared. She didn't like to be questioned. Well, too bad.

"Of course I did." She stirred whatever was in one of the pots. "But I didn't want to come on too strong, so I gave him a little time to get used to having me around."

"Not come on too strong?" He scoffed. "You expected to move in with us on day one."

She waved a hand, dismissing his comment. "Dylan," she called. "Darling, will you come here for a moment?"

"Don't drag him into this."

"Why not? It's *his* birthday." Dylan came in slowly, his expression saying he was all kinds of nervous. His mother didn't let that stop her. "Dad and I have been discussing your party. I suggested we hire live entertainment and ship the best people over from Auckland. Wouldn't you like that?"

Dylan's gaze leapt from one of them to the other, and he wet his lips. "Um."

"No pressure," Shane said, hating she'd put him on the spot. "Whatever you want, you just tell us. No one will be insulted." He sent his ex a meaningful look. "Right, Diana?"

"Exactly right," she agreed. "So, what's it going to be? A band and the best food the city has to offer, or your dad's barbecue and a game of cricket you could do any weekend?"

This wasn't fair. Shane took Diana by the arm. "Excuse us, bud. We'll be back in a moment." Drawing her into the hall, he turned to face her. "Why are you putting this on his shoulders?"

She raised her chin. "It's his decision. He's old enough to make his own."

"Perhaps," he acknowledged. "But you're throwing him in the middle of our problems. That's not good parenting." Her eyes formed slits, but then she smiled cattily and pulled Shane into his bedroom. "What are you—?"

She closed the door with a click, and then removed her dress with a couple of deft motions. It whispered to the floor, and she stood before him in a black push-up bra and a matching thong.

"Dear God." He averted his eyes. This couldn't be happening. What was she thinking? The boys were just down the hall, and he'd made it clear he was dating Faith and couldn't be less interested in her. "What are you doing? Put your clothes back on."

Her fingers feathered over his back and snuck around his chest. She pressed herself to him from behind, her breasts squishing into him. He yanked free of her and skirted around the bed, putting it between them and trying desperately to look anywhere other than at her. "Diana, get dressed. This isn't funny."

"I'm completely serious." He could hear the pout in her voice. She'd always been able to do that. It was part of the reason she was such a good actress. "You and I used to have fun together. We were compatible, and there's no reason we shouldn't be that way again."

He buried his face in his hands and groaned, wishing he could rewind the clock and hash it out with her in the kitchen instead of letting her manipulate him into taking her somewhere private. Because he had no doubt this was what she'd intended all along. While he was preoccupied, she rounded the bed and cornered him. The only chance at escape was to either push past her or leap over the bed, which was growing more appealing with each passing second.

"Back off," he said, looking at the space to the side of her head. "I'm with Faith now, and she makes me happy. If you don't leave immediately, I'm banning you from the property. I'll change the locks and file a restraining order. How would that look to your Hollywood big wigs?"

"You don't mean that." But Diana retreated and grabbed her dress, shimmying back into it. "I'm not going to let that little nobody take my family."

He threw his hands up in exasperation. "We haven't been your family for years, so she isn't taking anything from you. If you remember correctly, you traded us in for fame and fortune. You can't expect us to wait when we didn't hear anything from you for months at a time." He strode forward, escorting her from the room. "We're divorced, and as far as I'm concerned, divorcing you was the best decision of my life. Now get out."

"But what about dinner?" she asked, glancing over her shoulder.

"You can take it with you or leave it for us. Up to you."

She sighed, sounding truly put out. "I'll leave it. I'd hate for the boys to miss out."

"Great. So if you'll just grab your purse and say good-bye...." He led her into the kitchen, where Dylan was still waiting.

"What's happening?" he asked.

"Your mum is heading back to her hotel. She'll call you tomorrow to discuss what you want for your birthday, and neither of us will be bothered by what you decide. It's all about you, okay?"

He nodded. "She's not staying for dinner? Because I thought—"

"So did I," she said sadly. "But your dad said it would be best for me to go."

Dylan glared at him. "Why can't she stay? She's the one who made the food."

Shane sighed. Here she was, making him the bad guy again. He could hardly admit what she'd done. Not to their son. "It's better this way. Trust me."

Dylan shook his head and stormed away. Diana gave Shane a sly smile as she left. He walked her all the way to the door, then locked it behind her.

A small voice caught his attention. "Daddy, is the scary lady gone?"

He turned to find Hunter behind him and hugged him tight. At least he had one person on his side. "Yeah, she is. Let's finish dinner, shall we?"

THE SUNDAY OF DYLAN'S BIRTHDAY PARTY ROLLED around, and Faith collected the cake from Megan and transported it to the Walker house. Dylan had opted to keep most of his plans as they had been—with one exception. Diana had made a call, and two members of the Black Caps—the New Zealand men's cricket team—would be coming to mentor the kids and play a game with them. Everyone seemed happy with the result. Dylan got what he wanted, and Diana had the opportunity to flaunt her connections.

For her part, Faith was nervous. She hadn't met Shane's parents or his sister, and today would set the tone of their relationship going forward. If they picked up on Dylan's uncertainty toward her, or decided she was unworthy of Shane, it could sway him. She knew he held his family in high esteem. Especially his sister, Gabrielle, who had never liked Diana, and to whom he believed he should have listened all along.

What if Gabrielle didn't like her?

Pulling up outside, she took a moment to gather her wits and her courage, then got out of the car and eased the cake off the passenger seat. The door to the house was ajar and she nudged it with her foot until it opened.

"Hello," she called, letting herself in. She could hear voices but couldn't see anyone. She found three strangers in the kitchen, along with the world's most adorable pair of children.

"Faith!" Hunter cried and hurried over for a hug.

She set the cake on the counter and bent to embrace him. "Hi, cutie pie." She ruffled his hair, laughing when he squirmed and pulled a face. She waved to his companion. "Hi, Iz."

Izzy Cane was a little older than Hunter, but they had been fast friends. She bounced over, her cloud of dark hair bobbing behind her. "Can I have a hug too?"

Faith grinned. "Of course you can, sweetheart." She

scooped her up, breathing in the sweet strawberry scent of her hair. Then she straightened and met the inquisitive gazes of Shane's family. "Hunter, why don't you tell me who you're hanging out with?"

Hunter crossed the floor to stand beside the older woman. "This is my Granny June, and my Grandpa Dennis, and my Aunt Gabby."

"Hi." Faith hoped she didn't look as scared as she felt. She wanted to make a good impression. "I'm Faith St. John. I'm not sure if Shane has mentioned me, but we've just started seeing each other."

"Oh, he's mentioned you, all right," Gabrielle said, and Faith wasn't sure if she meant it in a good way or a bad way, but she wasn't smiling. Faith studied her. Shane's sister was a striking woman of average height with thick dark hair and eyes that were more golden than brown. Her features were delicate, her skin flawless, and she rocked jeans that showed off long legs. "It's nice to meet you. I'm Gabrielle."

Faith noticed she introduced herself by her full name, not her nickname, which was how her family referred to her. Based on Gabrielle's expression, the move was totally intentional. She didn't want to invite familiarity until she'd figured out what Faith's intentions were with her brother. Much as she'd have loved a warmer reception, Faith approved. It was nice that Shane had someone watching his back.

"Lovely to meet you." She looked at the couple behind Gabrielle. "You too, Mr. and Mrs. Walker."

At this, a smile eased across Mrs. Walker's kindly face. "Please, call us June and Dennis. We're all adults here."

"I'm not," Izzy reminded them, and they laughed.

"Okay, June," Faith said. "What can I do to help with lunch?"

June gestured to a mound of boiled potatoes beside her. "Dice these for the potato salad?"

"No problem." Faith rolled up her sleeves and got to work. "So, did you enjoy the drive over?"

"Yes, the scenery is spectacular."

"We stopped a few miles down the road for one of those real fruit ice creams," Dennis added. "Damn tasty."

"Not as good as mine," Faith told him confidently. "You'll have to try it. I brought a box of Russian fudge flavor because it's Dylan's favorite."

"I might just do that."

"No, Dad." Gabrielle's tone was stern. "You know you're not supposed to have one ice cream, let alone two. Not with your cholesterol levels."

He grumbled, and Faith laughed. "Maybe next time."

Her hands moved quickly as she chopped. She was deft in the kitchen because she'd spent so much time in her own, perfecting ice cream recipes.

June watched her with a raised brow. "You're doing that in half the time I'd take."

"I've had plenty of practice."

Gabrielle sidled over, effectively sandwiching her. Faith sensed something big was coming. "Now for the real question," Gabrielle said, her voice low. She glanced over her shoulder, and Faith did the same, noting that Dennis had taken the children away. "Do you love my brother?"

She felt both women's eyes on her, and her stomach bottomed out. Did she love him? Shane was everything a man should be: handsome, kind, a great dad, and willing to stand up for the people he cared about. It would have been impossible not to love him. But she hadn't admitted as much to him yet.

"Well?" Gabrielle demanded, hands on hips. "It's a simple yes or no question."

"Gabby," June cautioned. "You're coming on a bit strong. They haven't been dating for long."

"No, that's not the problem." Faith's heart was beating so erratically, she was certain they must hear it. Opening her mouth, she spilled the truth. "I do love him. I'm crazy about him. But I haven't told him that. We haven't said the words."

Gabrielle's mouth dropped open, then she snapped it shut and beamed. "Well, okay then. Thanks for being honest. All I want is for Shane to be happy."

"I know," Faith said. "I appreciate you looking out for him."

June tutted. "Don't you feel guilty for pressing the matter when Shane should be the first to hear it?"

Gabrielle shrugged. "Not at all, Mama." She turned to Faith and added, "If you hurt him, I'll hunt you down and shave off your hair."

Faith's eyes widened. "Um." How was she supposed to take that? "You do what you need to, but I don't intend to hurt him. He's had enough of that from Diana."

Gabrielle pulled a face. "Ugh, that woman. I can't believe she's back in town. What a bitch."

June clapped a hand to her mouth, and Faith thought she was affronted by the cuss word until she realized the older woman was trying not to snort with laughter. She grinned. Perhaps she'd fit in with the Walkers after all.

"ALL RIGHT, BOYS. HOP IN."

Dylan and three of his friends loaded into Shane's car while the other boys got into the van driven by Dylan's friend Caleb's father, who'd volunteered to help out. The kids were sandy and damp, with towels wrapped around their waists to prevent the water from their swimming trunks soaking into the car seats. Shane waited for the doors of the other vehicle to close, then led the way back to his place. When he spotted Faith's car parked alongside his parent's, his chest tightened. He'd hoped to be there for their first meeting. Had it gone well? His family's opinion of her meant a lot, considering his disastrous previous marriage.

He parked across the road and gave the boys time to climb out, then locked up and headed inside. His stomach was a tangle of nerves as he sought out his family. He found his dad in the living room with Izzy and Hunter.

"Your girlfriend is in the kitchen with June and Gabby," he said.

Shane winced. It had taken Mum and Gabby no time at all to corner Faith. A few more steps took him to the kitchen, where all three women were a whirlwind of activity. Faith didn't seem to notice him until he settled his hands on her hips from behind. She leaned back and tilted her face up, smiling. Desire fisted in his gut, along with something else. Something far more complicated.

He kissed her. "Hi, beautiful." Softly, he asked, "How's it going?"

"Everything is great," she replied too loudly, because that's how Faith was. "Gabrielle was just telling me about the time you jumped off the top of a playground with a plastic bag, thinking it would work like a parachute."

Really? They'd already gotten to the embarrassing stories?

"Thanks, guys." To Faith, he explained, "I was eight. You'd think they wouldn't hold it against me after all this time."

Her bright pink lips curved up. "It's adorable."

"Adorable. Great, just what I was going for."

Shouting outside interrupted their conversation, and Faith cocked her head. "My guess is, the cricket players just arrived."

"I'd say you're right," he agreed. "Shall we go say hello?"

He was nearly as excited to meet them as the boys were. While he didn't approve of the way Diana wielded her money and connections, he loved the Black Caps. Hopefully, he could keep his cool more than it sounded like the twelve-year-old boys outside were doing.

"I'm coming too," Gabby said, rinsing and drying her hands. "One of those cricketers might look at me and fall madly in love."

Having been as good as married to her job as a rural veterinarian for most of her twenties, his sister had recently decided she should try to find a life partner before she ended up alone with her four cats, two dogs, one horse, and half dozen goats. Unfortunately, "subtle" was not a word in her vocabulary, which sent most men running for the hills before they'd finished a single conversation. She claimed this was a tactic to weed out the weak links, but he wasn't convinced.

They left his parents in the house and watched the boys line up for the chance to say hi to a Black Cap. Shane waited until they'd finished, and then introduced himself and thanked them for coming. One of the men assured him it was their pleasure, seeing as Diana had offered to attend his daughter's birthday party in return. Shane had to smile. She may be self-centered, but at least she was trying.

Gabby deflated upon hearing the man had a family

but turned to the other with a broad smile and stuck out her hand. "Gabrielle Walker. I'm a massive fan."

"Dylan's aunt?" he asked, and she nodded to confirm. Shane noticed him check out her left hand, and the man's grin widened. Perhaps Gabby would reel one in after all.

Together, he and Faith set up the barbecue, then left another parent in charge of cooking. The boys set up their cricket equipment, and Faith returned inside to help his parents. Twenty or thirty locals had wandered in off the street to celebrate, as was the Haven Bay style. Diana had assumed a prime position on a sun chair she must have brought with her, lying back with her sunglasses on. Gabby and Shane stood side by side and watched the coaching session.

"What do you think of Faith?" he asked, dying to hear her opinion. His sister wasn't the smoothest when it came to her own love life, but she was shrewd and a good judge of people. She'd told him all along that Diana wasn't right for him, and he'd ignored her. He wouldn't go as far as to say he regretted that, seeing as Diana gave him their sons, but he certainly didn't want to repeat the mistake.

"I wondered how long you'd take to ask." She checked her watch. "Twenty minutes. Solid effort."

He sighed. "Gabs…."

"She seems nice," Gabby allowed, although her tone was cautious. "I can't say I was surprised to hear you got together. You've always talked about her more than most people would about their babysitter."

Relief swamped him. "So, you like her?"

"I reserve judgment. I need more time to get to know her."

He nodded. "Fair enough."

He watched as Dylan prepared to bat with guidance

from one of the Black Caps who stood behind him and off to the side. Another boy bowled, and Dylan smacked it and leapt into action. His relaxed expression told Shane he was having a good time. Seeing him like that after he had spent so much of the past few weeks tense and uncommunicative was a balm to Shane's soul. Hopefully, things would only get better from here.

24

WHEN LUNCH WAS READY, THE BOYS TOOK A BREAK FROM their cricket game and swarmed the tables Faith and June had placed near the barbecue, which were laden with salads, bread rolls, barbecued meat, tofu sausages, and a couple of sweeter options. Faith grabbed a roll and filled it with chicken and slaw. She looked around. Shane was heading back inside for something, so when she spotted Gabrielle near the back of the yard, she headed over to join her instead.

"Hi." Gabrielle shaded her eyes with her hand as she looked up. "You come to keep me company?"

"I sure have." Faith lowered herself to the ground and tucked her legs beneath her. "It's so sweet that you guys came for Dylan's birthday. Things have been hard on him lately, but he seems to be having a great time."

"He does," Gabrielle agreed. "What makes you say things have been hard on him?"

"Having Diana back, and me changing roles in his life. It's a lot to take in, especially if he was hoping for his mum and dad to get back together."

Gabrielle scoffed. "If Shane was stupid enough to take

that she-devil back, I'd disown him. But yeah, I can see where you're coming from. I have no doubt that by the time we leave, he'll be trying to shove us out the door."

"I thought you were only here for the weekend."

Gabrielle gave her a quizzical look, and she flushed. Apparently, she was out of the loop on something. "We're here until after Christmas. I'm surprised Shane didn't tell you. We all took leave from work, and I hired someone to housesit and care for my animals."

"Oh." She should have known that. "He mentioned Christmas would be here, but I didn't realize you were staying all the way through."

Gabrielle smiled, the expression gentler than what Faith was beginning to consider her usual. "Don't take it personally. He probably forgot. In some ways, his mind is like a steel trap, but in others, he's completely useless."

"I'm sure that's it," Faith murmured. She bit into her bread roll so she could mull things over without having to talk. At that moment, a glass clinked loudly, and someone tapped on a microphone. *Who'd brought one of those?*

What's more, who'd given it to Diana?

Faith shifted uncomfortably, but Gabrielle just rolled her eyes. "Seems like the queen is going to make a pronouncement."

"I'd like to call for a toast," Diana said to the crowd gathered on the lawn. She'd reapplied her vivid red lipstick and changed into a form-fitting dress that she hadn't been wearing earlier. She was right at home in front of everyone. "To Dylan: happy birthday." A few people cheered. Faith sought Dylan out in time to see him blush and duck his head. Famous or not, mothers could always embarrass their children. "And to Shane. Dylan is lucky to have him for a father."

228

Faith and Gabrielle exchanged a look. Faith didn't know where this was going, but she feared it was nowhere good. She scanned the crowd and didn't see Shane. Was he inside?

"I'm sure almost everyone here knows what a steady, kind man Shane is. In fact, he's such a nice guy that he recently pretended to be involved with someone to save her from humiliation. Faith, are you here?"

Oh, no.

Faith shrunk in on herself. Diana knew. Somehow, she knew everything, and Faith was frozen with a lump of undigested food in her stomach that she wanted to hurl back up. Fortunately, her revelation wouldn't be a surprise to most people from the bay, but what would Shane's family think?

"There you are!" Diana exclaimed, giving her a little wave. Everyone present turned in Faith's direction. "For anyone here who didn't know—most of you, I'd assume —back in high school, Faith sent naked pictures to a boy who had a girlfriend, and it blew up in her face." She pouted, as though she actually pitied Faith, whose teeth ground together. She wanted to rip the blonde bitch's extensions out by the roots. She got to her feet and took a step forward, but then she noticed the murmurs. Her friends and neighbors were whispering. About her? She froze in place. Opened her mouth to say something, but nothing came out. She searched frantically for someone to help, and at that moment, Shane appeared in the doorway and beelined toward Diana. Thank God.

"Drop the microphone!" he yelled.

Diana sped up her words. "Flash forward to this year. Darling Shane pretended to be her boyfriend to cover for her so she wouldn't have to face up to her past. Isn't he such a great guy?" She raised a glass. "To Shane."

Shane reached her as she finished the toast and snatched the microphone from her hand, but the damage was done. Diana leveled her gaze on Faith and smirked. She'd won, and she knew it. Faith wanted to take the bitch down a notch. To tell her exactly what she thought of her. But Shane's family were still watching, and the buzz around her was growing. She scanned the faces, noting their curiosity. Did they believe the story?

She heard her name and flinched. She should take the microphone from Shane and tell her side of the story. But how could she handle it if her friends and neighbors thought the worst? What if Shane's family decided she was just another woman who wasn't good enough for him? She closed her eyes, her heart sinking, and wished the ground would swallow her up. She'd put her life back together so carefully over the past few years and built her confidence up until she could be proud of herself. And now this.

"Please ignore everything my ex-wife said," Shane called across the gathering. "Faith is the same person you've always known her to be." He extended a hand in my direction. "Will you join me, sweetheart?"

Faith took another step forward. She could do this. She could. But then, as she moved toward him, she heard June asking what Diana meant about the naked photos and cold sweat broke out on her palms. They'd never welcome her into the fold after this, and with Shane's past and the way Diana had painted her, she couldn't blame them. Still, she wouldn't take this lying down. She strode to the front and took the microphone from Shane but shrugged off the arm he tried to place around her waist. If he comforted her right now, she'd break down. She needed to activate her internal badass.

"I did send naked photos to Mason Delphine when I

was eighteen," she said, staring into the space above the audience's heads. "We dated in secret because he was embarrassed to be seen with me. Not that I knew that at the time. He told me it was because he wasn't allowed to date. He lied, and then he lied again to Gigi when she found the naked photos after we'd broken up."

"You don't have to do this," Shane murmured.

"I really do." Whatever happened next, she wouldn't let the lies about her stand. "So yeah, when I found out Mason was coming to Erica's wedding, and Mom had set me up with a blind date, I pretended to be dating Shane instead. But nothing about it is pretend anymore, and that's the truth."

She thrust the microphone back into Shane's hands and bolted. She couldn't face his family after this. Whatever they believed, they wouldn't accept her. He deserved to be with someone they approved of. She stumbled over the lawn toward the road.

"Faith," Shane called.

Several people reached out for her, but she shied away. When she reached the driveway, she yanked her cute pumps off and left them behind. She could hear someone chasing behind her—Shane, maybe?—but she sprinted to her car, threw herself into the driver's seat, and took off before he could catch her.

SHANE BENT OVER, BREATHING HEAVILY. HE'D BEEN TOO slow. He reached into his pocket for his keys. He needed to go after her and make this right. He started toward his car, but someone grabbed his arm from behind. He swung around and came face to face with Caleb's father. For a moment, Shane wanted to shout at him because if he hadn't gotten back together with his ex-wife, Dylan might not have gotten those crazy ideas about a reunion between him and Diana, and then they might not be here.

"Let her go," Frank said. "Give her some time. Dylan needs you now."

Dylan.

Hell.

Diana had just said something completely inappropriate in front of both of their sons, all of Dylan's friends, and a number of their parents. At a kid's birthday party, for God's sake. Frank was right. He needed to do damage control.

He glanced at Diana. She stood, hands on hips, looking pleased as punch. When she saw him, she winked. His head spun. He started back toward her, ready to pull her and Dylan aside to sort this out, but before he could get there, Gabby rose to her feet and cleared her throat. His sister's eyes were hard, and if looks could kill, his ex would be a goner.

"You are out of line, Diana." Gabby raised a glass of juice. "I'd like to propose a counter toast. To Diana, the woman who abandoned her babies and her husband to pursue a life of fame and fortune and now won't let the people she left behind move on with their lives. Cheers, you raging bitch." She tipped her glass back and drank.

Diana's mouth dropped open and she made a sound of disbelief, her gaze darting from one person to another, as though trying to discern how much credit they were giving Gabby's words, and who they'd side with. When a number of people followed Gabby's lead and drank, she took a step back.

"I suggest you leave before you do anything else to embarrass yourself," Shane told her.

"No." She crossed her arms and threw her head back defiantly. "This is Dylan's day, and as long as he wants me here, I'm staying."

Dylan.

Shane searched for his son amongst the sea of faces, feeling like a failure for not thinking to check on him sooner. His son's cheeks were pale and his hands fisted at his sides. As the audience's collective attention settled on him, he rocketed to his feet.

"I want you to go," he cried, tears shining in his eyes. He looked absolutely distraught, and it gutted Shane. This was supposed to be a happy day, but his mother just couldn't let it happen. And Shane, in seeking his own happiness with Faith, had given her a reason to behave poorly. "I told you that in secret!" Dylan's voice rose shrilly. "You're a user, and I don't care if you go back to Hollywood and stay there."

Diana looked so crestfallen that Shane would have felt sorry for her under different circumstances. She hadn't expected his family—including their son—to rally around Faith. "You don't mean that," she said.

"Yes, I do. Get out. Just go!" Kicking the cricket wickets, he muttered a few curse words he shouldn't have known and stormed into the house. Shane hurried after him, heading straight to his bedroom, where he had no doubt Dylan intended to hole up for the foreseeable future. He arrived in the hall as the door slammed and approached cautiously, pausing to knock outside.

"I don't want to talk," Dylan snapped.

"It's Dad," he said softly. "Can I come in?"

There was a moment of silence, but then the door opened. Dylan's eyes were bright with the tears he hadn't wanted to shed in front of anyone, and his face was flushed with anger. He let Shane inside and sat on the floor, drawing his knees up to his chest.

Shane sat on the edge of the bed. "Are you okay, bud?" he asked. "That was pretty rough out there."

"I meant everything I said," he replied. "I don't care if it was mean."

Shane shook his head. "I didn't mean you. I meant your mum. She shouldn't have done what she did. Especially not if you shared things with her in confidence and trusted her not to mention them."

Dylan hung his head, his fringe flopping forward and hiding his face. "I'm sorry. I shouldn't have told her anything about you and Faith. I just wanted to make her happy. Do you think Faith will be okay?"

He wished he could brush away Dylan's concern, but he really didn't know. Faith might have put on a brave front, but she may not want anything to do with them after this. She'd managed to move on from the awful things that had happened when she was younger, and he'd dumped it all back on her doorstep with a hefty helping of more. He knew how much it had meant to her to make a good first impression on his family, and Diana had hit her where it hurt.

"I don't know," he said honestly. "It might not seem like it on the outside, but she's sensitive." He sighed, wishing he didn't have to say this when Dylan was obviously already struggling with what he'd done. "I know you didn't mean any harm, and I understand why you told your mum what you did, but you need to be careful the next time you're asked to share private information about someone, because people can get hurt."

"I know." He sounded so ashamed that Shane wanted to gather him into a hug, but Dylan was at that awkward age where he wasn't big on hugging and might not welcome it. Shane ran a hand through his own hair. Why did parenting have to be so damn hard?

"Can we go find Faith?" Dylan asked. "I need to tell her I'm sorry."

Despite everything, a sliver of pride lodged in his heart. His boy wanted to make things right. Maybe he wasn't screwing up the solo parenting gig as badly as he feared.

"I'm sure she'd like to hear that, but maybe not right now. She's upset and needs time to calm down first."

Dylan wiped his eyes on the heel of his hands. "But you're going to go get her, right?"

Shane nodded. "I'm going to try. But first, we need to talk to your grandparents. Do you think you're up for that?"

Dylan scrambled to his feet. "Yeah, okay."

They found June, Dennis, and Gabby talking quietly in the kitchen.

"Diana left," Gabby said when she saw them coming. "I saw her off the property myself."

Relief made him weak in the knees. At least that was one mess he didn't have to deal with. "Thanks, Gabs. And thank you for what you did out there. I appreciate it."

She scoffed. "I just said what I've been dying to for a fucking long time." She glanced at Dylan. "Excuse my French, Dyl."

"Would you care to explain what that was about?" Dennis asked. "We got the gist of it, but we'd like the full story."

"CliffsNotes version? Faith's parents were in town for her cousin's wedding recently, and they tried to set her up with some guy she didn't know because her ex was going to be there, and they didn't want her to feel vulnerable. She didn't like being set up, so we pretended

235

to be an item to make everyone back off. I recently learned that the ex was someone she'd dated in secret during high school, and then he dumped her for another girl but kept intimate photos of her on his phone, and when his new girlfriend found them, he claimed Faith had sent them because she was desperate to be noticed. The girlfriend shared them with some of the girls in their year, and they bullied her for it."

June covered her mouth with a hand. "How awful. That poor girl."

"How did Diana find out?" Gabby asked. "What kind of bitch uses another woman's pain for her own gain? Sorry, Dyl, I know it's your mum we're talking about."

"I don't care," he spat. "I'm the one who told her that Dad was only pretending to be with Faith for the wedding. I didn't know she'd do something like this."

"We know you didn't." June wrapped an arm around him and drew him to her side.

"Well, son," Dennis said, having taken all of this on board more smoothly than anyone would have expected. "You'd better hurry after your girl, or you might be too late."

Shane nodded and did just that.

25

FAITH PARKED BEHIND THE SHACK AND LET HERSELF IN the rear entrance. She opened the cupboards and tossed ingredients on the counter, not even pausing to think about how they might work together. Orange and cardamom—why not? While she was at it, how about double-chocolate fudge with a salted caramel swirl? Mm, that sounded like comfort to her. She grabbed cream, eggs, sugar, and was about to begin an all-new recipe— completely off the top of her head—when Megan came in from the shop. Faith froze, caught in the act.

Megan's brow furrowed. "Shouldn't you be at Dylan's birthday party?"

"I was," she replied, unable to hold eye contact.

"Is it over?"

"It's—it's...." Faith trailed off, and then the dam burst. Tears streamed down her cheeks, smearing her mascara and eyeliner. "It was so bad, Meg. I don't know—" She hiccupped. "—how I'm ever gonna show my face again."

"Oh, sweetie." Megan's expression softened, and she pulled Faith into a hug. "Do you want to talk about it?"

"Not yet." Maybe not ever. Although she'd have to

eventually, or someone else would break the news to her best friend. "I just need to be alone to make ice cream and stuff my face."

Megan released her and nodded. "We can do that. You wait right here." She went to the fridge and returned a moment later with a bottle of wine, which she uncorked and used to fill a glass. Then she headed into the shop and came back with one of her locally famous cocktail cupcakes. She handed it to Faith. "Eat a cupcake, drink wine, make ice cream, and we can talk whenever you want—or not, if that's what you'd prefer. I'll be in the shop if you need me."

Faith took Megan by the shoulders and planted a kiss on her cheek. "Thank you, gorgeous. I love you."

Who needed men when they had friends like this?

She set to work, but no matter how she tried to distract herself, she couldn't forget the way Diana had outed her in front of everyone. And yeah, most of the town had already known she and Shane started out pretending, but not everyone. His family hadn't. What must they think of her now?

And then there were the photos. Enough people had known about those to make her life unpleasant back at high school, but hardly anyone who'd been there today had been in the loop. Now her biggest secret was out.

Whisking cream furiously, she felt a burning ache in her arm and tried to focus on that rather than the tearing sensation in her heart. God, the party had felt like history replaying itself with the mean girl tearing her apart— only this time she'd truly been in love with the guy involved. She'd only had an idealistic teenage infatuation with Mason, and she'd long outgrown it. Her feelings for Shane were real, but she was stupid to have believed it could ever work out between them.

She peeled the wrapper off the cupcake and bit into it, savoring the sweetness of frosting as it exploded on her tastebuds. Normally, Megan's cakes could make her forget almost anything, but now, no matter how tasty they were, they felt empty. She sighed. Surely a woman should only have to live with one great embarrassment in her life. Why did she have to suffer through two? It wasn't fair. But maybe that was what she got for being idiotic enough to let her guard down.

Her tears renewed themselves, and she wiped her cheeks on a napkin, not caring that the smudge of color on the paper indicated her face was probably a mess. She collected the cardamom and sprinkled it into the cream mixture. It occurred to her that using powdered spice was probably a bad choice, but she didn't have the energy to do better. She frowned at the mixture and jerked in surprise at the sound of a knock on the back door. Glancing over, she saw the outline of a dark-haired man against the frosted glass, and her heart shredded itself even more.

Shane.

She didn't want to talk to him now. Her makeup was wrecked, her eyes were red, and she probably had remnants of cupcake on her face. Knowing he couldn't see into the kitchen any better than she could see out, she ignored him. He knocked again, and his outline didn't move. He must have seen her car, otherwise he'd have left. She grabbed her phone and sunk to the floor. She couldn't face him. It would only be salt in the wound, showing her what she couldn't have.

She tapped out a text to Megan.

Faith: *Please make him leave.*

She waited, and a few minutes later, a second figure joined Shane outside. They conversed briefly, and then parted ways. Shortly after, she heard his car engine start and he drove away. She flopped back against the cupboard in relief. Thank God.

BY THE TIME DUSK FELL, FAITH HAD PULLED HERSELF together enough to leave The Shack. Armed with goodies from Megan, she headed home. She'd just gotten out of the car when Betty appeared from next door—where she *didn't* live—puffing as she hurried down the path.

"Faith, I'm glad I caught you."

Faith sighed. "This isn't a good time."

"I know." Betty glanced at the carton of cupcakes. "I just wanted to make sure you heard what happened at Dylan's birthday party after you left."

Faith looked longingly at her front door. She should have realized Betty would know everything by now. The woman had a finger on the bay's pulse at all times. "I'm sorry, but I'd rather not talk about it."

Betty drew herself up to her full—and unimpressive —height. "Faith St. John. Be quiet and listen to what I'm trying to tell you. I've been waiting in Maude's house for hours for you to come back."

"Okay." Chastened, she fell silent.

"I don't know whether you've talked to Shane, but considering how upset that poor boy was last I saw him, I'm guessing you haven't. He and his family all stood up for you after you left, and nobody thinks the worse of you because of Diana's little stunt." She reached out and touched Faith's hand. "Do me a favor and go to his place. You don't have to talk to anyone. Just go there. Promise?"

Faith ran a hand through her hair. The last thing she wanted to do was face up to anyone, but if Betty was telling the truth and Shane's family had supported her, she owed it to them to go. Hope flickered in her chest. Maybe they didn't disapprove of her after all.

"I will." She bent and kissed Betty's cheek. "Here. Take these. I've had enough for a lifetime." She handed Betty the carton of cupcakes. "Thanks for making sure I got the message."

———————

"Do you think she'll come?" Dylan asked, glancing out the window to the front yard. Shane followed his gaze, knowing he was anxious to apologize. It had been his idea to reuse the birthday banner as a gesture for Faith. They'd turned it around and scrawled a message on the back: *The Walker family love Faith St. John*. Now they just had to wait for her.

"I don't know, buddy. Betty said she'd do her best, and she's a determined woman, so I guess we just have to hope she pulls through."

After clearing up the party, the family had gathered inside, unusually subdued. He'd caught his parents watching him several times and knew they were concerned. He couldn't ease their minds though. They were all balanced on a razor's edge.

"I want Faith," Hunter said, climbing onto Shane's knee.

Shane commiserated. "So do I." He ruffled his son's hair. "Why don't you go brush your teeth? It'll be time for bed soon."

"Hey. Shane." Gabby stood in front of him, and she nodded toward the window. "Look out there." He spun around in time to see a car pull up at the curb. "Go," she said. "We'll stay in here."

He nodded. "Thank you."

He straightened his clothes and went outside, moving slowly so as not to startle her. Faith got out of the car and stared at the house. He knew the moment she caught sight of the banner flying proudly and stamped with his, Dylan's, and Hunter's hand prints. Her hand flew to her mouth, and she gasped.

"Hi, sweetheart." He stuffed his hands into his pockets so he wouldn't reach for her.

Her eyes darted from the banner to him. "Is it true? Even after today?"

"It is." He stood in front of her, taking stock of her bare face and reddened eyes. She'd been crying, and that ripped him apart inside.

"I'm sorry for running," she said, her chest rising and falling rapidly. "And for shutting you out. I just needed some space to think."

"Don't apologize." Every single one of the painful emotions he'd experienced over the course of the day lodged in his throat. "I'm the one who's sorry. Diana shouldn't have said what she did. She shouldn't even have *known* it, but Dylan told her about how we started out, and he's very, very sorry." He hoped she could hear the sincerity in his voice. Dylan was riddled with guilt over sharing what he knew with his mother.

She swallowed. "I didn't realize he hated me so much."

"No, baby. He doesn't. He's just blind where Diana is concerned. He's furious at her, and he's waiting inside to apologize if you feel like speaking to him." He pointed to the banner. "This was his idea."

"That's sweet." Her expression softened slightly. "Sorry about the party. I hate to imagine what your parents must think of me now."

"Faith," he said softly, moving closer and reaching out

a hand. "My family like you. What Diana said doesn't change that. In fact, after you'd left, Gabby tore her down in front of everyone.

"Really?" she asked, her voice small. "Betty said your family had stood up for me, but she didn't share the details."

He let everything he was feeling show on his face. Every bit of love he had for her. "Yes, Gabby did that. You shouldn't be surprised. Everyone who knows you adores you. Once they got over their shock, they sided with you, but you ran off so quickly that you didn't see it."

He took a deep breath, ready for the biggest leap of faith he had ever taken. It terrified him, but he couldn't stand to see her in pain, and while he feared she'd reject him because she had so much more to offer than he ever could, he was prepared to bare his soul and pray for the best.

Curving a hand around her cheek, he said, "I love you, Faith. I love you, and I never meant to bring any of this down on you, and I'm sorry."

She blinked rapidly. "It's not your fault. Everything she said is true."

His heart squeezed. Was she not going to acknowledge the other part of what he'd said? The part that was far more important. "If it helps, I don't think she'll be staying in the bay for much longer. Even if she does, it doesn't matter. Not to me, and not to my family. Did you hear me, sweetheart? I said I love you. I'm out of practice at this dating thing. I...." He studied the green flecks in her hazel eyes and swallowed hard. "I haven't wanted anything for myself in so long, but I want you. I *need* you. And I have to believe that you love me too, whether you've said it or not, because otherwise you wouldn't have gone through everything you have for my sake. You don't have to say the words. If you need me to, I'll believe in our love strongly enough for both of us."

"Oh, Shane," she sighed, and then pressed her lips to his before pulling away. The brief taste of her wasn't nearly enough, but he suspected it was all he'd get for now. Then her lips curled up at the edges. Only very slightly, but she was trying to smile, wobbly as it may be, and hope pierced his heart. "I love you too."

He caressed her cheekbone with his thumb and scarcely dared to breathe. "You do?"

"Yes." A glimpse of teeth peeked from between her lips. "Is that so hard to believe?"

"Well, yeah," he admitted. "You're smart and funny and beautiful. I'm a tired, single dad with a bitchy ex and a son who's not far off being a teenager."

She shook her head. "You're so much more than that, and I love your whole crazy family. Well, except Diana. I don't think I'll ever like her."

He laughed. "Fair enough. Come inside? My parents want to see you, and I promise they don't think worse of you for what she did."

He half expected her to refuse, but she shrugged one shoulder. "Okay."

"Thank you." He kissed her, tasting the saltiness of dried tears on her lips, and wished he could erase every event that had ever made her cry. "Let's go in."

26

AS THEY HEADED INTO THE HOUSE, FAITH COULD HEAR voices inside. She slowed, reluctant to deal with the Walkers. Regardless of what Shane had said, she couldn't help but feel that they must blame her to a certain extent. He threaded his fingers through hers, raised her hand to his mouth, and kissed the back of it. His gaze was warm and reassuring.

"It'll be all right," he said. "I promise."

God, she hoped so.

They entered the hall, and he led her to the living room. The moment they walked in, the conversation halted.

"Um, hi," she said, giving a little wave and feeling excruciatingly awkward.

Gabrielle rushed over and wrapped her in a hug. "I'm so glad you came back."

"Oof." Faith gasped. "What's with this? Not that I mind. I do love hugs." She dropped Shane's hand and hugged Gabrielle back, then released her.

"I'm sorry for what that heinous bitch did to you." Gabrielle placed her hands on Faith's shoulders. "To go through that and come back for more, you must love my brother. So, thank you for being strong enough to withstand Hurricane Diana. We're happy to welcome you to the family."

"Wait.... What?" She'd expected pointed questions, if not outright hostility. She *had* indirectly ruined Dylan's birthday party and been outed as a fake, after all. "But what about—"

"None of us care what that good-for-nothing woman says," June added as she joined them. "You were betrayed by someone you trusted when you were young, and Shane helped you keep a brave face in front of him. As far as we're concerned, he was the best person for the job, and we're pleased he was there when you needed him. That's all there is to it."

"I never liked Diana," Dennis remarked, and Faith glanced over Gabrielle's shoulder to smile at him. He gave her a nod. "A little ambition is a fine thing, but she makes a habit of stepping on people along the way."

"That she does," June agreed. "She could have had a steady career here in New Zealand television, but that wasn't enough for her, and look what happened as a result." She shook her head. "Would you like a glass of wine? We've all been indulging while we waited to see whether you'd come back."

Faith nodded, shock and relief making her heart flutter like a butterfly in her chest. "Yes, please. The bigger the better."

Gabrielle laughed. "I like you already."

"If I'd known this was all it would take to get accepted into the family, maybe I'd have beaten Diana to the punch."

An arm wrapped around her waist, and Shane kissed her temple. "Don't even joke about that." His hand settled on her hip, drawing patterns over the fabric there. "I think there's someone who needs to say something to you. Dyl?"

Everyone turned to face the corner, where Dylan had stood largely unnoticed until now. His hands were stuffed into his shorts, and his eyes were as red as hers. Despite everything, she wanted to comfort him.

"I'm sorry," he said in a low voice that she struggled to make out. A tear tracked down his cheek, but no one acknowledged it because he was at that age where he'd rather they pretend not to see. He scuffed his shoe on the floor and raised his head, expression distraught. "Like, so effing sorry."

"Dylan!" June exclaimed.

"Sorry, Grannie. I mean, I'm really super sorry. I was stupid to tell her, but I didn't think...." He trailed off miserably. "I *hate* her," he exploded, clenching his fists at his sides. "I hate her so much. I wish she'd stayed away." He paused for a moment, a hiccupping sound coming from the back of his throat, and then he was openly sobbing. He crossed the floor and stopped in front of Faith, tilting his face up to look her in the eye. In that moment, her heart bled for him. He may have messed up, and she'd been hurt as a result, but what kid didn't screw up sometimes? All he'd ever wanted was his mother's love and affection.

"I didn't want things to change," he admitted. "And I knew everything would be different if Dad had a girl-friend. But maybe that's a good thing." He glanced at Shane. "He smiles more when you're around. Anyway, do you think you could maybe forgive me? It's okay if it takes a while. I can make it up to you somehow."

Oh, man. She was toast. If Shane himself hadn't sealed the deal, this stricken boy would have. She opened her arms, waiting for him to come to her, if he wanted to. He stepped forward, and she enveloped him, resting her cheek on the top of his head and smelling grass, sunscreen, and sweat on his skin. It wouldn't be long before he was too tall for her to do this, so she'd enjoy it while it lasted.

"It's okay," she murmured. "I don't hold it against you. I also don't want to replace your mum, but I hope you can make room in that big heart of yours for both of us."

He nodded. "I can do that."

They let each other go, and Faith glanced up at the ceiling, taking a moment to wipe the underside of her eyes. A shaky breath eased from her lips. "Have you had cake?" she asked.

He shook his head. "No one has."

"Well, that seems like an oversight." She affixed a smile in place. "I promise you, Megan's cakes are out of this world. I reckon we should all grab a piece and stuff our faces. What do you think?"

His expression lightened. "Yeah. Can we, Dad?"

Shane chuckled. "I guess so. We shouldn't let it go to waste."

They assembled around the counter while Dennis retrieved the cake and handed Dylan a knife to slice it. He cut a massive hunk for himself and a bunch of smaller pieces for everyone else. They plated the cake and took it outside, where they sat in a ring around a brazier and started anew. Hours later, Faith was still smiling.

THAT NIGHT, SHANE INVITED FAITH TO STAY IN HIS bedroom. It was the first time they'd been open with his family about her sleeping over, and he hoped they'd made the right choice. As he lay with her cheek resting over his heart and her arm draped over his waist, all he could think was how lucky he was to have a second chance. She breathed softly, stirring his chest hair, but he didn't believe she'd fallen asleep yet. Not after the romp they'd just had.

He dipped his chin to kiss her forehead. "You have no idea how long I've wanted to be with you."

She tilted her face up, her lips curving into a lazy smile. "Probably only half as long as I've had a crush on you."

"I doubt it." A feeling of contentment settled over him, filling him with warmth. He could scarcely believe she was here in his arms. His very own miracle woman. "Back when you first started babysitting the boys, I wanted you. But I was so bitter and angry, I knew it would be wrong to make a move. Even now, I'm amazed you return my feelings. It makes no sense, but I suppose love rarely does. I'm just glad you're here." Cuddling her close, he dropped another kiss on the end of her nose.

Her eyes shone in the dark, as open and unguarded as ever. "I've liked you for just as long. Do you know how impossible it is to see a single dad who loves his two little boys with all his heart and not fall for him?" She nuzzled his throat. "I've wanted you to bend me over the couch and have your way with me from day one."

His eyebrows shot up. "Oh, really?" Had he thought he was done for the night? Because he could definitely rally. "What else did you like about me?"

"Your smile, your protective streak, your kind heart. Oh, and don't get me started on how hot you looked cradling Hunter."

"I'll cradle him any time you want, baby."

She laughed, the corners of her eyes crinkling with

humor. "He might protest these days. What about you?" She smoothed a hand up his chest. "What was it about me that made you have babysitter fantasies?"

"Honestly? I think it was how genuine you were." He cleared his throat and hastened to add, "You're beautiful, anyone could see that, but you never made pretenses. You were yourself, and people could take you as you came. After everything with Diana, that was a very attractive trait."

"Huh." She sounded surprised. "So, it wasn't my bangin' body or great rack?"

"They sweeten the deal," he conceded, "But other women have those too. However, other women are *not* Faith St. John, and that's who I fell in love with." Perhaps it was the dark, and the fact they'd built a cocoon of safety around them, but he couldn't stop himself from adding, "I hope you know I'm thinking long-term. As in, I want to put a ring on your finger one day."

"Is that supposed to scare me?" she asked. "Because you'll have to try harder. In fact, I might not let you out of this bed until you make good on your promise."

He relaxed, tension easing from his body. "I wouldn't mind if you did."

They kissed as though they had all the time in the world. Their tongues touched and dragged against each other. Their caresses were slow and unhurried.

Something creaked in the hall outside, and they both froze, but then footsteps padded past and into the bathroom. Faith giggled, muffling the sound in his chest. But the interruption had reminded him of something.

"Hey, I always meant to tell you that my family would be staying for a while, but I just got sidetracked."

She nodded. "I figured as much." She kissed the

underside of his jaw. "I know you have a ton of things to think about."

He groaned. Hell, he could hardly think at all with her kissing him like that. "Join us."

She drew back. "What?"

"I know you probably have plans, but I'd love it if you could join us for Christmas. As part of the family. Where you belong."

"Hmm." She appeared to mull it over. His heart hammered. Then she cracked a grin. "I'd love to. As long as I can invite Charity, because without me, she'll probably spend the day alone. My parents will be away with friends."

"Absolutely," he agreed. "I want you to think of yourself as part of our family, and that means Charity is family too. She always has a place with us."

Her expression softened. "You are the sweetest. I love you so much. Let me show you."

She did. And by the time she finished, Shane had never felt more appreciated in his life.

EPILOGUE – CHRISTMAS

"Are you sure I'm welcome?" Charity asked as she and Faith made their way down the drive toward the Walker's home.

"Totally and completely," Faith assured her, flipping her hair over her shoulder and checking the gift wrap on her stack of presents once again. She'd brought something for each of the boys, a gift for Gabrielle, one for Shane's parents, and two for Shane—one he could open in public, and another she'd give him later, when they were alone.

"I'd hate to intrude," Charity continued. "This is a family Christmas after all."

"Yes, and you're family." They reached the door, and Faith knocked. Beside her, she sensed Charity stiffen. Her sister hated being in the bay, but Faith had threatened to blow off her first Christmas with the Walkers if Charity didn't turn up, because she couldn't handle the thought of her sister passing the holiday alone.

"Faith!" Hunter cried as the door swung inward. He stopped short of flinging himself into her arms when he spotted Charity and hid behind Dylan instead.

"Merry Christmas, boys," Faith said, handing them each a present. "This is my sister, Charity."

"Hey," Dylan said and pointed down the hall. "Everyone is through here."

Hunter glanced over his shoulder as they entered, but he didn't say a word.

"He's shy," Faith said. "Don't take it personally."

"I should have brought a present," Charity muttered. "What kind of dimwit doesn't bring a present to a Christmas with kids?"

"Mine can be from both of us." They'd been over this. "And I promise, everyone will be nice."

"Faith is here," Dylan announced as they arrived in the living room, which had been decked out with a real tree in the corner, tinsel hanging from the ceiling, and lights around the walls.

"Hi, beautiful." Shane came out of the kitchen, wearing a Santa Claus suit and a fake pot belly. He swooped Faith into his arms and dipped her low for a kiss. The touch of his lips stole her breath, and a sizzle ran through her from that tiny bit of contact.

When he let her go, she knew her cheeks were red. "You make Santa look good, sugar. Can I be one of your elves?"

He grinned devilishly and mouthed, "Later." She shivered, having no doubt he meant it. Then he looked over at Charity and his smile broadened. "Great to see you." He gave her a hug so quickly that no one other than Faith noticed the way Charity's eyes widened. "Mum, Dad, this is Charity. Faith's sister."

"Lovely to meet you," June said.

"Yeah, you too," Charity replied, casting her eyes down.

Faith wished her sister would loosen up for long

enough to enjoy herself. "Char, I'll introduce you to Gabrielle. You're going to love her."

Once everyone had a drink and a snack, they gathered around the tree to open presents. The boys went first, taking turns to tear into gifts with the kind of enthusiasm reserved for youth.

When they'd finished, Shane called them to attention. "How'd you boys like to show Faith her gift?"

Faith frowned, confused. Hunter took her hand and urged her to get up. He buzzed with excitement. "Come on, come on."

"Where are we going?" she asked as Dylan grabbed her other hand and tugged her down the hall. They stopped outside the bathroom, and Dylan went to the vanity and opened the second drawer from the top. It was empty.

"This is for you."

"Excuse me?"

"But that's not all." Hunter yanked her sleeve and guided her into Shane's bedroom, where Dylan opened the closet. Half of the rack had been cleared.

"And this." Shane stepped forward and gestured to a small cabinet on the side of the bed. "This is yours too."

Her mouth dropped open. "Wait, wait, wait. Hang on a minute. Are you...?"

"Move in with us," Shane said, beaming from ear to ear.

"We wanna see you all the time," Hunter added, apparently not wanting to be left out. "I want you to read me bedtime stories every night."

"And what about you?" she asked Dylan softly.

He ducked his head, his fringe flopping over his eyes. "I kinda like having you around."

"Aww!" She grabbed him and hugged the crap out of

him. Tears prickled in her eyes. "I kinda like you too, weirdo. And you." She pulled away and peppered kisses over Hunter's face while he giggled. "And you." She paused to take a long look at Shane's freaking gorgeous face, and then she kissed him. He wound his arms around her, and she heard Dylan usher Hunter from the room.

"Is that a yes?" he asked against her lips.

"Yes," she replied, kissing him. "Yes." Kiss. "Yes." Kiss. "Yes." Kiss.

"Good." His features softened, and he rested his forehead on hers. "Because I don't like having you away from me, even if it's only for short periods of time. I want all of you, all the time."

Faith's heart sang. For someone who'd always been told she was too much, too loud, too out there, his words were what she'd been waiting her entire life to hear.

"I want as much of you as I can get too." She angled her mouth over his. "Don't you worry, handsome. I'm not going anywhere. Not ever."

Why would she, when she finally had everything she'd ever wanted?

All she had to do was say yes.

THE END

BEGIN AGAIN WITH YOU

"WELCOME TO HAVEN BAY," CHARITY ST. JOHN MUTTERED
to herself as she drove past the brightly colored sign
announcing she'd arrived in the quaint beachside holiday
destination that was her hometown. "Where everyone
hates you, and flaming pitchforks are at the ready."

When Charity moved away three years ago, she'd
vowed never to return. Unfortunately, that vow hadn't
lasted as long as she'd have liked. First, she'd been
summoned back for her cousin Erica's wedding—which
she'd happily have ignored if not for the less-than-subtle
threats from her parents to drag her there kicking and
screaming—then she'd been talked into spending
Christmas with her sister's new family, and now the
simple fact of the matter was that she had nowhere else
to go.

Okay, amend that. She could move in with her
parents, who'd left the bay a while ago in favor of the
bustle of Wellington, but much as she loved them,
they'd drive her crazy within a week. Plus, Samuel
would expect that, whereas after everything that had
happened here, he certainly wouldn't think to look for

her in the bay. So here she was, with a crappy car that was lucky to have survived the trip, and all of her worldly belongings crammed in the back seat and trunk.

Jobless, homeless, and penniless.

"Oh, Samuel," she murmured. "If you could see me now."

How her ex-husband would laugh, knowing what had become of her. His buddies had been messing with her head for weeks, ever since her former roommate, Simone, sold out her location to them. They'd been messaging her constantly—creating new social media accounts each time she blocked them—and had turned up at the café where she worked and made a scene more than once. Not to mention the days they'd staked out her apartment building and jeered, or tailed her in their car when she was forced to leave for work. They'd driven her to the point where she could hardly sleep, was too distracted to do her job—hence getting fired—and felt like she was going crazy. Then, without Simone around to help pay the rent anymore, she hadn't been able to keep her apartment. And frankly, no landlord wanted to take a chance on a broke, unemployed woman with a patchy work history. Her one consolation was that Samuel was rotting in a prison cell. As far as she was concerned, he could stay there.

Charity indicated and pulled onto one of the roads leading to the town square, which was the thriving hub of Haven Bay, especially during tourist season. She glanced over at the neatly printed papers on the passenger seat. Her resumé. Nerves clustered in her stomach and her fingers tightened on the steering wheel. The sooner she found a job, the sooner she could earn enough money to get the hell out of here again. But she wasn't fooling herself. Convincing anyone to hire her would be a mission.

She parked on a side road, grabbed her resumé, and got out of the car, locking it behind her. Most people would consider it safe enough around here that everything could be left unlocked, but when you were on the residents' shit-list, it didn't pay to take chances. She ducked her head and walked toward the square, not making eye contact with anyone and hoping they wouldn't recognize her. She'd changed a lot since she stopped being Mrs. Charity Hagley. Not enough to conceal her identity from people who knew her, but enough that the general public often didn't realize who she was.

The square had a cobbled center and Old English-style lampposts, which she'd once found charming. She went directly to Cafe Oasis—the only cafe in town—and let herself in. A bell chimed as she entered, and she joined the line waiting to order. She kept her face lowered until she reached the cashier, then she sucked in a breath as she raised it and looked into the familiar eyes of Lana McQueen. *Damn it.* Lana had owned the cafe during Charity's youth, but she'd hoped the older lady might have sold it and moved on. Apparently not.

"Well, look what the cat dragged in," Lana drawled, a chill in her green eyes. "Charity Hagley, fancy seeing you here."

Charity managed not to squirm. "Actually, it's Charity St. John. I'm divorced."

Lana huffed. "That doesn't surprise me. I guess you couldn't get anything more out of him after he was convicted. But shouldn't you have found another con artist to attach yourself to by now?"

Charity tried not to show how much Lana's words

affected her, and she didn't protest. She deserved every ounce of censure she got. After all, she'd married a man who'd defrauded dozens of people by persuading them to invest in a non-existent real-estate scheme. "I'm moving back to the bay," she said, getting to the point. "I've worked for the past three years as a barista in Auckland. Is there any chance you're hiring?"

Lana snorted and put a hand on her hip. "Let me get this straight. *You're* asking *me* for a job? After your husband tricked me into investing my retirement savings and then stole them out from under me? You've got some nerve, girl."

Closing her eyes, Charity reminded herself not to snap back. There was no point in arguing that she'd been oblivious to Samuel's shady dealings. Even though she hadn't faced charges—and had actually testified for the prosecution—she'd been tried and convicted in the court of public opinion.

"Yes," she said, opening her eyes and swallowing her bitterness. "I am."

At this point, a good number of people were watching them, and the cafe was strangely silent.

"It isn't happening," Lana told her. "Get out of here. I wouldn't so much as sell you a scone."

Tail between her legs, Charity nodded and left before she could spit a retort that would only make the situation worse. She'd always been a little fiery, but she'd tried to rein it because nothing good ever came of it.

Once she got back to her car, she started the engine and drove to Sailor's Retreat, the local restaurant. Unfortunately, they had no more interest in her than Lana did. Deflated, but not surprised, she wandered across the beach-side pavilion that separated Sailor's Retreat from The

Shack, the ice cream and cupcake parlor owned by her sister Faith. A gust of wind stirred the black skirt she'd picked up from the Salvation Army shop because she'd hoped it would make her look more professional. She smoothed it back into place before pushing open the door to The Shack.

"Charity!" Faith exclaimed from behind the counter, her vivid red lips spreading in a grin. "You're here! I wondered if you'd come by." She rushed onto the shop floor and swept Charity into one of the best hugs ever. With her curves, bubbliness, and the scent of cream and sugar that clung to her like a second skin, Faith's embraces could make the worst days seem better. Charity sank into her, squeezing her eyes shut and wishing everyone was as forgiving as Faith.

"God, I missed you," she said. "You're the one good thing about being back here."

"Come on, there must be more than just me," Faith said, releasing her. "What about the lack of traffic? The warmth? The beach?"

"The lack of traffic is nice," Charity allowed, and glanced around the store. She'd only been here once before and thought her memory must have exaggerated how cute and funky the parlor was, but it hadn't. The color scheme was pink and green, very retro, and Faith wore a fifties-style polka dot dress to match. Behind her, Charity noticed another woman. Slender, with dark blonde hair and eyes that were brownish-gold. She assumed this was Faith's business partner, Megan, who she'd heard a lot about but not met yet.

"Hi," she said, approaching her. "I'm Charity, Faith's sister."

"Nice to meet you." The woman came around to join them and offered her a smile. "I'm Megan. Faith has told me so much about you. She's really excited to have you here."

"She's the only one. If looks could kill, I'd never have made it this far."

Faith grimaced. "That good, huh? Sorry, Char. Where have you been?"

"First to Cafe Oasis, then Sailor's Retreat. I was hoping to find work, but they're not interested." She shrugged, trying to pretend it didn't bother her, but based on Faith's sympathetic expression, she wasn't fooling anyone.

"You might need to target people who weren't around three years ago," Faith suggested.

"Actually," Megan said, and they both turned to her. "There's a job posting board near The Refuge. You should have a look and see if there's any you might be able to apply for."

Charity nodded. At this point, she was willing to try anything that would allow her to build a nest egg and escape. "I'll head over there now and have a look. Thanks, Megan."

"No problem."

"Once you're done there, feel free to go straight to my place and get settled in," Faith said, reaching into her pocket and extracting a key, which she handed over. "We've cleared space for you in the spare bedroom. It'll probably be easier to unpack before the boys get home from school."

"Great, thank you." Charity slid the key into her purse and zipped it shut. "I really appreciate everything you're doing for me. Did you tell Shane I'm happy to chip in once I start earning some money?"

Faith rolled her eyes. "Yes, and he said the same thing

I did. You're family, and we're happy to have you until you get back on your feet. No payment necessary."

Charity made a mental note to find out their bank account number so she could transfer something into it on the sly. Faith and her new family were being more than generous, but with two young boys around, they couldn't afford to put her up indefinitely without some kind of repayment.

"If you say so, sis. I'll let you know how things go. Fingers crossed."

"We'll cross ours for you too," Faith said. "See you later, gorgeous."

"Good luck," Megan said, as Charity exited the shop.

She returned to her car and drove to The Refuge, which was the local retirement village. Halfway down the block, she noticed what looked like a newsstand on the side of the road and pulled up beside it. She headed over and scanned the scraps of paper pinned to the board. Many were old, but one looked to have been added recently. It was a job advertisement for an assistant librarian role. Charity quirked her brow and considered that. She liked books. She had no experience, but if it was only an assistant role, perhaps that wouldn't matter. It was worth a shot, anyway.

She took a photo of the advertisement on her phone, then tucked it away in her pocket. It was a short drive to the library, and she managed to find a parking spot right outside. Resumé in hand, she headed through the main entrance, aware that she could be walking into another potential confrontation. She'd barely made it five steps before she smacked into a solid wall of man. Her papers scattered on the floor, and she dropped to her knees to gather them up, fingers trembling because she had no doubt everyone was staring at her. As she straightened, her forehead knocked against the man's as he bent to help her. He grunted in shock.

"Oh, my God, I'm so sorry," she exclaimed, backing away so quickly she tripped over her own feet. The only reason her ass didn't hit the ground was because the stranger grabbed her by the arm before she fell.

"Are you okay?" he asked in a deep, velvety voice.

"I'm fine," she assured him, afraid to look up in case she'd given him a black eye in addition to making a fool of herself. But what she could see of him was very nice. A broad chest and tapered waist. He smelled good, too. Like lemongrass. "I'm not normally so clumsy. I hope I didn't hurt you."

He chuckled. "No, you just took me by surprise."

Finally, Charity dared to lift her eyes to his. Her heart stuttered.

Just freaking typical.

She'd bowled into the hottest guy she'd ever seen. With dimples, golden hair, and eyes the vibrant blue of the water in the bay, framed by sexy glasses, he knocked the breath right out of her lungs. He grinned, revealing straight white teeth set in a brilliant smile. Charity melted. Her brain lost its capacity for rational thought. All she wanted to know was whether his body was as gloriously muscled beneath his button-down shirt as it appeared to be.

Because of course, *of fucking course*, she'd steam-rollered into the most attractive specimen of a man in Haven Bay.

ALSO BY ALEXA RIVERS

ACKNOWLEDGMENTS

Thank you to my husband. This will be the last book I publish as an author with a day job, thanks to your unflagging support. You are incredible and I love you so much.

Thank you to the crew of people who helped me bring this book to life: Kate, for your astute suggestions and fine eye; Serena, for honing the final product; Shannon for the gorgeous cover; and my wonderful readers for reviewing and enjoying the story. You are all amazing and I couldn't do it without you.

XO

ABOUT THE AUTHOR

Alexa Rivers writes about genuine characters living messy, imperfect lives and earning hard-won happily ever afters. Most of her books are set in small towns, and she lives in one of these herself. She shares a house with a neurotic dog and a husband who thinks he's hilarious. When she's not writing, Alexa enjoys travelling, baking cakes, eating said cakes, cuddling fluffy animals, drinking copious amounts of tea, and absorbing herself in fictional worlds.